BLOODY PAGES

A Kim Jansen Detective Novel – 2

BRUCE LEWIS

Black Rose Writing | Texas

ISBN: 978-1-68513-004-6
PUBLISHED BY BLACK ROSE WRITING
www.blackrosewriting.com

Printed in the United States of America
Suggested Retail Price (SRP) $19.95

Bloody Pages is printed in Garamond

*As a planet-friendly publisher, Black Rose Writing does its best to eliminate
unnecessary waste to reduce paper usage and energy costs, while never
compromising the reading experience. As a result, the final word count vs. page count
may not meet common expectations.

Bloody Pages is dedicated to my great aunt, Mildred Frazier,
for teaching me the meaning of persistence,
and my wife, Gerry, for making this a
better novel in so many ways.

Special Thanks

Author **Mary Ellen Bramwell** (*the Apple doesn't Fall Far*), editor extraordinaire, who fixed my timeline and so many other mistakes. She made everything better.

Author and life-long friend **David Haldane** (*Nazis and Nudists* and *Jenny on the Street*) for introducing me to Black Rose Writing.

Author **Ginny Rorby** (*Like Dust, I Rise* and *Hurt Go Happy*) for her 20-year friendship and support.

Authors **Chris Patchell** (the *Lacey James Mysteries*), **Susan Clayton Goldner** (the Winston Radhauser Mysteries), and **Martha Pound Miller** (*Child of Fate Series*) for their guidance and moral support.

Black Rose Writing: Creator and Founder **Reagan Rothe**, Social Media Jedi **Chris Miller** for his book promotion ideas, Design Director **David King** for his amazing cover and book layout, Sales Director **Justin Weeks** for smoothing the book distribution process, and **Minna Rothe** for her behind-the-scenes marketing work on behalf of all Black Rose Writing Authors.

BLOODY PAGES

BLOODY PAGES

CHAPTER 1

Colin Byrne skipped through the living room, into the kitchen, kissed his mom and said, "I'll be at Jimmy's." His mom smiled, tousled his hair, and told him to be home by 8 p.m., just before sunset. He was reaching for the door when the knob rattled and the door swung open, nearly knocking him down. Standing on the porch was his father, Peter, carrying a dented black metal lunch bucket, looking wobbly.

"Where do you think you're going, Squirt?"

"Over to Jimmy's."

"The hell you are. You're going to get me a beer and set up a tray for me in the living room. Your mother is going to bring my dinner. And we're all going to sit and watch TV like a proper family."

Tears filled Colin's eyes. His lip quivered as he prepared to protest. It was summer and he should be able to go out and play with his friends, shouldn't he? Anytime his dad came home drunk, he knew he and his mom, Mary, would be forced to sit and listen to dad call people on TV losers, then turn his verbal blowtorch on them. It seemed like his dad was angry all the time. There was no way to predict when he might slap him or his mother across the side of the head, telling them to "wise up" or "shut up."

"What are you yammering about, kid?" Peter asked, snarling at Colin.

"I… I… just want to go play… at Jimmy's. Can I go, Dad?" His plea came out as a squeak. Mary Byrne didn't wait for her husband to answer. "Go, honey," she said.

Father and son shared Black Irish genes with wavy, thick black hair, milk-white skin, freckles, and deep blue eyes, but little else. Colin Byrne, 10, was 4-feet-5 inches and 70 pounds. Peter was 6-feet-1 inches, 350 pounds, with a stomach so big six inches of fat protruded below his wife-beater T-shirt. Sweat stains had spread under his armpits. Manual labor jobs had built massive arms and chest, while beer had created the exploding gut. He had bounced around from one job to another, drinking up so much of his paycheck each week there was barely enough money for food, let alone rent. For a time, the family lived in a homeless camp, sleeping in a rusty station wagon with torn seats.

Peter was a serial abuser, physically and mentally. He regularly hit Colin and punched his wife. It happened when he was drunk. Like most nights. Like tonight. Looking at his son, who was defying his order, his cheeks were scarlet against his light skin, his fists opening and closing.

"Where the hell is my dinner?"

Mary turned around, opened the refrigerator, pulled out a plate of food covered with congealed gravy, and slapped it down. A chunk of stiff mashed potatoes leaped off the plate and onto the flowered tablecloth. "Here's your dinner," Mary said, frowning and folding her arms. "If you had come home after work, it would be hot."

Peter closed his eyes. When he opened them, they appeared to have rolled back in his head with only the whites showing—like a Great White Shark about to close on its prey. He pushed the boy out of the way and swept the food to the floor. He reached up, grabbed Mary by the hair, and slammed her against the wall. There was a crack. Her arms dropped to her sides, her eyes fluttered, and she slid down the wall onto her tailbone, her head dropping toward her lap.

Colin ran to his mother, hugging her, screaming, "Mommy, Mommy, are you okay?" There was no answer. "Leave the worthless bitch alone," Peter commanded. Mary's eyes opened. They were glassy, like a boxer just knocked to the canvas. She shook her head, trying to bring the world back into focus. She finally pushed herself into a sitting position, then reached up and touched the blood trickling down her cheek. Her head was pounding. Her fingers found a dent in her head, which matched the apron hook on the wall.

"Colin, get out of here. Go play," she said, the words barely audible.

Colin rose and looked toward the door. He had witnessed this scene dozens of times and knew he was no match for his father. "Get me a fucking beer, put it in the living room, then sit on the couch, and keep your mouth shut." It appeared the standoff was over. Colin sighed, expelling the air from his lungs like a deflating balloon. He took a beer from the refrigerator, set it down in the living room, and walked back to the kitchen. Colin looked at his mother, who waved him away. "I'm okay," she said. "Don't worry about me." She clearly wasn't, her eyes closing, her chin dropping to her chest before lifting it up again. Blood seeped from her wound.

"I'm leaving," said Colin, his head up, shoulders back, his mouth a tight line. He clenched his fists and said, "You better leave Mom alone or I'll call the police." Peter Byrne cocked his head as if his son were speaking a foreign language, his brain wrestling with the translation.

"You're a useless drunk," Colin screamed as he stepped up to his dad and began punching wildly, hitting the big man in the belly, and slapping his face before trying to push past him. Colin didn't know where he got the courage to confront, let alone hit, his father. A dam of emotion had burst. As little as he was, he needed to fight back. He couldn't allow Dad to push them around for no apparent reason other than being a mean drunk.

Peter shoved Colin down and prepared to retaliate. He unbuckled the 60-inch monster belt he called Big Brownie, a vicious weapon that had left a thousand welts on Colin and Mary. He snapped it like a whip. Colin moved away, farther into the living room. His dad followed.

Holding the leather end of the belt, with the massive steel buckle touching the floor, Peter whipped it high in the air and brought it down hard, the buckle knocking off the corner of the cheap wooden coffee table. Rage rose in the back of Peter's throat as he screamed, "You'll pay for what you did." Colin looked at his father, trying to figure out what he, Colin, had done to deserve a whipping. But his dad's warning seemed aimed at something unseen, a ghost.

What he didn't know was that a lifetime of pain from Peter's own beatings as a kid was surging through his dad's arms and into his hands and fingers. The belt was rising like a rattlesnake about to strike. Gritting his teeth, Peter Byrne swung the belt down on his son as hard as he could. Colin had fallen back onto the sofa, like a turtle helpless on its back, his feet churning uselessly in the air as he attempted to fend off the blows. He screamed as the buckle struck his foot and broke two toes. Colin was twisting and kicking wildly to escape.

The second strike ripped a hole in his thigh, blood spurting from the wound and onto the thin, coffee-stained carpet. Choking on the pain, Colin couldn't talk, cry, or scream. Two more strikes ripped holes in his back near the spine and cracked a rib. His father took no notice, a snarl contorting his face. Colin rolled off the sofa and pushed himself up against the wall. Unable to escape, he put up his hands, but he had no chance against his father's attack. The next strike broke a finger.

Colin was barely conscious when the metal ripped into his cheek. The buckle prong pushed into the middle of his eye, puncturing his cornea, pushing through the iris, and shredding the retina and nerves. Colin screamed from the pain, pleading for his dad to stop hitting him, but Peter didn't seem to notice as he continued to rain blows with his belt.

When Mary heard her son's agonizing yelps, she fought to stand up, barely conscious. Hanging onto the door frame as she entered the living room, she looked at the carnage. Adrenaline took hold. She flew at her husband, grabbing the belt in mid-air. Jolted out of his fury, he let go of the belt. Mary grabbed it and started hitting him. The buckle ripped across Peter's ear, a piece tearing away as Mary yanked the belt back for another strike. "Take this and this and this," she hissed. Peter, bloody from Mary's attack, stumbled into the kitchen to escape. Tripping over a step stool, he crashed to the floor and then began spinning and twisting to get away. It was no use in their small kitchen. She had him pinned down.

"Get the hell out of here, you monster," she screamed, before dropping the bloody belt and running toward Colin's painful sobs in the next room. Surveying Colin's injuries, she yelled, "You bastard, you've blinded our son." Ignoring the damage to her own head, she staggered into the bathroom, grabbed a towel, and returned to her son's side. She surveyed his wounds and began dabbing at this eye. Even her gentle touch sent waves of pain through Colin as she attempted to staunch the bleeding.

In the kitchen, Peter rolled onto his knees and pushed himself into a standing position. He struggled to open the kitchen door, then staggered outside, taking the car keys with him.

Mary scooped up Colin and ran outside to get help, their only car burning rubber and fishtailing down the street. With nothing left to do, she let out a blood-curdling scream for help. Neighbors began peeking out windows. Then Colin's world went dark.

CHAPTER 2

1

A Red-tailed Hawk's screech awoke Colin. His body was vibrating. Knots spasmed in his legs. He felt a wave of nausea as he reached up and felt the deep scar on his face. It pulsed with pain. The pain was phantom, like an amputee who feels their missing limb long after doctors had removed it. Lying on his back, Colin opened his eyes and looked up. The carved beams were just as he remembered them from the night before, the ceiling fan turning slowly. The warm air felt chilly against his sweat-covered face. He took deep breaths to reassure himself that he had escaped his never-ending nightmare, if not the scars of his father's attack.

Like he had every morning during 30 years of marriage, Colin Byrne, 58, reached his hand out to touch his wife, Angela, next to him. They started the day holding hands while they woke up. On mornings after his recurring nightmare, her warm, gentle touch and soft voice would slow his heart rate and breathing, pulling him back to reality. Now, when he reached out, there was no hand.

Although a year had passed since his wife died of cancer, her absence was nearly as painful for him as his recurring nightmare. He took a crumb of solace in her quiet passing. Oregon's death with dignity law let her choose her last moments, to avoid the growing pain before it became unbearable. The day she ended her life, Angela swallowed the doctor-prescribed pills. Then she and Colin held hands, lying side-by-side in the same bed he was in now, as she drifted away.

Colin looked at the clock by his bedside and rolled up to a sitting position. He had suffered bouts of mild vertigo and, at his physical therapist's suggestion, took more time climbing out of bed into a standing position. His doctor diagnosed the unsteadiness as "normal for a man your age."

Like he did every day, Colin stood in front of the mirror, confirming his existence and identity. Not as a tortured boy of 10, but as a successful Oregon vintner in the Willamette Valley, one of the state's major wine-producing areas. His once jet-black hair was salt and pepper. The belt buckle-shaped scar below the missing eye was smoother. Colin could have gotten a prosthetic with perfectly matching color. Instead, he kept the slightly off-color glass eye with no iris or pupil. Pure white and creepy.

Over the mis-matched eye, he wore a patch. The patch was a reminder of his father's brutal attack. Years of therapy had done little to boost his self-esteem. Still, women loved the patch. They said he looked like a pirate. Although a personal trainer helped him keep his body buffed, he rarely took off his shirt in public to avoid questions about the scars on his back and chest. When asked once on a beach vacation, dressed only in a swimsuit, he said he had been in a car accident that killed his father.

In fact, Peter Byrne died the night of his attack on Colin in 1973. According to witness interviews in the police report, Peter left the house, drove to his favorite bar, and drank until the bartender refused to serve him more alcohol.

Peter reportedly got up from the barstool and weaved his way out the backdoor into the parking lot, the whole time talking to himself, saying something about how sorry he was. No one knew what he was sorry about. Peter's apparent plan was to climb into the back of the family station wagon— as he had many times before—to sleep it off. Unable to find his keys, he walked over to a grassy area nearby to lie down. Instead, he tripped and slid into thick bushes at the bottom of a hill. He passed out where he landed and never woke up.

The coroner said Peter Byrne had died from hypothermia and severe alcohol poisoning. He was just 34. His death was a godsend to Colin and his mother. She never remarried, but had many good friends she met as a library volunteer. Colin and Angela always included Mary on vacations and holidays. Mother and son never again mentioned the name Peter, nor discussed what happened the night he died. After cremation, a family friend dumped the ashes into the Columbia River, which emptied into the ocean. No trace of the man existed except terrible memories.

2

After his shower, Colin pulled the patch over his head, dressed in jeans and a white short-sleeve cotton shirt, and strapped on his Hermes Apple Watch. When he entered the password to unlock his watch, connecting it to his smart phone, a notification popped up on the screen: wine buyer meeting begins in one hour. He grabbed a cup of coffee in the kitchen, took the stairs to the tasting room below his living quarters, and walked out a set of French doors onto a terrace. Even with one eye, the beauty of the rolling hills that made up his 28-acre vineyard usually renewed his energy and carried his thoughts away to better times. Today, however, his mind couldn't escape the belt-beating. Arthritis on the two toes broken during the attack was a constant reminder. Along with the scars.

Why the hell had his dad savaged him with the belt? Colin was an obedient kid who rarely defied his father. How did his drunk dad's normal verbal taunts and slaps turn into a fury neither he nor his mother had ever experienced before? What flipped the switch, turning everyday abuse into pure rage? Colin had asked himself that question a thousand times and never heard an answer. With both of his parents dead, who else could he ask. He had resigned himself to never knowing the answer.

CHAPTER 3

1

History Professor Bryan Byrne, 36, had set up his tent in a shaded area near the trailhead to Little Death Hollow, an eight-mile slot canyon in Escalante National Monument. He spent the cool morning by a fire, drinking coffee as he watched the sun rise. He also used the quiet time to review photos and video of the area he had taken the day before. They would be part of a multimedia presentation to his graduate students at Canyon College in Tucson. His dog, Dino, lay by his feet, half asleep.

"Dino, are you hungry?" The black and white border collie's head snapped up. "Okay, let's eat," Byrne said.

Byrne prepared a bowl of food for Dino, then placed a grate over the fire, moved the coals into a mound beneath, and set down an iron frying pan. After it heated, he dropped in a half dozen pieces of thick-sliced bacon and watched as it crackled and popped. The smell of cooking bacon caused his stomach to rumble and his mouth to water.

When the bacon was crisped, he removed some of the grease, leaving just enough to cover the yolks of the eggs he gently placed in the skillet. Ten minutes later, he was wolfing breakfast with his third cup of black coffee. When he finished eating and cleaning up, he loaded his day pack with snacks and water for himself and his dog.

After dousing the fire, he clipped a leash on Dino before heading off for another day of hiking and photography. From his campsite, they walked two miles into Little Death Hollow, marveling at the high, red sandstone cliffs. Byrne let Dino off the leash to run—a violation of park rules—figuring no one else would be hiking in the canyon since they had been alone in the campground and no cars were parked at the trailhead. Layers of rock revealed eons of geologic formation, the undulating walls a tribute to nature's artistry. The canyon was so narrow he could stretch his arms wide and touch opposing cliffs.

Byrne closed his eyes, leaned his head back, and pulled in a deep breath of cool, dry air. When he opened them, he was looking into an azure sky punctuating the multi-colored canyon walls. The light and color were glorious. Overwhelmed by the beauty of the moment, a surge of emotion rose through his chest into his neck and face. He burst into tears of pure joy, sobbing and smiling at the same time. He wiped his face on his sleeve, then pulled out his phone to take more photos while Dino ran ahead, disappearing around a twist in the trail.

A faint crack of thunder sounded in the distance. Before getting on the trail, Byrne had tuned into the U.S. Park Service radio station and listened to a weather report. "It's monsoon season," a park ranger noted. "And that means a danger of flash flooding." The ranger explained that flash floods occurred when heavy rain—channeled through streams or narrow gullies—turned instantly into a torrent, often overwhelming unsuspecting hikers caught in narrow canyons with no escape route.

"Okay, I'm warned," Byrne had said to the man on the radio. Byrne knew about flash floods. He also had read a recent story in a backpacking magazine about a woman hiker's harrowing, near-death experience: trapped in quicksand, about to be drowned in fast rising water in a slot canyon—just like the one Byrne was walking.

He was putting his phone back into his pocket and tightening the strap on his day pack when he heard a second crack and then a third, each nearer than the last. When a fourth lightning strike thundered nearby, a danger alert sounded in Byrne's head.

"Dino, come boy," he said urgently. The dog came racing back. "Let's get out of here." They turned and took only a few steps before Bryan realized he was too late. Around the corner, out of sight, he heard a deep rumbling. He stopped to listen. That's when he saw an unidentified object coming at him — a spiky green mass. A second later, a tumbleweed impaled him, its thorns sharp enough to puncture a bicycle tire. It tore at his legs and arms as he fought to untangle himself. Dino barked as Bryan struggled with the invader. Despite the pain, he grabbed the twisting plant with both hands, spun it around, and let a blast of wind carry it away.

Barely free of the tumbleweed, Byrne realized he was standing in water swirling around his feet. In an instant, it was up to his knees, then his waist, then over his head. His arms were pinwheeling to keep his head above the water—now a muddy churn which threatened to carry him away. Byrne clawed his way up, opening his mouth to gulp in precious air a second before the roiling stream pulled him back down. He was losing the fight. Dino's four legs furiously fought the surge, terror in his eyes. When Bryan surfaced a second time, he saw Dino and tried to close the distance between them a moment before he slammed against the rock wall, his leg shattered, driving him under water. His hands punched through the surface, but he could not raise his head for one more breath. Finally, his hands slipped out of sight and his body went limp, nothing more than flotsam pushed along by the flood.

2

Bryan Byrne's lids fluttered open, terror in his eyes. Sweat covered his body. Cotton sheets tangled his feet. Dino was licking his face. He looked around and realized he was home. The flash flood had been a dream. "Off, Dino," said Byrne, grimacing. His canine companion's attempt at play electrified his hip. A shock of pain shot down his leg into his foot. "Damn hip," he yelled. Confused by the sudden outburst, Dino sat down and looked at him. "It's okay, boy," he said, rubbing his dog's ears. Peeling the damp sheets from his legs, Byrne sat up and planted his feet on the floor. He reached for a pill bottle on his nightstand and rattled the contents. In search of relief from a deteriorating hip in need of replacement, hydrocodone had hooked him. Now, faced with a series of classes, term papers, and mentoring, three pills remained, hardly enough for 12 hours. He would never survive the day unless he could find more relief. Next to the pill bottle, a message flashed on his smartphone screen. A text from Dean Stanley Watkins, president of the Canyon College, said, "Come at 9. My office. B on time. Mandatory!!" A frowning emoji followed the message. Not a good sign.

Watkins' text must have rescued Byrne from his nightmare. Now, he guessed, he faced the academic equivalent of an ass kicking.

Byrne reached for his metal cane, struggled up into a standing position, another shock of pain freezing him in place. His orthopedic specialist had urged him for the past two years to get replacement surgery. When Byrne resisted, the doctor smiled and offered, "You'll know when the time is right." Byrne had claimed he was too busy. What an idiot. Now, he was a tenured college professor with a medication use disorder—the politically correct term for "drug addict."

"I'm ready for surgery," he emailed his doctor. "Please! ASAP. In a lot of pain." Unfortunately, his surgeon, Michelle Allen, had a long waiting list. "My earliest appointment is in four months," Dr. Allen wrote. There was neither a 'sorry' nor an offer to work him into her schedule. He could visualize her smirking as she wrote the response, no doubt thinking, 'I told you so.'

3

Hobbling over to his coffee maker, Byrne poured a cup, hoping a rush of caffeine might distract him from the pain. Pain had made him miss faculty meetings, come late for class, or not show up at all. Today, he would launch the semester with twenty-four undergrad students who signed up for U.S. History: Trails and Travails of Western Explorations. The class required rigorous field trips along the routes of emigrating pioneers and early Spanish explorers. His department head had reprimanded him for failing to show up for classes and not alerting anyone in administration. Had he listened, he would not be in this predicament. He looked at the time and realized he had one hour to shave, shower, and get to campus for the meeting. In his full-length mirror, he saw the reflection of a man 6-feet-1 inches tall. Like his father, Colin Byrne, he was Black Irish with thick black hair, pale skin, and blue eyes. Unlike his dad, who was always trim from working out, even now in his late fifties, Bryan was overweight at 200 pounds. Too little exercise, too much dessert, and excessive drinking— after his wife left him for a teaching assistant 10 years her junior—added to his weight, and the pressure on his ailing hip.

4

"I got a call from Tim Ellington, and he isn't happy," Dean Watkins said before Bryan could settle into the chair in front of the dean's giant mahogany desk. "Tim says you jumped the line, ducked into his prescription filling area and began rifling through other people's prescriptions while he was ringing up a customer. He said you grabbed a bottle of painkillers intended for a cancer patient, which was not you. What the hell do you have to say for yourself?"

Tim Ellington was the owner and chief pharmacist at the local GoodMeds. He also was Dean Watkins' best friend.

"It was all a mistake," Bryan lied. "I asked my doctor to call in a prescription. He didn't call back, but I assumed he had done it. I needed the pills and thought the prepaid prescription was mine. My hip was pulsing with pain and Tim had a line of customers. I knew I shouldn't have but figured I could take what was mine."

"I know that's what you told Tim, but we both know that's bullshit." Watkins' language surprised Bryan. He was normally a mild-manned guy who never spoke an unkind word.

"Luckily," Watkins continued, "Tim will let it go rather than call the police— a favor to me after I explained your health problem. I assured him I would make you get your hip fixed and your head straight."

"My hip is getting worse."

"Fix the hip. Go to rehab for the pill addiction."

"I promise I will. But I need the pain meds until I get my hip fixed. The earliest surgery date I can get is four months from now."

"Professor Byrne," Watkins said, suddenly formal, sitting up straight and leaning forward. "Unfortunately, you are getting a poor reputation. When a teacher gets into trouble, it's a black mark on the entire institution. Which leaves me with no other choice. I'm putting you on an indefinite sabbatical, starting the moment you walk out of this office. I'll cancel your classes. If you have time off coming, you'll get paid. Otherwise, you won't get a paycheck."

"You can't do that. I need this job. And I need the health insurance."

"If you keep up this behavior, you won't have a job. Right now, we'll pay 100 percent of your healthcare costs. Come back when you're ready to keep your commitments to this college and our students, whose parents pay a small fortune for them to study here."

Bryan struggled to his feet, thanked the dean for maintaining his insurance, and limped out of the office. The cane provided little support. As he stood in the hallway outside the dean's office, he wondered what he would do while waiting for a new hip? No doubt he would be chasing fresh supplies of pain pills if his primary care doctor cut him off. He pushed away the thought. "I know what I'll do," Byrne said to himself. "I'll visit Edward Curtis."

About 1924, Edward S. Curtis had hired his great grandfather, William Bryan Byrne, a gifted young photographer, to assist him in capturing North American Indian portraits. The photos were part of Curtis' 30-year quest to record and preserve fast-disappearing North American Indian culture. William Byrne worked for Curtis, according to family lore, for six or seven years. Because of Bryan's family connection, creating a history class around his relative would enhance his professional reputation and give him some fresh material to teach. Besides online research, Bryan decided he would visit the Portland Central Library's rare book room to see the Curtis masterpiece first-hand. Called *The North American Indian*, it wasn't a single book, but a 20-volume set of photos and text about native culture. Bryan would visit his dad, Colin Byrne, during his Portland stay — a visit Bryan dreaded. But he needed his dad's help.

5

On his trip from Tucson to Portland, Bryan Byrne drove dusty pioneer roads, visiting rural towns and historic sites while collecting information for future classes. Near the end of his trip, Byrne entered the Oregon Trail. Hundreds of thousands of American pioneers in the mid-1800s emigrated west along the 2,000-mile route from Independence, Missouri to Oregon City, a half hour south of Portland. Of course, there was little remaining of the original trail, mostly roadside monuments and museums memorializing what had been.

A week from the end of his trip, Byrne made an appointment with Bill Bowman, the curator of a rare book room at the Portland Central Library to view *The North American Indian*, Bryan could never meet Curtis, who had died before Bryan was born. But he might reach across time and meet him through his great-grandfather.

CHAPTER 4

1

The nightmare of the beating by his father, Peter Byrne, had jerked Colin awake eight hours before. The resulting agony was still fresh in his mind despite a hectic day of vineyard management meetings, equipment malfunctions, and a private tasting for a half dozen wine buyers. Colin walked across the tasting room, which had just closed, and onto the terrace overlooking acres of ripening pinot grapes. He had oriented his home with outdoor seating areas to take advantage of east and west views so he would never miss a sunrise or sunset. As he sank into a plush high-back chair to soak in the view, he felt like a king overlooking his realm. Unlike a king who inherited his wealth and status, Byrne had earned his. He had been awarded degrees in viticulture and enology from the University of California at Davis, one of the nation's premier colleges for wine education. Then he worked his way up the ladder, performing every winery job, from field hand to winemaker. Along the way, he saved money and made small investments in up-and-coming wineries until he partnered with two men and a woman to form Four Friends Vineyards. Eventually, he bought out his partners and changed the winery name to Byrne. In the 20 years since becoming sole proprietor of Byrne Estate Vineyard, he had amassed a small fortune.

Colin closed his eyes and listened to a screeching hawk circling above. "Colin, would you like a glass of wine and a cheese tray from today's tastings?" Byrne's stomach leaped at the interruption. Opening his eyes, he saw his tasting room manager and personal assistant, Stella Mason, smiling at him.

"I would love both, Stella. Please join me."

Occasionally she did. Tonight, she had to get home to help her teenage daughter with a class project due in the morning.

"Kids always leave these things until the last minute," she said.

"I know all about it," Colin said. "My son, Bryan, who is now a history professor, never completed his assignments on time. My wife and I alternated in the all-too-frequent, frantic last-minute race to deliver Bryan's projects on time. I imagine he is getting payback as he attempts to manage college students who are among the world's best procrastinators."

"I know Bryan," she reminded Colin.

"Of course you do. The two of you were a thing one summer when he worked here." Stella turned red.

"I never guessed you knew about us," said Stella. "We tried to be sneaky. But as a parent now, with observation superpowers all parents have, I understand how you knew." They both smiled.

Stella brought over a glass of Byrne's best pinot noir and a charcuterie plate, said goodnight, and left.

Today would end like every day when it started with a bad dream. Colin would take a few gulps of wine to settle his nerves, then think about the nightmare. Before Angela died, she would distract him from his negative thoughts with stories about the day's winery tours, including silly tourist questions, which made them laugh. They would eat dinner, take a walk, then settle in to read or gaze at the flickering fireplace. After her death, Colin ate dinner alone most nights. Occasionally, his chef, whom he hired to manage food presentations for winery parties and special dinners, would join him. Tonight, he was having leftovers. And he was caught in a mental merry-go-round about what had fueled Peter Byrne's anger, abuse, and alcoholism.

From many years of counseling—something Colin resisted until he accidentally blackened his wife's eye when she woke him in the middle of the dream about his father's attack—he learned that mental and physical abuse often passes from one generation to the next. 'It's learned negative behavior,' his therapist said, 'ingrained as deeply as a gene for hair color.' Of course, you couldn't change your genes, but the behavior could be unlearned. Unfortunately, when Colin was a kid suffering his father's abuse, there was no such thing as "family therapy."

"When did the abuse begin?" Colin Byrne asked himself again, as if someone were listening. "Does it really make a difference?" Only he could decide. No matter how hard he tried, he remembered nothing after he passed out following the attack. What he remembered came from the scars on his body. They told their own horror story. His father's death was a fitting end for a tormented man.

2

A vague memory scratched at the edge of Colin's mind. When his mother died, he had inherited several bankers boxes. The top of one had been secured with several layers of tape, as if something evil might escape. Colin put his wine down, got up, and walked down two flights of stairs. At the bottom, the path to the right led to his 2,000-bottle wine cellar. A path to the left led to a nearly forgotten room, a storage space little bigger than a broom closet.

He opened the door, scanned the contents, and stopped. There was the box with his mother's handwriting. In large black letters were the words "P. Byrne's Personal Effects." Seeing the name jolted Colin, as if his father had come to life and punched him in the chest. His eye ached. His heart raced. Dizzy, he fell against the wall. When his recovered, he reached for the box, his hands shaking. He pulled back like he was about to wake a poisonous snake.

Colin took a deep breath, pulled the tape off the box, lifted the lid, and looked inside, ready to jump away. On top was the tan cap his dad always wore. Beneath the hat were a pair of khaki-colored pants and matching shirt, both part of a drab uniform. There was also the wife beater t-shirt he wore under his uniform top. These were the clothes his dad was wearing the day he died. Dried blood spatters, now a dark rust color, covered the pant legs. Was that Colin's blood? He stepped back as a wave of nausea washed over him.

Colin moved back to the box, removed the clothing, and found several smaller items: a pocket-knife with a worn blade his dad had used to whittle and to clean his fingernails, a plain gold wedding band, and a wallet. Colin picked up the worn brown leather wallet, holding it with two fingers, as if contaminated. He opened it, found his dad's lucky $2 bill, a yellowed driver's license with a picture of his dad, and a family photo. His mother and father stood facing the camera with smiles on their faces. They each put an arm on Colin, who also was smiling. Seeing his father's face for the first time in decades, except in his nightmares, made him cringe—as if the photo might come alive and grab him.

The sight of his father smiling, appearing to share a happy moment with his family, made Colin tear up, then burst out in anger. "Damn you," he said to the man in the photo, "Why couldn't you have been like this all the time?"

At the bottom of the box were seven leather-bound journals embossed with the letters WBB. Who the hell was WBB? Colin wondered. He opened the first page and read the inscription: "This is my humble account of my journey as a photography assistant to the great man, Mr. Edward Sheriff Curtis, on his mission to preserve the cultures of native peoples."—William Bryan Byrne, April 10, 1924.

Colin realized he had discovered a family treasure. They confirmed that family lore was true: his grandfather worked for Edward Curtis, not just as an unidentified assistant—a gofer of sorts—but as a trusted, essential assistant photographer. The journals had been sitting in the box for ten years since his mother's death, a few steps from the wine cellar he visited every day. He wondered if the journals contained intimate details of his grandfather's experiences during the seven years he worked for Curtis, from 1924 until 1930. Curtis published one book in each of those years. Did they include photos taken by Grandfather Byrne?

Colin removed the journals, put the lid back on the box, and dropped the box on the floor. He carried the journals upstairs and placed them on a table next to the chair where he sat every evening reading until well past midnight. After pouring a double cognac, he settled in for the night and began paging through the 1924 journal. The detailed entries reflected his grandfather's enthusiasm for working with Curtis. The first year, especially, was a wonder for William Byrne, who revealed his dream of earning his living as a full-time photographer. He was on a grand adventure, seeing natural wonders few had experienced, learning something new every day from Curtis, his idol.

During the fall of his first year with Curtis, William wrote: "Curtis is down, sick today. He seems feverish. Insisted that we not cancel our planned photographs of Tolowa Tribe members. He asked me to stand in for him and capture the images. The enormity of the challenge scared me. In the end, I think I did a journeyman's job. I await Curtis' judgement."

What a revelation, Colin thought, to read William Byrne's first-hand account of his adventures a hundred years ago. His heart raced as he flew through the journals, absorbing the details. He felt like he was nearing the end of a murder mystery, frantic to know the conclusion. Then he was sorry. He picked up journal seven, dated 1930, and opened it to the last page. There was nothing. The back page was blank. Turning to the middle of the journal, he saw a rant written by his father, Peter: "Curtis, damn your soul to Hell." Colin's heart skipped a beat. His chest tightened. His breath came in gulps. He hesitated before flipping back through the journal, then scanned the pages as fast as he could. The answer to his question about why his father had been an alcoholic and a mean son of a bitch, Colin felt, must be in the journal pages. In entry after entry, Grandfather William Byrne expressed his disappointment in Curtis and the lack of recognition for his supporting role as assistant photographer.

When Colin reached the last entry in the journal—a page or two before his father's rant—he read the haunting words of his grandfather: "Death is coming for you, Edward Curtis." Puzzled at the threatening tone, after reading earlier positive accounts of the expedition, Colin feverishly turned pages to find the source of William Byrne's anger. Halfway through this last journal, Colin read an account of an interaction with Curtis that deflated him like a balloon stabbed with an ice pick. The next pages laid bare a 100-year-old family secret—the reason his sadistic father, Peter Byrne, had nearly beaten him to death, blinding him in one eye. It was the reason nightmares had tortured him for decades and why he jumped anytime someone reached toward him to shake hands—as if they were going to strike him. Grandfather Byrne's story stunned Colin.

A moment later, he screamed, "Fucking Curtis," and began sobbing. "You will pay for what you did to my family." Of course, Curtis couldn't hear him. He had been dead for decades.

Gripping the journals so tightly his fingers hurt, Colin lifted them overhead and slammed them down on the slate floor before kicking them into the fireplace, then yelled, "Curtis, I hope you are in Hell."

CHAPTER 5

1

The team was down six points with 15 seconds left on the clock—time for one play. Quarterback Mike Teller said to the huddle, "Guys, this is it: our chance to win the first league championship in the school's 50-year history. We can do it. Val, this one is coming to you, buddy." The huddle broke, and the offense settled on the line of scrimmage. Teller took the hike from the center. An instant later, a 275-pound defensive back crashed through the line, coming right at Teller like a locomotive on full throttle. When his offensive tackle threw a block, Teller positioned himself for the biggest throw in his college football career. He rolled out, found his wide receiver, Valentine "Val" James, running astride a linebacker. Teller threw a high-arching pass, which came over Val's right shoulder perfectly and into his hands. Val tightened his grip on the football and sprinted for the goal line 10 yards away. On the one-yard line, three defenders simultaneously brought him down like a high-powered rifle bullet striking a buffalo. Pushing the ball ahead just before hitting the ground, Val broke the goal plane. The fans exploded as the referee's hands went up. Mike Teller had just thrown the winning pass, assuring his place on the rookie roster of a professional team and a place in school sports history. He raced across the field to Val, ready to lift him, a hero, for everyone to cheer. When the tacklers crawled off Val, he was inert, his left leg twisted in an unnatural angle. His eyes were closed, his body lifeless.

2

Val James opened his eyes and looked up. His beagle, Mac, was inches from his face, sniffing his morning breath and licking him. "Off, Mac," he said, and pushed the hound gently aside. The touchdown play that made him a local hero—ending his college football career and any hope of going professional—was a recurring nightmare. Thankfully, it wasn't nightly. Some years, the dream only surfaced once or twice. It seemed to plague him when his life was filled with uncertainty, like now; he was homeless, living in his car. Pulling his sleeping bag over his head to delay getting up, he heard his phone ringing, playing Aerosmith's "I Don't Want to Miss a Thing."

Val knew it was Colin Byrne calling. He didn't answer. The phone stopped for 15 seconds and then started ringing again. Byrne, his former college roommate, was persistent. Val poked his head out of the sleeping bag, reached for his phone, and opened it.

"Hey, Colin, kind of early, isn't it?

"No, Val. It's ten."

"Had a late night," said Val.

"Where are you?" Colin asked.

"At a roadside inn near Grants Pass," Val lied. "A couple of days ago, I drove up from the Bay Area on a business trip. I planned to stop by and surprise you." They hadn't talked in more than a year. The last time had been a two-minute call the day of the memorial for Colin's wife.

"Come at 6 pm for a sunset lounge," said Colin. Sunset lounge was the name Val and Colin gave to cocktail hour get-togethers—buddy bullshit sessions.

"Looking forward to it, old buddy," said Val. "It's been a while."

"See you later," said Val, who ended the phone call, and looked up at his car roof, a foot from his face. His "roadside inn" was the back of his Subaru Outback, jammed with camping gear. Val was a vagabond, running from poor decisions and bad people. If he hadn't hit rock bottom, he was close. He had come to Portland to connect with Colin with the hope he could borrow desperately-needed cash to stay alive and create breathing room while he found a new job—a new beginning.

3

When he had pulled into Portland the night before, just after sunset, Val drove to the Union Station train depot and found a parking space under a roadway. Dressed in sweats and sneakers, he climbed out of his car to walk Mac and discovered he had parked at the end of a long line of tents. Small groups of homeless were talking, swearing, and laughing. Several dogs ran over to Mac, sniffed him, and returned to their owners. Was he really one of these losers? He would look for another parking space later in the day. But first he needed to dig out clothes for the dinner with Colin.

Just ahead of the line of tents was a green van. Painted on the side was a line of white paws with the name *Have Paws—Will Travel*. Below the paws were the words Loving Canine Health Care, James Allen Briggs, D.V.M. Was the guy living out of his car, like Val? Was he homeless? A moment later, a very tall man with a red beard, red hair, tan legs covered with red hair—wearing a red Hawaiian shirt, shorts, and sandals—emerged from the van. The man lifted a dog with a bandaged leg off the table in the van and placed him on the ground. Val walked over. "Hi, I'm Val James. This is my dog, Mac."

"I'm Jim Briggs," the man said. "I'm a veterinarian and this is my office. I come down here a few times a week to care for the dogs of homeless people. The service is free. Does your dog need something?" Val was about to say he wasn't homeless, but who was he kidding—he was living out of his car, his clothes ragged. His hair covered his collar. Mac jumped up on Briggs and sniffed. Briggs rubbed his ears. "Mac," said Briggs, "let's look at you." He listened to the dog's heart, checked out his eyes, his coat, feet, and ears. "Mac appears to be in good shape. By the way, his collar is missing."

"I've been meaning to get him one. Not sure how long I'm going to be in town."

"That doesn't matter. I'll inject him with a rice grain-size chip that anyone anywhere in the country can scan to identify him. Here's a tracking collar I can register as well."

"Good idea," said Val. "Please go ahead."

Briggs injected Mac with the chip and strapped on a tracking collar with a PupFinder GPS chip that would allow Briggs to log onto his laptop to locate Mac and Val, assuming Val would be nearby his dog. "Homeless people move around a lot," said Briggs. "The GPS collars allow me to locate their dogs when I need to provide follow-up care."

"A great idea," said Val. "I work in security and GPS devices are a wonderful addition to protecting all kinds of things. Why not a dog?" He felt no need to tell Briggs the security firm had fired him for stealing pills from clients.

"You're good to go," said Briggs, giving Mac another pat.

"Thanks Doc," said Val. "Do you know where I can find a dry cleaner?" Briggs directed him to a place six blocks away, then turned his attention back to a line of homeless waiting for help with their dogs.

4

With his clothes cleaned and pressed, Val locked Mac in the car, put his pants and shirt into his backpack and headed toward Union Station. When he walked in, two dozen people were scattered on benches across the massive lobby. No one registered his presence. He walked across the room and down a hall to the men's bathroom, locked himself in a stall, and got dressed. When he came out, he looked like a different person: pressed khakis, a polo shirt open at the neck, and tan suede oxfords. Although he was running out of cash, he had splurged on a haircut, so he looked the total package: well-turned-out, successful—a man without a care in the world. It was the image Colin Byrne, his best friend, expected. He even got his car washed, something he hadn't done in a year.

Looking back at himself in the mirror was a 58-year-old man, 6-feet-2 with broad shoulders and long arms. In high school, he played varsity baseball. Gifted at any sport he tried, he switched to football, which was a huge mistake given the horrific injury he suffered. Thick brown hair and liquid brown eyes gave him a look that women found "dreamy." His square jaw with cleft chin and a physique requiring little or no exercise added to his attractiveness. In high school, the student body voted him the graduate most likely to succeed. In college, Val managed a B average, but could have done better with a little effort. He wasn't a genius, but smart enough. He rescued Colin Byrne, his roommate, from flunking out in his senior year. Byrne was a lady's man who partied more than he studied. Val kept Colin academically afloat by sharing class notes and drilling his friend on expected test questions. The test preparations were always last minute. When the test results were published, with a B or even C grade in hand, Colin had a reason to party. And he and Val partied plenty.

During college, Val fell in love with horse racing. He would scrape together every dollar he could get—including cash to make bets for friends—and spend Saturdays at Golden Gate Fields in Albany, across the bay from San Francisco. He devoured the racing sheet, handicapping the horses, and placed bets. Initially, his bets were $2, but as the gambling bug burrowed deeper, bets grew to $25 and $50 per race. Years later, marriage and a family provided a vaccination to the growing threat to his life and finances. A daughter and high-paying jobs in sports broadcasting and TV advertising gave him something else to do. His looks and high school football heroics made him a star in the local market.

In the end, his gambling addiction returned with a vengeance, beating him down until nothing remained. He was divorced, estranged from his daughter, with threats to his life for failure to pay up the money he had borrowed for making big bets. Now he hoped Colin Byrne would rescue him—if not from his addictive behavior, at least from his crushing debt.

5

After one more hair check in the car side mirror, Val drove 45 minutes south from Portland to the Willamette Valley, the heart of Oregon's wine country, to Byrne Vineyards. He followed the signs to the tasting room, stopping at the top of the hill to take in the estate house and surrounding rolling hills covered with vines. Clearly, Colin was the one who had hit the jackpot.

Pulling into a space in front of the tasting room, a young woman stepped out and waved. Colin was rolling out the red carpet for his first visit to his friend's vineyard. Val climbed out of his car and let Mac out to do his thing.

"Hi! I'm Stella Mason, Colin's estate manager. He said you've best friends going back to college days."

"That's me," said Val, who offered a blazing smile, his teeth the whiteness you would expect from someone who had spent a decade as a local TV sportscaster.

"And that's Mac," said Val, as the dog peed on a grapevine. "Sorry."

"No need," she said. "We use sheep to eliminate the weeds rather than applying pesticides. They pee everywhere. A little dog pee won't raise an eyebrow. In fact, Mac is free to wander around and is welcome in the house when he wants to come in. Follow me."

Stella led Val into the house. "The tasting room is over there," she explained. "We have conference rooms through those wooden doors. Colin lives upstairs."

Exiting the house through double French Doors, Stella took Val onto a terrace overlooking the vineyard where Colin was standing. Colin turned around and looked Val up and down as if doing a uniform inspection. "You look great, Val," Colin said.

"And you're as big a stud as ever," Val said. They smiled and moved in for a hug.

"Try this." Colin handed Val a glass of red wine. "This is our best pinot. Nothing is too good for my pal."

"Been too long, Val. I miss our college days—the carefree, wild days of youth. And I miss all the times we sat around talking half the night about life and the future, drinking until we nearly passed out. Studying together. Competing for girls."

They sat quietly for a few minutes, looking across the vineyard as the dipping sun's golden rays illuminated the vineyard rows.

"Wow, Colin, this is a masterpiece—the house, the view, the life, and the wine."

"Thanks, Val." When the sun dipped below the hills, they lingered a few minutes longer before Stella came out and announced dinner was ready.

"Is Stella your chef, too?"

"No, she manages VIP dinners like this one, and group retreats. Really, she manages everything except the winemaking process. I also have a full-time chef who oversees the menu for tastings and keeps me from starving. When Angela was deteriorating with cancer, our chef kept both of us alive."

Stella brought in a plate of charcuterie and opened another bottle of wine.

"Colin, I'm so sorry for your loss. Angela's death devastated me," said Val. "I wanted to come to the memorial service but was in the middle of a life crisis with my family and couldn't leave them."

"Although Angela passed more than a year ago, I still reach for her in the morning, only to land my hand on an empty pillow. It's said time heals all wounds. That's a load of garbage. I like Rose Fitzgerald Kennedy's view, after losing three sons. She's quoted as saying, 'The hurt becomes covered with scar tissue and lessens the pain. But it never goes away.'"

Colin changed the subject. "Val, last I heard, you had transitioned from sportscasting and TV ad pitch man to a security job."

Val looked down, trying to decide if this was time to drop the bomb on Colin. He had never kept secrets from his friend. He took a gulp of wine and put the glass down. "Colin, I could bullshit you, but best friends don't do that." Colin sat up in his chair, cocked his head, and waited for what was coming next. "I'm at the bottom of a valley—emotionally, physically and financially," said Val. "At the moment, I'm homeless, sleeping in my car down by Union Station with my dog, Mac."

Colin drew back from Val with a puzzled look on his face. "Okay, I get it. Today must be April Fool's Day. You could always get me going."

"It's no joke," said Val.

Colin looked at him for what seemed like a long time, searching his face for deception or a smirk that would give away that he had made up a wild story. When Val's shoulders fell and his head dropped toward this his lap, Colin knew Val's story was true.

"Do you remember in college when I fell in love with the ponies and used to win regularly out at Golden Gate Fields or Bay Meadows racetracks?"

"You won often enough to inspire other students to trust you with their money, hoping to hit it big," said Colin.

"When my daughter went to college, the expenses were staggering. I was making six figures, but our budget was tight. I wanted more and thought I might still have the golden touch for picking winners. I didn't. Online betting and bets through a bookie wiped me out. I gambled away my house, my daughter's college savings account, and our retirement. I was always trying to go bigger with the idea I could make it all back—the loser's lament."

Colin waited for more. "Gail divorced me, and Cindy is working extra jobs to stay in college. Neither one of them will answer my phone calls or texts. I came here hoping you could help me out, in the name of friendship." Val cleared his throat and said, "And there is more."

"Oh my God, Val, what can I say?"

"My life is in danger," said Val. "I owe my bookie $57,000 and he's trying to collect. So far, I've evaded his grasp."

Colin had sensed something was wrong the past few months when Val didn't return his repeated calls, but he hadn't imagined Val's tale of personal destruction.

"Val, I'll always be your friend. I'll be there for you, no matter what."

"I really appreciate that, Colin," said Val, a hitch in his voice as he fought back tears.

Colin got quiet for a moment, looking away from Val toward the sunset. Finally, he said, "I think we can help each other."

"How could I possibly help you?" Val said, considering everything Colin had.

"I have a story to tell you," Colin answered.

Colin told Val what he'd discovered in his grandfather's journals.

"Val, I want payback. I want recognition for the contribution my grandfather, William Byrne, contributed towards Edward Curtis' *North American Indian*. I will do whatever is necessary to make that happen."

"I'm not following you, Colin."

"You've seen my scars from when I was a boy, right? And you remember the story of my dad dying in the crash?"

"An awful thing to happen to a kid," said Val.

"It was a lie," Colin said. "It never happened."

Val fell back in his chair, stunned. "What are you talking about?" he said, frowning, his jaw visibly tightening.

"When I was 10, I was going out to play with a neighborhood friend. I opened the door and my dad, drunk out of his mind, was standing there. He demanded to know where I was going. When I told him, he said to forget about going anywhere. He told me to go to the refrigerator for a beer and set it down in the living room. Then he jumped on my mother about serving him a cold dinner, even though he had come home two hours after she had put it on the table. When mom told me to go out and play, and I started out the door in defiance of my dad's order, he pulled off his belt in a blind rage and nearly beat me to death. My eye injury resulted from his belt buckle prong ripping into my face. All these years, I have wondered why he did that to me. What could I have done to justify his brutal punishment? I did nothing to deserve it." Colin's voice was suddenly tinged with anger, his face red and the veins in his neck bulging.

"That's so sick and twisted," said Val. "Buddy, I am so, so sorry."

Val now understood why Colin was so frightened of conflict. In high school and college, if someone threatened Colin or tried to push him into a fight, Val had to step in and save him. It appeared Colin was asking him to step in again.

"I still don't see the connection between Curtis and what happened to you," Val said, taking another gulp of wine. His face was numb after three glasses, and he was struggling to focus on Colin's words.

"You wouldn't understand," Colin said, cutting him off. "Besides, I don't need you to understand. I just need you to do me a favor. And I'll help you in return." Val sighed. He knew no more explanation was forthcoming. He also knew he urgently needed money that Colin could afford to give him. Forget motives. Val was no social worker.

"What do you want me to do?" Val asked.

"I want you to break into the rare book room of the Multnomah County Library, Central branch in Downtown Portland, and steal the Curtis books which contain my great-grandfather's photographs. It should be a straightforward job for you, especially since you're a security expert. You can easily get in and out undetected. I want you to bring the books back to me and I'll take care of your debt and more. You'll have money and a secure future. I'll even give you enough to pay your daughter's tuition until she gets her degree."

Colin's offer stunned Val. And gave him a feeling of elation as he realized Colin was offering him a lifeline—a way to win his family back and escape his debts.

"What's the value of the books?" Val asked, expecting Colin to give him some number in the hundreds of thousands.

"As a complete set, three million," Colin said. Val whistled, astonished at the value. "That would be a major felony. If caught, I would go to jail for 20 years. You could get the same."

"I'll take the blame," Colin said. "I'll say I blackmailed you, threatened to turn you over to your bookie. You'll be off the hook or will do minimum time, if any."

"Still, it's an enormous risk to you, your reputation, and all you've built."

"I don't care. Edward Curtis ruined the lives of generations of Byrnes. If he were alive, I would strangle him." Colin straightened his arms and thrust them out in front of himself, moving his hands left and right violently, as if choking some invisible being. His face was a snarl.

Val had never seen Colin so angry. He wanted to know more. "Colin, you're not thinking straight. There has to be more than one set of Curtis books, right?"

"In fact, there are. About 300 sets, each with 20 books."

"How is grabbing a third of the books from one set going to achieve your goal of revenge? It makes no sense?"

Colin looked at him as if he didn't hear the question—or didn't care. He only wanted to know if Val was in, then realized he needed to explain more.

"I'll make this short and sweet. Grandfather Byrne worked for Curtis from 1924 to 1930. During those years, Curtis produced the last seven volumes of the 20 books that comprise *The North American Indian*. Those seven books include photos taken by my grandfather, yet Curtis took credit for all of them. He gave Grandfather Byrne no recognition. I can't let the record stand. I want to get the seven books from the Portland Central Library and burn them to gain attention of every museum, university and private library that owns copies."

Val shook his head in disbelief as he listened to his friend who clearly had slid off the rails. "There is something you need to know. I was arrested for stealing from the security firm's clients to get gambling money. The resulting 10 months in jail was hell. I can't go back there."

"Are you in or out?" Colin asked, ignoring Val's confession of prison time and his concerns about getting caught.

"I need to think about it," said Val.

"Val, I'm sorry to do this. I'm sure you would love to have days or weeks to consider such a big ask. But I'm not giving it to you. You need me and I need you. Now is the time to decide." Weakened by Colin's emotional appeal and the wine, Val gave in.

"I'll do it," said Val. He was desperate. What choice did he have? It was his last chance to get the bookie off his back and win back his family.

"I'll call and make a reservation for you in town at a decent hotel, at least for the next month," said Colin. "When I get the books, I'll wire the money to pay off your gambling debt. I'll give you a job here at the winery so you can make some additional money to get you on your feet."

"One more thing," said Colin. "You need to get your gambling addiction under control. I want you to attend meetings at The Alano Club in Northwest Portland. My foundation contributes to their work. They're the best in the city. They have gambling addiction meetings on Saturdays."

For the next two hours, Val and Colin discussed the details of their deal. Colin then offered Val a job as a wine cellar assistant. During summers in college, he and Colin had worked odd jobs at various wineries. Colin continued in the wine industry, while Val, unable to play professional football because of his knee injury, decided sports broadcasting was a better fit for him.

"I'll call and arrange for you to have a Byrne Vineyard debit card with $1,000 for a hotel room, food, and incidentals. Forget plunking any of it down on a hunch. Stella monitors all card expenditures. She gets an email for every charge. I'll know if you buy a pack of gum or a pack of rubbers. That's the deal."

Exhausted and overwhelmed with the task in front of him, Val said, "It's getting late, Colin. I've got to get back to the city and walk and feed Mac. We'll talk tomorrow."

When he got outside, Mac was sleeping on the tasting room porch.

"Come on, Mac, let's go home." The dog jumped into the car and took up his spot in the passenger seat. He put his paws on the dashboard, looking out the front window.

Despite his renewed connection with Colin and possibility of getting out of his financial fix, Val felt alone. "You're my friend, aren't you, Mac?"

Mac turned his head, looked at Val, then jumped into his lap and licked his face.

CHAPTER 6

1

When Val returned to Portland from his dinner with Colin, it was after dark. Rather than find a new parking spot for the night, he returned to Portland Union Station, next to a line of tents. He could have gone to the hotel Colin had reserved for him. He felt safer being outside with the residents of a tent city, which housed a tiny contingent of Portland's 4,000 homeless. Why not? Val was homeless, and the other homeless had welcomed his presence—if only for one night so far—rather than make him feel like an intruder.

The next morning, after Val walked Mac, he dressed in yesterday's outfit, which created an air of success, and walked to the train station where he again used the men's room to wash up and prepare for his day. A station agent entered the bathroom while Val was shaving and wished him a pleasant journey. The agent must have assumed Val was a traveler freshening up before catching a train. Val thanked him, lied that he was heading to Southern California to visit family.

He returned to his car, filled dog bowls with water and food, then watched Mac dive into his breakfast. Val prepared a bowl of cereal and pulled out a banana, which he planned to cut up for his cereal. Unfortunately, Mac heard the snap of the peel, ran over, and sat down. Ever since Mac had acquired a taste for them, he could be in another room of the Val's apartment and come running when he heard the peel coming off. Val broke off pieces of banana, gave one to Mac and ate one. Odd, Val thought, that his dog loved bananas.

Val looked at his watch and realized he needed to leave for his 10 a.m. appointment for a look at Edward Curtis' *North American Indian* at the library.

2

Val drove two miles to Downtown Portland and found a shaded parking space in a pay lot near the library. He gave Mac one more bathroom break, poured some water into a bowl, cracked the windows, locked the doors, and walked down the street and around the corner to the entrance of the early 20th Century, Georgian-design building that filled an entire block. Inside, he walked through an entry area, where volunteers managed a friends-of-the-library used bookstore and into the massive lobby flanked by checkout stations and library assistants. Ahead of him was a grand staircase with granite steps and carved wood bannisters leading to the second and third floors. Tempted to sprint up them, he looked down at his cane and limped toward a nearby elevator behind one of the checkout desks. His cane was part of his disguise. He took the elevator to the second floor, got directions to the rare book room, and worked his way through the stacks to a more remote corner of the building. It was the perfect location for a valuable book collection, out of the way of everyday library traffic.

Lined up single file at the bottom of steep stairs leading up to the Wilson Room were nine people waiting for the tour. Val made ten. A few minutes later, a man stood at the top of the stairs. Without coming down, he introduced himself and read off the names of those who had signed up.

"Welcome everyone," he said. "I'm Bill Bowman, the curator of the John Wilson Collections and your guide for today's visit. Like all special collections, we must use care with the rare items you will see. No materials may leave the room. We cannot allow purses or backpacks. These security procedures help us protect the collection, which includes some of the rarest books in existence. Everyone clear on the rules?" They nodded. "Okay, come on up. When you get into the room, station yourself around the table. And don't touch!"

Val held back a few steps and used his limp and cane to give him the extra time he would need to assess the security systems. Toward the top of the steps, he noted a camera positioned to see anyone on the steps, checked the door and made a mental note of the lock. In his online research the previous evening, Val had determined Paragon Security Systems was the library's security provider.

Paragon was one of the best in the corporate security business. Its team, equally divided between men and women, were all ex-FBI agents, former detectives, or decorated cops who had retired early or had accepted buyouts offered during downsizings. Despite Paragon's powerhouse image, the library security measures were standard industry stuff. Effective, but not challenging for an individual schooled in counter-security measures, like Val. A good quality door lock secured the main door, while locked book cabinets would discourage pilfering, but would be easy for a security pro to defeat. Disconnecting the power supplies, including a back-up battery, would shut down the alarm system. With a screwdriver, Val could bypass it in less than a minute. Bowman looked out the door and saw that Val was still a few steps from the top. "Do you need some help?"

"I am almost there. Give me 30 seconds."

"Please close the door behind you when you come in," said Bowman.

"No problem."

3

Once inside the Wilson Room, Val moved into the circle of observers, gawking at a half dozen rare books laid out for viewing. Standing at the head of the table, Bowman displayed a broad smile, like a proud man waiting to introduce a daughter or son chosen as valedictorian. Before going to bed the night before, Val had logged onto his laptop to learn about Bowman as part of his security assessment. Bowman, 45, had earned a master's degree in library science. After a decade working his way up the library chain of command, he won the coveted job as curator for the library's John Wilson Special Collections.

Bowman's blue eyes stood out against prematurely white hair, like a speck of color in a black-and-white photo. No doubt he was serious about his job and protecting the collection at all costs. The job won out over fashion.

Laid out on the tabletop was a rare first edition of Dicken's Christmas Carol, a one-inch square book that contained the complete text of the King James Bible, and a book from Edward Curtis' *North American Indian*. Val's eyes locked on the Curtis book. When Bowman picked it up and opened it to a page with a haunting photo of a Salishan Indian Chief, the tour group gathered around. Val squeezed in behind them. The paper, quality of the printing, and the artistry of the portraits transported you 100 years into the past. You felt like you were in the room when the pictures were taken. Bowman closed the Curtis book and put it in a cabinet behind him and locked it up before moving on and describing the next book. Asked how a public library could afford rare books worth millions of dollars, Bowman said, "With generous book lovers, like John Wilson, whose donations helped grow our collection to 10,000 titles."

After 45 minutes, Bowman wrapped up his presentation and escorted everyone out. Exaggerating his limp so Bowman noticed his cane, Val turned around and introduced himself. "Hi, Mr. Bowman. I'm Robert Hill. Wonderful presentation. Thanks for taking time to share these amazing books with us."

"You're welcome," said Bowman, beaming.

During Bowman's presentation, Val's eyes had swept the room, assessing the security. He observed there were no additional cameras to record an intruder. Paragon apparently felt the remote location, in a far corner of the library, along with the high-quality entrance door camera and cabinet locks, provided ample protection. The on-site security guards were minimum wage staff with little more than basic training. Bowman escorted Val to the door and said goodbye. Val had taken two steps down when he heard Bowman lock the door behind him. Out of sight and alone, Val reached into his messenger bag and pulled out a jar of a petroleum jelly. He opened the jar and dug out enough to cover the end of his finger. He returned the jar to his bag, took two steps up, reached for the camera and coated the lens. Any recording would appear blurry. You wouldn't be able to recognize anyone who passed under it. If someone were monitoring it, which he doubted given small library budgets, their initial thought would be there was a software glitch or hardware malfunction. Getting someone to come in from the security company would probably take a couple of days. Val and the books would be long gone by then.

4

After lunch and another short walk with Mac, Val located a hardware store where he bought a screwdriver, a bump key, and latex gloves—standard burglar tools. Val loved the simplicity of the bump key. You insert the key into the lock and bump the end with a mallet, forcing the tumblers into the open position.

Once he had the needed tools to break in, he headed across town to Next Adventure, a popular outdoor store in Southeast Portland, to buy a dry sack, a waterproof bag used in water sports to keep personal items dry. He also bought a ski mask, ski pants and hooded sweatshirt in a basement full of used gear. Back at his parking spot near the train station, he reviewed his plan, assembled his gear in a backpack, and headed for the library.

CHAPTER 7

1

Standing at the entrance to City Park in The Dalles, a Columbia River town an hour from Portland, Bryan Byrne snapped a photo of a brown wooden sign with gold letters declaring it the end of the Oregon Trail. After a month on the road, suspended from his job—which his boss called a sabbatical—Byrne wondered if he also was at the end of his own trail. Would Canyon College take him back after attempting to steal pain pills at a pharmacy, then trying to cover it up?

City Park was as drab and dark as he felt. A little grass, a few trees, and some cement walkways. Nothing inspiring or special. Not a trace of the thousands of people, filled with hopes and dreams for a better life, who emigrated through The Dalles from Missouri to the Oregon Country in the mid-1800s.

Bryan was trying to make the most of his suspension, gathering new material for his popular course on pioneer trails of the west. Before his hip deteriorated, his sabbaticals, some lasting six months, rejuvenated him, boosting his enthusiasm for teaching. This time, his career was in a ditch and hiking in his favorite places was too painful, his hip screaming with each step. Mostly, he observed from his car or explored historic sites where a monument or scenic view was close by.

After a brief visit in Oregon City, the actual end of the Oregon Trail, Byrne drove into Portland, checked in at a hotel near the Portland Union Train Station, and headed downtown for lunch and a tour of a new Oregon history exhibit at the Oregon Historical Society. He had a 2 p.m. appointment at the John Wilson Special Collections at the Portland Central Library. Normally, he would include his border collie, Dino, in the day's activities. However, he knew his appointment to look at Edward Curtis' 20-volume *North American Indian* and other rare books could take up the afternoon and he didn't want to leave Dino in the car all day. Instead, he checked his companion into Noah's Arf, a doggie day spa.

Given his limited mobility, Byrne chose a taxi for his trip to the library, rather than search for parking downtown. The cab let him off at the library's front entrance. Looking at the ten steps to the front door, he gritted his teeth, locked his cane in his left hand to support his right hip, and fought his way up. Even 10 steps left him sweating—from the pain rather than the effort. He would need to double up on his hydrocodone. Inside the library, his eyes swept the lobby and locked on the grand staircase. That was a no-go.

A library staffer, who spotted his limp and cane, silently pointed to a corner of the lobby, and mouthed, "Elevator." On the second floor, he exited and asked for directions. Another jolt of reality for the disabled struck him when he arrived at the entrance to the Wilson Room: fifteen steep steps up. "I've got to do this," he said to no one.

He inched his way up to the Wilson and knocked. A moment later, the door swung open and Bill Bowman greeted him. "You must be Professor Byrne," said Bowman, smiling. Bowman liked showing off the book room to the public, but he especially loved interacting with historians and educators, people he felt could fully appreciate the collection.

"I recognize you from the picture on your *Trails and Travails* textbook. The men shook hands and Byrne followed him in.

Bowman, like he did with all visitors, reviewed the rules of handling books and other materials in the collection. They were not unlike the rules created to protect art and antiquities in public and private museums. "You mentioned in your registration note that you're gathering material for your history class," said Bowman.

"That's correct," said Byrne. "I have twelve students enrolled in my graduate course in *U.S. History: Trails and Travails of Western Explorations*. We use my textbook by the same name. I build a lot of the curriculum around my personal experiences following pioneer routes, documenting sights, sounds, historic markers, and museum exhibits in big cities and towns. I'll interview descendants of famous pioneers or explorers and include their pictures and oral histories. Most of the actual routes have been obliterated by modern highways or have deteriorated badly, disappearing after they were no longer used. The Oregon Trail is an example."

"No doubt you've visited The Dalles City Park," said Bowman. "Until 1846, the Oregon Trail ended in the Dalles, where emigrants loaded their belongings onto rafts for the trip down the Columbian River to Oregon City, the actual end of the trail."

"What a sad little place," said Byrne, shaking his head at the memory. "I was there this morning."

Bowman and Byrnes continued an academic version of small talk, trading knowledge about history, explorations, and settlements in the West for another fifteen minutes before the conversation came around to Edward S. Curtis.

"Tell me about your connection to Edward Curtis," Bowman said.

"Our family wasn't big on genealogy, family photos, or records of any kind," Byrne explained. "What I have is oral history. My great-grandfather, William Bryan Byrne, fell in love with photography after viewing Curtis' photos of Alaska. You may recall that railroad magnate Edward Harriman embarked on an epic journey in 1899, hiring two dozen scientists to explore and document their observations in the Alaskan wilderness. Curtis and an assistant were part of the expedition."

"Where does your great-grandfather fit in the Curtis story?" Bowman asked.

"He got himself hired as Curtis' photography assistant around 1924 and worked for him until 1930, when the last of edition of *The North American Indian* was published. Or so our family lore would have you believe." Bowman and Bryan traded knowledge of Edward Curtis' quest. With major financial support from J.P. Morgan, Curtis had hired a legion of men to assist him, among them William Bryan Byrne.

When they finished chatting, Bowman went to a locked cabinet, opened it, and pulled out volume 1 of *The North American Indian*. He placed the book in front of Byrne.

"It's beautiful," said Byrne, admiring the cover and binding. They were nearly 100 years old and in perfect condition.

"If your hands are clean and dry, touch it, turn the pages, and take your time looking at the photos," said Bowman.

"Don't I need gloves?" Byrne asked.

"Contrary to popular belief, you don't. The Library of Congress advises against it. And I've learned from experience that gloves dull the sensation of touch and make it easier to tear a page. Of course, your hands should be clean."

"Hang on," said Bowman, jumping up from the table, disappearing into another part of the room. When he came back, he opened a folder and handed it to Byrne. "This is my personal attempt at being a historian," said Bowman. "It's a list of all the people Curtis hired for his trips, along with their positions and background."

Byrne scanned through the list. "Here it is," he said. "I'll be darned. We always heard the stories, but we didn't really know if it was true or a family fable. William Byrne is listed. Great job, Bill. I wish I could award you a Ph.D. for your scholarship." Bowman beamed at the compliment.

"No doubt you've read Timothy Egan's Short Nights of the Shadow Catcher," said Byrne. "The subtitle of Egan's book is The Epic Life and Immortal Photographs of Edward Curtis."

"Of course," said Bowman. "The book details Curtis' passion to preserve Native American culture, along with the hardships he endured—including a failed marriage and money problems."

"I've read Egan's book twice," said Byrne. "Bill, I didn't mention this before because it could be hearsay, which librarians, history professors, and historians shouldn't pedal. I offer that caveat before I tell you. I've heard that Great-Grandfather Byrne may have kept journals during his seven years with Curtis."

Bowman's eyes got big. "Oh my God, wouldn't they be the find of the century."

Byrne told Bowman about dinner with his father, Colin, which was a few hours away.

"I'll ask Dad about the journals. Who knows, maybe he has them tucked away. I'll let you know what I find out."

Bowman smiled and nodded. He and Byrne knew the chances of finding personal accounts of the Curtis trek were a million to one.

CHAPTER 8

1

Bryan looked in the hotel mirror, cinched his tie, brushed off his coat, and hitched up his jeans over growing belly fat. "I'm presentable," he assured his reflection. He knew he was overdressed, especially with the temperature forecast to hit a high of 80 in the Willamette Valley. He also knew his father, Colin, would judge his appearance and comment on it. Bryan didn't want to give Colin another reason to disapprove of his only son. He had been bitterly disappointed Bryan chose teaching over following him into the wine business. Colin's dream was a father-son business with Bryan inheriting it all. But building a winery, producing wines, and marketing them didn't fire up Bryan's imagination. Not like history and the pioneers who settled the American West.

In college, Bryan had worked for his mother and father, helping wherever they needed it, from managing the tasting room to assisting the winemaker. The money was good. And he had learned the nuances of making excellent wine. One summer he fell in love—his first time. Memories of Stella Mason were still fresh. Before heading for the dinner with Colin, Bryan picked up Dino from Noah's Arf and tucked him in for the night at the Sniff Hotel, luxury canine accommodations in Northwest Portland. Bryan then drove 25 miles south to Newberg, Oregon, to Byrne Vineyards. Although Bryan and Colin talked on the phone a few times a year, this would be Bryan's first visit in nearly five years. When his dad invited him to come for a few days of rest and relaxation, he claimed that year-round classes and seminars left him little time to travel— beyond field trips which were part of his job. Some of that was true. Bryan preferred hiking and exploring remote and wild places over drinking wine and visiting tourist attractions. Thinking ahead to the expected multi-course dinner and abundant wine, Bryan figured he might stay overnight.

Driving up the long, winding road to the Byrne Vineyard Estate House, Bryan stopped at the top of a hill and got out of the car. He walked over into a row of vines, bent over, and picked up a handful of soil. With his eyes closed, he lifted the dirt to his nose. There was a sweetness to it. He stayed that way for a few seconds, then opened them. A sense of dread followed the moment of Zen. He and his father had gotten along except for a couple of Bryan's teen years.

After Bryan had pulled a prank that damaged a neighbor's prize rose garden, Colin had pulled out his belt and whipped it through the air. The chill of the memory came rushing back whenever he got close to his dad after an absence. His dad had appeared ready to explode and hit him with the belt. Instead, he rushed from the room and into his office down the hall. Bryan was stunned to hear his father sobbing through the closed door. His mother, who witnessed the incident, put her hands on Bryan's shoulders and said, "He's okay. He's suffering from a terrible memory." She didn't explain. Bryan didn't ask. Although Colin never again threatened Bryan with a belt, he yelled at him a lot. Once he put eight-year-old Bryan over his knee, pulled down his pants, and smacked him on the butt.

Bryan remembered one occasion when his angry father walked out to the garage and slammed his fist into the wall, creating a hole in the plasterboard, breaking his hand. Bryan never asked his mother what happened. He did not want to stir the dragon in the cave. Back in the present, Bryan pulled into a space in front of the tasting room. He walked up the steps, opened the door, and was face-to-face with Stella Mason, his dad's manager, and his first true love. So long ago, yet Stella's presence still made his heart race. Memories of secretly making love—losing their virginity together—in the old barn had him buttoning his jacket to avoid her seeing his growing erection.

"Bryan, how are you?" she said, hugging him. "Let me look at you." She held him at arms-length, quickly scanning him from head to toe. "You are as handsome as ever. How's the professor business?"

"Loving every minute," he assured her.

"Your dad is out on the terrace," said Stella. "I'll bring hors d'oeuvres in a few minutes." Before turning to leave, she turned and faced him, grabbed both of his hands, and said, "I'm sorry about your mom."

"Thanks. The grief hit me hard. I would have come but was in the backcountry collecting information for a course. By the time I got back into phone range and heard dad's message, Mom had been cremated and the memorial over."

"It hit Colin hard, too," said Stella. Bryan knew his father and mother were best friends and soul mates. Their marriage was rock-solid. He and his dad did not discuss the details of his mother's last days or taking her own life under Oregon's Death with Dignity Act. Given the pain her cancer was inflicting, he supported her decision.

"By the way," said Bryan. "You look great, too." They hugged again and looked into each other's eyes for a long moment before they snapped out of their daydream of what could have been. For two more summers, when Bryan was attending graduate school and came home to earn money for tuition, he and Stella were inseparable—and they fell in love. Bryan's decision to accept a teaching job in Arizona led to the eventual break-up. She wanted to stay in Oregon. They agreed to date other people rather than try to maintain a long-distance relationship.

Shortly after Bryan left for his new job, she found out she was pregnant. Bryan didn't learn about Stella giving birth until his dad mentioned it months after the fact. It didn't occur to him at the time that the child could be his. A year or two after Cindy was born, Stella briefly married, ending the relationship in an annulment. As far as Bryan knew, Stella had not remarried. For a moment, he wondered if he could convince her to move to Arizona and live with him, since he also was divorced. Of course, he wasn't sure he would even have a job to return to. His other choice was to quit teaching and join his dad in the business. He and Stella could pick up where they left off.

"How's your daughter?" Bryan asked.

"Cindy is fine. Full of energy. Doing very well in school. Outgoing. Cute. And, yes, boys have discovered her." Bryan smiled. Cindy could have been his, he thought. The time between Bryan's departure and the discovery of her pregnancy was very short. She had admitted that the pregnancy resulted from a one-night stand, her reaction to Bryan leaving, choosing the job over her. Bryan wanted her to move with him. She wanted to stay close to family.

"Guess I better go see dad," Bryan said. Their hands touched and then pulled apart as he turned and walked out to the terrace.

2

"You're looking sharp," Colin said as Bryan stepped onto the terrace.

"Thanks, Dad. Glad you approve." The words came out more defensive than Bryan intended. Colin raised an eyebrow but said nothing.

"So, how are you?" Colin asked, although he already knew.

"Not bad. I'm taking time off to smell the roses, exploring dusty backwaters and rural roads that were once the Oregon Trail—part of my plan for a new curriculum."

Bryan nervously picked up a glass of wine from the table and took two big gulps, hoping to dull the pain in his hip and reduce the stress he felt anytime he was in his father's presence.

"Whoa, partner!" said Colin. "That wine is $150 a bottle—a special pre-dinner taste." Colin and Bryan's eyes locked on each other. The resemblance was uncanny. As Bryan got older, they looked even more alike.

"How are you, really?"

Bryan thought about telling a story but knew instinctively his dad already suspected something wasn't right beyond the cane and the limp. Before Bryan could answer, Colin said, "I know all about your sabbatical, which is a forced leave of absence."

"How could you know about that?" Bryan asked, his jaw clinching, his face red, and the veins in his neck pulsing. "I didn't tell you."

"Easy, son. Dean Watkins is a friend of mine. He keeps me up on school happenings." Colin said it casually, as if to say, why shouldn't he know.

"I ought to bring a civil suit against Watkins for a major breach of my confidentiality. I'll bet a big fine would clamp his mouth shut," Bryan yelled.

"Since when did you become Dean Watkins' pal?" he added.

"Since I donated $250,000 toward development of a new history wing and offered help with a major fundraising campaign."

"You did what?" Bryan squeaked, choking on his words. He stood up and backed away from the table like his dad was a snake. Stella heard Bryan's cry and rushed into the room.

"Is everything okay?" she asked, her head swiveling from Colin to Bryan, waiting anxiously for a response.

"Dad just surprised me with his very generous donation to my college's fundraising campaign for a new history wing."

"Thanks, Dad," he said. Stella smiled. "Enjoy your dinner," she said, and left the room.

As he calmed down, Bryan remembered from faculty planning meetings that there would be enhanced digital capabilities for master's and Ph.D. programs at the college.

"You're spying on me?"

"No, the Dean offered to keep an eye on you as a favor. Call it a father's prerogative."

"A clear invasion of my privacy," thought Bryan. "I'll have a little talk with the dean when I return to school."

"I thought you hated my job—thought my career was a lost cause?"

"Hate is too strong. I thought it was a waste of your talents as a budding winemaker. Yes, I tried to discourage you. I wanted you to join me in the wine business. But I'm proud of what you've accomplished."

Bryan choked up at his dad's declaration of being "proud." He could not remember his dad ever using the word. "Okay, fair enough. I guess it's okay for a parent to worry," said Bryan. "I get parent inquiries all the time checking on the progress of their son or daughter, trying to squeeze me for information. Since I know these college kids reveal very little to their parents, I feel okay sharing. And every bit I have shared was a confidentiality break. I still think it was justified when a student was in academic jeopardy."

"You know the main reason the dean has kicked me to the curb," said Bryan. "This hip is so bad I can't get enough pills to quiet the pain. My doctor is cutting me off at the end of the month."

"So, you stole drugs from a pharmacy?" Colin said, frowning. "Why don't you get the damn hip fixed?"

Bryan winced at the criticism. At least his dad did not pull out his belt and threaten him.

Bryan told the story of the gossipy old lady in line, his impatience to get his pain meds, reaching over the counter to grab a bottle of hydrocodone. "When caught, I made up a story. Said I was sorry. I thought it was my prescription. Just in a hurry to get going. Luckily, the pharmacist didn't call the police. He called Dean Watkins, his best friend."

"Do you need money to get the hip fixed?", Colin asked.

"As long as they don't fire me, I'm okay. I've scheduled hip replacement surgery, but the surgeon is booked for the next three months."

With Colin's generous support for the new history building, Bryan felt he might be safe from being fired. In the meantime, he needed a reliable source of pain pills. "It would be embarrassing to the college if the person whose name will be on the building had been fired, don't you think?" Colin asked.

"My name will be on the building? I don't know what to say. Thanks, Dad. You're the donor, you earned the money, your name should be up there."

"Not interested. Besides, the deal is done," said Colin. Bryan knew that once his dad decided there was no changing it.

Colin smiled and said, "You're welcome."

While they were discussing Bryan's predicament, Stella walked in with hors d'oeuvres.

"Hi, guys, here's something to hold you until dinner arrives."

"I might be able to help with the pain issue," said Colin. "I give lots of money every year to Oregon Health & Science University to support research and other programs. I have a friend there. He's a professor of medicine and a member of the hospital board. He can connect you with a pain specialist. I'll text him this evening and ask for an urgent appointment."

Bryan let out a sigh of relief. He sat up taller, feeling the lift of optimism replace the recent angst. Bryan smiled at his dad's efforts to help. "I appreciate your help very much." Bryan said. Colin smiled back, a rare moment of father-son love. Colin rarely showed his feelings.

A moment later, Byrne Vineyard's chef set down two Caesar salads and announced the dinner menu: bacon-wrapped Harris Ranch filet mignon, potatoes au gratin, asparagus, and Crème Brule for dessert.

"My favorites," said Bryan, his face lighting up.

"I know," said Colin, smiling, his way of reinforcing the idea that he cared about Bryan and would not have forgotten what Bryan liked and disliked.

"Dad, this afternoon I visited the rare book room at the Central Library. It's called the John Wilson Special Collections and contains about 10,000 books, including Charles Dickens first editions from the mid-1800s. The collection has the complete *North American Indian* set. Because of our family connection, the curator, Bill Bowman, gave me extra time to page through Curtis' work. I remember you telling me that great-granddad Byrne loved photography. Any chance he took any of the pictures?"

"Damn right, he did," Colin shots back, his face suddenly red, covered with a scowl. Taken aback, Bryan waited for his dad to say more. Just as quickly as Colin had turned furious, the anger melted away.

"I might know something about that," Colin whispered, then abruptly stopped as he felt a sudden sharp pain in his eye—the missing eye. The one his father destroyed with his belt buckle.

"You okay, dad?"

"Give me a second."

"I probably never told you, but ever since I lost my eye in the car accident, I get phantom pains. The doctor isn't sure why." Colin had been telling the car accident lie his entire life. He wasn't ready to reveal the truth to his son. Describing what happened would be like ripping off a scab.

"I'm okay now," said Colin. "They go nearly as fast as they come."

Rather than jump back into the conversation about Edward Curtis, Colin turned to his wine business. "We've added 20 more acres of pinot grapes, doubled production, and have won five awards the past two years," said Colin, smiling, puffing out his chest.

"Dad, that's amazing."

"And, when I die, it's all yours.".

"Dad, you've created a great winery. I'm proud of what you have accomplished. I know you wish mom was here to share it. As far as inheritance, that's very generous. Of course, I would welcome it. I won't lie about that. By the time you die, I might be ready for retirement from teaching and happy to while away my days drinking superb wine and overseeing this estate." They both laughed. The tension over Bryan's career choice melted away.

Before Colin could say it, Bryan added, "Yes, I know I could come to work with you any time I want. I'll never say never. Right now, though, I'm content where I am—assuming I can ever get back to work." Despite Colin's donation, Bryan still worried about getting fired. His dad's donation to the college, he thought, was no guarantee he wouldn't get thrown out.

He could find a teaching job in Oregon and reconnect with Stella. He had met her daughter as a little kid years ago when he came for a visit. Bryan couldn't help thinking she looked like him. Was Cindy his daughter? Her hair was jet black like his. Her deep blue eyes were also a match. Both were Black Irish traits. He pushed the thought out of his mind with more visions of the last time he and Stella made love. Did Stella really have a one-night stand, or did she make up the story?

After Colin and Bryan finished dinner, they moved into the house for dessert. The warm day had turned to a 40-degree evening and Stella had lit a roaring fire in the massive stone fireplace.

"A few nights ago," said Colin, "I went to the basement, opened a box with a few of my dad's personal items. Inside, I found seven leather-bound books."

"What books?"

"They appear to be journals, describing Grandfather Byrne's life as part of the Curtis expedition."

Bryan couldn't believe his ears. "Where are they?" said Bryan, suddenly on his feet—the look on his face like a kid waiting to open presents on Christmas morning.

"I threw them in the fireplace."

"Oh my God, you did what?" said Bryan, his mouth dropping open. "Dad, they're treasure—a piece of history."

"I didn't think they were important," said Colin, trying to suppress a smirk.

Bryan dropped into a chair and said, "Those were the lost journals Bill Bowman and I discussed earlier today. I had heard they existed, but no one had any idea where to look."

Reaching down to the side of the sofa, Colin lifted a bag and handed them to Bryan. "They are right here. I read several passages that made me furious: how

Edward Curtis discounted your great-grandad Byrne's work. I got angry and did throw them into the fireplace, but Stella retrieved them before lighting the morning fire." Despite the revelation about Curtis and his grandfather, Colin wasn't ready to tell Bryan about the connection to his missing eye and scar on his cheek. Or the other scars.

"Take them with you," said Colin. "Read them and then let me know what you think. Share them with Bill Bowman, if you like. I have no use for them." Bryan gave his father a questioning look. When Colin offered no explanation, Bryan let the subject drop.

The journals were pure gold—the discovery of a lifetime for a history professor working at a small, private college. They could be the source of a future book that would give Professor Bryan Byrne's academic work national recognition.

"Bryan, I have one more thing to share," said Colin. "Val James came to dinner last night."

"Wow, there's a name I haven't heard in a long, long time," said Bryan. "How is he?"

"Sadly, he has a gambling addiction, lost his home and his wife. His daughter was forced to take a job to stay in school because he burned through the trust fund set up for her tuition. He was living in his car with his dog, so I had Stella rent a hotel room and give him a debit card with cash. I've also offered him a job here at the winery." He did not mention the deal to pay off Val's bookie or the plan to steal the Curtis books. Bryan listened and nodded, bringing Val's face into his mind.

"Sorry to hear about Val," said Bryan. "Nice of you to help. I know he's your best friend."

"He'll be okay," said Colin. "I've also enrolled him in a gambling addiction program. He's really a great guy and just needs a helping hand to turn himself around."

Bryan had considered spending the night. Now, he wanted to get back to his hotel room and dive into great-granddad's journals.

"I need to get going before dark, Dad. Just noticed a headlight out," he lied.

"Are you sure you're okay to drive?"

"I'm fine. I'll stay off the freeway. In 30 minutes, I will be tucked away safely in my room, reading. I'll text you to confirm my safe arrival." Bryan was already dreaming about the book he would write. An award-winning book. A book reaching across history, linking him with his great-grandfather, William Bryan Byrne, and Edward Curtis' plan to record disappearing native North American culture.

CHAPTER 9

1

Bryan Byrne struggled up the stairs, taking each step slowly as he climbed toward the Wilson Room and a second meeting with Bill Bowman.

Unlike the previous day, when each step sent a jolt of pain through his hip joint, new pain medication allowed him to relax and enjoy a few pain-free hours. His father had come through as promised. He had tapped his source at Oregon Health & Science University late the night before and got him an early morning appointment with a pain specialist, Madison Miller. When Bryan arrived, Miller ordered an X-ray and conducted a physical exam, confirming the diagnosis of a deteriorated hip.

After examining Bryan, the doctor prescribed a long-acting morphine derivative to eliminate the need for hydrocodone. The morphine, she said, would smooth the hills and valleys of Bryan's pain. Dr. Miller also convinced Bryan's surgeon—a friend from medical school—to move him to urgent status, scheduling the surgery in a month, instead of three. Good old dad. Colin Byrne knew how to make things happen.

At the top of the stairs leading to the rare book room, Bill Bowman swung open the door the moment Bryan knocked, a wide grin on his face. When Bryan called to tell Bowman that he had possession of the lost journals they had discussed the day before, Bowman cleared his schedule so he and Bryan could devour them.

Bryan pulled the journals out of a bag and carefully laid them on a massive oak table in the middle of the room. They were made of a well-worn, tanned cowhide, about six-by-eight inches.

Bowman couldn't take his eyes off them as Bryan talked. He was like a chocoholic within arms-reach of See's Candy.

"I started reading the first one last night," said Bryan. "The detail is staggering. Great granddad meticulously documented major activities—and some mundane ones, like an exotic dinner made with several species of wild game." Bowman sat up straight, waiting for Bryan to reveal more.

"In the first year, William Byrne took at least a dozen photos which were credited to Curtis. Apparently, he took on photography assignments when Curtis was sick or needed to leave to raise money to keep his expedition alive. At some point, the Curtis treks got so big and complex, they were more than even the fabulously wealthy J.P. Morgan was willing to support. The frequency of these requests for William Byrne to take Native American portraits increased with the strain of work and the financial stress, as well as family problems, plaguing Curtis. It's a new window into the creation of *The North American Indian*."

"Bill, in my meager research over the years into the Curtis expeditions, I recall reading a story about an incident involving Curtis and his brother, Asahel. Do you remember what happened?

"I know what I read in Timothy Egan's book on Curtis' life." said Bowman. "Egan details how the Curtis brothers had a row when Asahel complained to Edward that Edward was taking credit for photos Asahel took. Edward blew off his brother's complaint, saying all the work produced was his, and his alone."

"That's where I read it," said Bryan. "Remind me how the brothers' dispute played out?"

"Asahel dropped out of the business," said Bowman, "which was responsible for printing, binding, and distributing Edward Curtis' Indian portraits and his books. They never spoke again."

"I wonder if there's a mention of the Curtis brothers' dispute in William Byrne's notes," said Bryan. "So far, I haven't read about any conflicts. That may have occurred in later years."

Bryan handed Bill the first journal, dated 1924. Bill studied the front, turned it over, noting the stains and wear on the leather, like a well-worn saddle. When he turned to the first page, the writing was an elegant cursive. Perhaps to save space, Granddad Byrne had kept the writing small—the equivalent of 10-point type on the printed page.

"These are so beautiful," said Bill. "When can I read them?"

"Since I've read the first one, I'll leave it with you," said Bryan.

Bill's face bit up, his eyes big and his smile wide

"By the way, Bill, dad says he doesn't want the journals and told me to do what I like with them. First, I want to catalog key dates and locations mentioned and eventually use the information to create a new graduate-level class based on great-grandad's writings. Publishing a book of the entire work with commentary and historical perspective would be an incredible addition to any individual collector or institution holding a complete set of *The North American Indian*. Your collection could eventually make a suitable home for the journals."

"If I can help you collect and digest the information you need for a class, please ask," said Bill.

"That's very generous," said Bryan. "Would you consider co-authoring the book?"

Bowman was grinning from ear to ear. "Writing and publishing an important historical work is a lifelong dream," he said. "You won't have to twist my arm. I'm all in."

Bill and Bryan agreed to talk more after they both had time to review the journals.

"I'd love to stay here all day and speed-read through the journals with you and kick around the findings," said Bryan. "But I've got a meeting scheduled at the Oregon Historical Society research library in 15 minutes to help build my course on the Oregon Trail."

Working with Bowman on a history book taken from the William Byrne journals could speed it to press and give Bryan's career the boost he needed. National recognition might generate offers from larger, more prestigious universities. His spirits lifted by the thought, he could visualize a different future. He could move to a university in Oregon and marry Stella. If he found a teaching position at Oregon State University, they could buy a home halfway between the winery and the university. As he stood at the foot of the Oregon Historical Society steps, he wanted to run up, like the fighter Rocky Balboa, throw his hands in the air and yell. That will have to wait, he thought, until he had a new hip. It would be one more thing to celebrate.

CHAPTER 10

1

Val James was nearly ready to begin his new life—a life with no more debt, a daughter's tuition paid for, and hopefully a wife he could lure back with a solemn promise not to gamble. He wasn't sure he could make good on that last promise. He would sure as hell try. Colin had given him a lifeboat. It might be the only one he would ever get. Jump on or sink into the depths.

Val had no intention of sinking back into his ocean of guilt, anxiety, and failure, fueled by his gambling addiction. Now, all he had to do was steal the books Colin wanted and risk a hefty prison sentence, if caught. Of course, the value of the books was for a complete set, in good condition—not a partial set with seven volumes missing. A lower value, he thought, might translate to a lighter jail sentence.

As part of Val's pre-theft planning, he researched the Curtis book project. He wanted to understand the project scope and significance, as well as opening a window on Colin's motives for stealing them. Val discovered that with $75,000 from J.P. Morgan in 1906, Curtis launched a two decade-long quest to photograph, record, and document the people and culture of rapidly disappearing native peoples in Canada and the U.S. *The North American Indian* was the result.

Despite financial hardships and a divorce, Curtis would print nearly 300 20-book sets—one of which lived in the Portland Central Library, his target. A website dedicated to Curtis' 20-volume work stated that Curtis took 40,000 photos over 23 years. Along with thousands of pictures, the books contain 5,000 pages of text.

Curtis died penniless, living in a one-bedroom apartment in Seattle, Washington. The apartment, according to news reports, held a complete set of *The North American Indian*, which went to his family. At the time of his death, there was little market for his work. There was no mention whether the family sold it off for a few hundred dollars or a few thousand.

Val found the Curtis' New York Times obituary, dated October 1952:

> *Edward S. Curtis, internationally known authority on the history of The North American Indian, died today at the home of a daughter, Mrs. Beth Magnuson. His age was 84. Mr. Curtis devoted his life to compiling Indian history. His research was done under the patronage of the late financier, J. Pierpont Morgan. The foreword [sic] for the monumental set of Curtis books was written by President Theodore Roosevelt. Mr. Curtis was also widely known as a photographer.*

2

Over the past 24 hours, Val had scouted the library's rare book room where the Curtis books were located, bought the clothes and tools he would need for the break-in, and had assessed security. He knew the routine of the two guards on duty, the location of the single security camera, and the schedule of Bill Bowman, the John Wilson room curator. Val was nearly ready to carry out the plan. He needed to complete one more important task: contact his wife and daughter. Call them one more time in case something went wrong. It might be the last time they communicated.

Before calling, he texted each saying he had important, life-altering news to report. He wrote he would really appreciate the opportunity to speak to each of them for a few minutes. He noted their lives would be affected by a decision he had made.

A few minutes after sending the text, Val dialed his wife, Marion.

"Hi, Val," she answered. Nothing followed. He knew she didn't care how he was doing. He couldn't blame her after the public humiliation he had put her through once the media revealed that their local hero had stolen from the clients of his security company employer. "Hi, babe. I'll make this quick. I've turned the corner on my gambling. Colin Byrne and I just met, and he has pledged to help me. Rather, he will help us in exchange for me working at his winery. He's agreed to pay off the debt I owe to my bookie, provide you with a no-interest mortgage that will come out of my paycheck, and provide Melanie with full college tuition that will take her through graduation. The tuition will be a gift. Colin said the deal is only valid if I join Gamblers Anonymous. He has arranged for that to happen. That's all I have to say."

Marion didn't interrupt.

"I love you, Marion, and I'm really sorry."

"It's too late for sorry," she said. "But I don't want to be negative. Good luck in the new job and your effort to quit gambling."

"I know you need to wait and see if this will happen as promised. I'm hoping. I'll try my best."

"I have to go, Val. Bye." She hung up.

Next, he dialed his daughter, Melanie. She did not pick up the phone or answer his text. Given what he had put her through, he wasn't surprised. Losing her tuition money and the need for her to take a full-time job to pay for school nearly resulted in her flunking out. With two small scholarships and tips from her waitressing job, she had pulled her grades out of basement and had remained in school. Val texted, "Call Mom. I talked to her just now. She can tell you why I was trying to reach you."

3

Dressed in a ratty jacket and backpack, Val blended in with other patrons, many of them homeless people using the library's computers, charging their phones, and hiding from the weather—air conditioned in the summer and warm on wintry days. He waited until 6:30 pm, a half hour before closing, to enter the library. Before entering, he packed his cane away and strolled into the main lobby. He smiled and nodded to a staff member at the check-out desk, then took the stairs to the second floor.

Val inconspicuously moved among the stacks, out of the sight of the reference librarians. A few minutes later, he was standing below the Wilson Room and the steep staircase he had ascended for his tour. He looked at his watch. He pulled out a book and pretended to read. At 7 p.m., Bill Bowman locked up, walked down the steps from his book room, and turned toward the grand staircase that led to the first floor and outside.

Val looked around, saw no one, and walked to a classroom in a corner, 25 feet from the Wilson Room entrance. He checked the schedule on the door and confirmed there were no evening classes. He jimmied the lock, stepped inside, relocked the door, and closed the blinds. He pulled out a black t-shirt, black jeans, black hooded sweatshirt, black balaclava, and his metal cane—an adjustable hiking pole he used for backpacking. If caught in the building, he could claim he was disabled and unable to move fast enough to get out before closing time. He could hope they would not ask to search his backpack. If they did, they would find dirty underwear and socks, greasy rags, a roll of toilet paper, paper cups, and canned food—enough to discourage their need for him to dig under the detritus where the Curtis books would sit in his massive backpack.

When he finished dressing, he turned out the classroom lights and reopened the blinds. He didn't see anyone, so got down on the floor and pushed himself and his pack into a dark recess under a long table. Val determined that around 7:30 p.m. a guard would make a last check of the area, peer into the dark room, see no lights—and no evidence of stragglers—and move on.

Like clockwork, the guard arrived on time, looked in, rattled the door to make sure it was locked, and moved on. Val waited five minutes before climbing out from under the table, exiting the classroom, and moving to the bottom of Wilson Room staircase. His tennis shoes were silent on the wood steps as he climbed up. Before moving under the security camera, which he had smeared with petroleum jelly on the previous day, he put his head down so only the top of his black hoodie was visible. Even with a clear lens, the camera recorder would have a hard time registering images, with almost no light coming in. At the most, the recording would show a blurred, dark form near the Wilson Room door.

Val pulled out a bump key, inserted it into the lock, and bumped the end with the mallet. The internal pins lined up, allowing him to open the lock. As he stood at the room entrance, he reached into his bag and pulled out a pair of infrared goggles, and looked around. With the goggles, the dark room appeared brightly lit. He walked to the cabinet with the Curtis books and used a screwdriver to force open the locked wood cabinet. He located volumes 14 to

20 of *The North American Indian*, pulled them out of the bookcase and placed them on a table. He stopped for a moment and wondered if he should grab an 1894 first edition of Charles Dickens' Great Expectations, worth $40,000, that he had spotted on his tour of the rare book room. If Colin failed to come through with his promised deal, Val could use the Dickens' book as a source of cash. He pulled the Dickens book off the shelf and then put it back. "I don't need more trouble," he said to himself.

Just as he was about to put the last Curtis book into his bag, a light went on. The light momentarily blinded him; the infrared goggles turned the room's normally soft overhead light into a flood lamp. Val threw off the goggles, spun around and looked toward a blurry figure.

"What the hell are you doing in here?" said an elderly, gray-haired guard with a bushy white mustache and a pot belly. "Looks like it was a good thing I returned to check the Wilson Room door."

Val squinted at the guard while his eyes fought to adjust to the light.

"Bill Bowman arranged for me to come by and pick up these books for the Oregon Historical Society," stammered Val, who then identified himself as Robert Hill. Regaining his composure, Val insisted he was following instructions.

"And why were you wearing infrared goggles when you could have turned on the light?" the guard asked. "Not to mention the library is closed. I'm not buying your story, fella."

"I'm an amateur sleuth and always wanted to try out the goggles. They're a hobby."

The guard wasn't convinced.

"Mr. Bowman is very particular about what goes in and comes out of this room. He would have planned weeks before, alerted security, and had one of us accompany you. More likely, he would have delivered the books himself."

"I can explain," said Val, trying to stall with one more story before he could figure out how to get out of the room and avoid jail.

"You can explain to the police," the guard said, picking up his radio and thumbing the mic to call for backup and the Portland Police Bureau.

Panicked, Val grabbed his metal hiking stick. He swung it like a baseball bat, aiming for the radio in the guard's hand.

The guard saw the pole coming but couldn't get his hands up fast enough to protect himself. Instead of knocking the radio out of the guard's hand, Val swung high, the sharp metal tip of the pole slashing the guard's neck. The guard's eyes went wide as he touched his neck and realized blood covered his hand. "You've killed me," the guard cried. Val's momentum from his poor aim sent his hand smashing through a glass-front cabinet door, slicing open two fingers.

Val looked at the surprise on the man's face and the words coming out of his mouth, but had not yet processed what it all meant. One minute, he was in the dark finishing his task, ready to move onto new and better times, the next he was watching the guard's legs buckle and his eyes closing as he fell.

For a moment, Val thought about calling 9-1-1, administering first aid to stop the bleeding and wait for the police and ambulance to arrive. Turn himself in. Confess. Take Colin down with him. In that same moment, he visualized death row or death in jail from friends of the bookie he had stiffed. No matter how he looked at it, his life would soon end—and the end would not be pretty.

Val knew he had to make a run for it. He grabbed the books, including one on the floor next to the bleeding guard. There was blood on the bookbinding. And on pages from Val's cut. He pulled off his cloth mask and wrapped it around his hand to help stop the bleeding. He wiped the blood on his pants, trying to clean off the bloody pages the best he could. There was no more time if he wanted to escape. He put the last book into his backpack, closed it, and climbed under the 50-pound weight. With the waist belt and chest straps secure, he headed down the stairs.

Val's heart was racing, his head spinning. He took a last look at the guard, blood spreading out onto the carpet, and then at his own fingers under the bloody mask he wrapped around his hand.

"What have I done?" he cried. "What have I done?" The guard was dead. The rare, precious Curtis books had blood on them. And now he had blood on his hands, literally and figuratively. Once again, he had lived up to his reputation in recent years as a loser.

Thinking about how he had harmed Marion and Melanie, tears streamed down his face. Wiping his eyes and nose on his sleeve, he knew the only way to help his family was to get the money from Colin. Whether he was executed or locked in a jail cell the rest of his life, his wife and daughter, at least, would live a comfortable life. He would never know. He knew he would never see his wife again.

Walking quietly through the library toward a side exit he had scouted, Val stopped to watch the second guard move up the stairs and enter a room across from his location. Once the guard was out of sight, he moved down the marble stairs, creating a wisp of sound with his sneakers. A minute later, he was on the street and headed away from the library.

CHAPTER 11

1

She was floating in a cool, deep pool of calm water on a warm summer day. A few feet away, the gurgling stream rushed past. Hovering in the water, she moved her fins just enough to maintain her position. From above, a wiggling form appeared, drifting toward her. A primordial memory in her primitive fish brain created a surge of energy, propelling her toward the dangling creature, food to sustain her.

With three tail thrusts she was on the worm, swallowed it, then relaxed for just a second before moving away, back into the deep. Suddenly constrained, her head jerked up, a force pulling her through the water, away from her safe place below. She broke the surface, leaping into the air for a moment before crashing back into the water, racing to the depths of the pool. She was desperate to get away. Her long, sleek body was fighting against the upward pull. With another tail thrust, she pushed herself down. Again, the counter force steadily pulled her upward.

Terrified, she fought the pull for another minute until she was exhausted. As her will weakened and energy drained from her body, a web of foreign material entangled her, digging into her flesh, then lifted her from the water. Her gills, hungry for oxygen, were useless in the air.

A massive thing she couldn't comprehend encircled her body, pulling her free of the webbing. Her eyes wide open, an alien creature came into focus, turning her this way and that, admiring the slashes of pink, greenish-blues, and cocoa browns on her skin. The thing squeezed her so tight she couldn't move or breathe.

A moment later, pain electrified her body as an object was inserted into the opening below her anal fin. Her lips opened and closed, gasping for air. The pain was searing as her chest exploded from the force of the object inside her, pushing out along the length of her body. Now she recognized it. It was a knife. The alien creature she saw was a human, a fisherman. After cutting her open, the man grabbed her insides and pulled them out. She screamed, but the language she spoke was not a language the man understood. Holding her in one hand, he looked at what he had pulled from her body. It was the fetus of an unborn child.

2

Kim Jansen screamed, still in the grip of her fish-gutting nightmare. Now, a new alien thing wrapped itself around her body. She tried to swat it away. It was no use. She couldn't move.

Jansen's eyes flew open. The thing grabbing her, she realized, was her husband, Jim Briggs. He was holding her arms to her sides, hugging her.

"Kimmy, it's okay. You had a nightmare," said Briggs. Her body relaxed.

A familiar ringing sound on her nightstand brought her fully awake. Briggs let Kim go so she could reach for her cell phone. Instead of picking it up, she waited until it went silent. A flashing light showed a waiting message, time of call: 11:03 p.m. Jansen dialed voicemail and listened to the message, put down the phone, and rolled on her side, away from Briggs.

Her boss, Capt. Michael Melrose had awakened Jansen, a detective for the Portland Police Bureau. "Call me," he said. "It's urgent. A possible homicide. I need you to go to the scene. Det. Alice Munson called in sick tonight. You're next up on the duty roster. A guard was critically wounded during a burglary at the Central Library on 10th Avenue downtown."

"Don't touch me," she warned Briggs as he moved in to hug her. "I feel hollowed out. My entire body is tingling."

"The same dream about the angler?" Briggs asked. She nodded.

Her nightmare was always about her as a beautiful rainbow trout, pulled from the river, then gutted. The bloody fetus she saw in the dream was that of the unborn daughter she had lost when a suspect jammed a knife into her pregnant belly, impaling her. Lily Mary Briggs had been days from being born.

Doctors saved Jansen, but the knife had fatally pierced Lily's heart. A team of surgeons worked for hours to repair the damage and keep Lily alive before moving her to the neonatal intensive care unit. Initially, they were optimistic she would survive. Briggs could touch Lily's hand through the opening in the incubator. Kim never had the opportunity. She didn't regain consciousness until 10 days after the emergency surgeries. That was a year ago, just days after Jansen had been promoted from patrol sergeant to detective.

What started as a routine traffic stop had turned into a tragedy. Jansen had responded to a call for help after another officer pulled a man over for running a red light. When the officer checked his computer for wants or warrants, an alert appeared, "Caution, 211 suspect should be considered armed and dangerous." The car matched one seen leaving the scene of a fast-food store robbery.

When Jansen arrived, the patrol officer covered the suspect with his gun while she approached. With her own weapon in hand, she commanded him to put his hands on the car roof. When he complied, Jansen holstered her weapon, pulled out her handcuffs, and moved behind him. Normally, she would have patted him down. All she could remember from that day was how her pregnancy made bending over for a search difficult. Instead, she had cuffed one wrist and had told the suspect to put his other hand back. Instead, he pulled a eight-inch hunting knife from his belt, swung his arm backward, plunging it into Jansen's abdomen. The other officer shot and killed the suspect, called for an ambulance, and attempted to stop Jansen's bleeding. His efforts and the emergency crew kept her alive long enough to transport her to a nearby level 1 trauma center.

After recovering, she suffered through months of psychological counseling and physical therapy before she was cleared for duty. To the untrained eye, the scar on her abdomen appeared to have resulted from a Caesarian Section.

Known among her fellow officers for her fearlessness in the field, Jansen suppressed her emotions. Inside, she was shaky. The invincibility she had once felt was gone, along with some of the optimism she had about life. Still, Jansen convinced a department therapist she was fine, ready for duty. The scary dreams told a different story. She wouldn't share those with the department shrink.

While she continued to suffer the nightmares, Jim Briggs suggested getting pregnant again might help deal with her grief, changing her focus from what will never be, to what could be. She wasn't ready to give him an answer because the answer would be, "No, never, not in this lifetime." She never wanted children. Had no maternal instinct. When she found out she was pregnant, her first thought was to get a prescription for abortion pills. But her husband wanted children. When she told Briggs she was pregnant, he was excited and proposed marriage. Jansen was caught up in the moment and never told him about her intention to end the pregnancy. Now, after she had lost Lily, her feelings about not having children had returned stronger than ever. She just hadn't figured out the right time to tell Briggs.

CHAPTER 12

1

Thirty minutes after Chief Melrose called, Jansen was at the public library. She had walked the mile from her and Briggs' condo in the Portland Pearl District to unwind after the fish-gutting nightmare. Crime scene tape blocked the front steps of the library with a uniformed officer protecting the entrance. Jansen ducked under the tape and greeted the officer with a fist bump and said, "Hey, Jeff, how are you?"

"Great Kim, how about you?"

"Fine, thank you," she lied.

Jansen had been Jeff Maddox's supervisor in the patrol division. "Kelly is about to have our first baby," said Maddox.

"Great news," said Jansen, her stomach clenching, managing a smile despite her own misfortune.

Inside the library, Jansen admired the beauty of the place, soaring ceilings and grand staircase. She had been in the Central Library many times with Briggs, who was a genealogy nut and spent time every week researching his family. He could easily access online databases from his laptop at home. But at 6-feet-6, Briggs loved the airy feeling of the 27-foot-high ceilings. And he had made friends with several reference librarians who helped him with searches.

Taking her time on her walk up to the crime scene, Jansen stopped along the way to enjoy artwork and book displays. She was a voracious reader and loved hanging out at the library. Before the stabbing, she would have raced to the scene, pushing people out of the way to get there first. After her near-death experience, she had adopted a new philosophy, one she thought was best expressed by a phrase she read in the book of one of her favorite authors: "Carpe diem, every damn day." Yes, she would seize this day and every other day. Life really was too short. After 10 minutes, she stood at the bottom of the stairs to the Wilson Room, the crime scene.

She was gasping for air by the time she reached the top step. "Damn, I'm out of shape," she thought. "I've got to start working out again." Since losing her baby, she hadn't been back to the gym. Naturally thin and athletic, 5-feet-8 and 120 pounds, she used to be able to life her weight five times over her head. Now, she'd be lucky to get the bar off the floor. Her fitness program had gone to hell.

Inside the room was a massive wooden table with chairs. Glass-front wood cabinets and metal file drawers with rare books filled the room. Crime scene techs were taking photos and collecting evidence. An ambulance had taken the wounded guard to a nearby hospital where he was in grave condition. The weapon used in the attack had nicked his carotid artery. He was lucky to be alive, an officer told her, relaying information from an officer stationed at the hospital.

One of the CSIs pointed at the metal pole on the floor. "There is something on the tip," she told Jansen.

Jansen put on a pair of sterile latex gloves, got down on her knees, looked at the end of the pole, and saw what looked like skin; there was also a spot of what could be blood. The pole was a popular adjustable brand hikers and backpackers used. "We need to photograph and bag this," Jansen told an evidence tech standing nearby, waiting for instructions. "Have it analyzed for DNA," Jansen said. She made a note of the brand so she could check their availability and sales records at Next Adventure and REI, major outdoor gear stores in Portland. Connecting the pole to a specific buyer was a long shot, Jansen knew. Still, she would try.

Standing over to the side was a man with white-blond hair, beige clothes, and deep blue eyes. His arms were folded, his lips pulled back in a grimace as he watched the evidence documentation process.

Jansen pulled off her gloves, introduced herself, and shook hands with Bill Bowman.

"What is this place?" asked Jansen.

"This is the library's rare book room," he said.

Bowman gave her an overview of the collection, where the books came from, and their value at market.

"Anything missing?" she asked.

"Seven volumes of *The North American Indian*," said Bowman.

Jansen cocked her head and raised her eyebrows, waiting for more explanation. She didn't know what he was talking about. She could tear through a novel in a day or two but wasn't much for non-fiction. She found memoirs—full of sad, desperate people—just plain annoying.

Bowman gave her a brief history lesson.

"What's the value?"

"Detective Jansen, you're asking an excellent question. Fewer than 300 20-volume sets were printed. A complete set, like the one we owned until yesterday, auctioned in 2012 for nearly $2.9 million. Most people would say they are priceless because they are so rare—such an important effort to capture vanishing Native American culture."

"How can a public library buy books worth millions?" Jansen asked.

"We can't," said Bowman. "It was a donation by wealthy Portlanders 100 years ago."

Doing the calculations in her head, Jansen answered her own question. "Each book is worth $100,000. The seven would be valued at $700,000."

"There is nothing wrong with your math," said Bowman. "However, the value drops precipitously when you break apart the set. Its value is in having all 20 books in good condition. On the black market, each book might bring $10,000." And a pawn shop would pay $2,000, Jansen thought.

"Why would a person steal part of a set?" she asked.

"It puzzles me," Bowman admitted. Jansen figured the perp wanted all twenty books but panicked and took what they could grab on their way out.

"Mr. Bowman, what time did you leave last night?"

"I closed up, locked the door, and walked out at 7:00 pm sharp. Like clockwork. Same time every night." Jansen knew allowing a burglar to pinpoint the exact time Bowman left the book room empty was a basic security breach.

"Besides roaming guards, do you have a provider who manages overall security?"

"Paragon Systems. The president of the company is a member of the library board of directors and provides services at a huge discount."

"You get what you pay for," Jansen thought, but didn't say it. Of course, it wasn't Mark's fault. The system was in place before he assumed his current senior management position at Paragon. She loved Mark Larson, who had been her Portland Police Bureau patrol partner and a former homicide detective. He was also her best friend. He had jumped ship after his first investigation turned into a fiasco. Larson's girlfriend, Helen Williams—a woman he had fallen in love with—turned out to be a serial killer he was chasing after six homeless people went missing without a trace. Mark and Helen made love, enjoyed cooking elaborate dinners together. They often discussed the case—and his progress. Love apparently is blind because Larson never saw her as a suspect, even after coming face-to-face with various warning signs. Even his cop intuition alarm failed to sound.

"Could an individual hide here until after the library closed?" Jansen asked Bowman.

"If you look around, there is no place to hide. I review and approve all requests for visitors, as well as logging them in and out. No one would ever be in here alone."

"The library is a big place," Jansen said. "Isn't it possible they hid after the library closed and waited?"

"It's possible," Bowman admitted, frowning as he thought about nearby hiding places.

"You mentioned a visitor log. Can I get a copy?"

"I'll copy it first thing in the morning and walk it over, if that's okay? I'd give them to you now, but I'll need the library director's approval. It's policy. I'm sure there won't be a problem."

"That's fine, said Jansen. "Has anyone come in recently asking about the Curtis books?"

Bowman thought about it for a minute.

"I've had quite a few visitors this past week. One man, Bryan Byrne, is a history professor from Arizona who said his great-grandfather was an assistant photographer who helped Edward Curtis with Native portraits. Professor Byrne couldn't possibly be a suspect."

"Why do you say that, Mr. Bowman?"

"He's an educator. Books are his currency. He teaches history of the West and would do anything to preserve books and papers that illuminate our past. Besides, we just agreed to work on a history project together. *The North American Indian* would be a key resource in our work. What reason would he have to steal them?"

"Three million bucks is a lot of reasons for anyone to steal the books," Jansen said.

Bowman shook his head vigorously. "No way," he said, verbally confirming his doubt, as if his head shakes weren't enough. Jansen pulled out her notebook, scribbled Byrne's name and wrote *Professor Byrne is suspect number 1.* "Anyone else who might have an interest?"

"None come to mind," said Bowman. "But I'm exhausted and it's late."

"We'll talk again tomorrow when you bring by the sign-in log."

Jansen walked over to the area where the body had lain and got down on her hands and knees. Next to the blood from the guard's neck was the imprint of a book, its outline marked in blood.

Bowman looked down at the carpet and saw the outline.

"Oh my God," said Bowman, looking over her shoulder. "Looks like a book fell in the blood."

"Bloody pages—another clue," Jansen thought, jotting down a note for follow up.

"Detective Jansen, you need to find the books as soon as possible or they will be gone for good. There's a huge black market for rare books, with a long line of collectors willing to pay big bucks to get that one special first edition. Once the middleman has the books, they could be halfway around the world in a week. No one would ever find them."

"I'll do my best," said Jansen. "My team will give it top priority."

"I'll do anything I can to help you recover and save the books," Bowman said.

2

A man in a security guard uniform appeared at the door to the rare book room just as Jansen was about to leave. "I'm Daryl Epley," the guard said, reaching out to shake Jansen's hand. His hand was sweaty, like a person trying to cover up their guilt. He said he was the one who found the victim and dialed 9-1-1 to summon an ambulance and the police. "Any news about my friend?" Epley asked. Not waiting for an answer, he said, "Elliot was about to retire for a second time. He had been a college librarian. He saw an advertisement to work as a guard in the library, so he joined our company. He loved books and interacting with library patrons. Once he was on the job, he figured part of his job was giving people advice on finding books and other resources at the library. Normally, he worked day shifts. However, when another guard took off a week for vacation, Elliot volunteered to take the evening shifts. The job was also a way to earn money to pay for vacations. He and his wife loved cruises."

"Why would anyone hurt him?" Epley added. "It is so unfair. The library is supposed to be a safe place—a haven of calm."

"Mr. Epley, I realize you're upset about Mr. Delaney. I wish I had good news to report on his condition. As far as I know, he is still in surgery. In the meantime, I'll do everything I can to catch the individuals or individual who did this. You can help by telling me where you were when the attack occurred."

Epley explained he was at the other end of the library. He and Elliot started their rounds in the first-floor lobby and then they each took a floor, checking locked doors, and looking for anyone who might have fallen asleep or was hiding. "Elliot had completed the second-floor, then realized he hadn't climbed up the stairs to the Wilson Room to check the door. He said he would be right back. The Wilson Room check isn't part of his day shift routine. When he didn't call after about 10 minutes. I radioed him and got no response. That's when I knew there was a problem and went to investigate. I found him and called 9-1-1."

From Epley's description of their routine, Jansen figured Delaney could have been lying injured for up to five minutes—long enough for the attacker to slip out of the library.

"So, you didn't get a call from Delaney alerting you to the intruder?"

"I thought I heard static on the radio that might have been Elliot thumbing the call button. It's easy to do. Nothing much happens on our rounds. I didn't give it another thought—until Elliot didn't check in. That was around 8 pm."

"Thanks for your help, Mr. Epley. If you think of anything else, let me know," said Jansen, handing him her card. He nodded and walked away, shoulders drooping, no doubt the sign of a man feeling failure—failure to help his colleague and friend who may die from the vicious attack.

Walking back over to Bowman, Jansen said, "We will do our best to find the books."

With Elliot Delaney's life in the hands of doctors, she needed to jump-start her investigation.

CHAPTER 13

1

A doctor had inserted a needle in Mark Larson's vein and taped it into place. His arms were outstretched like Jesus on the cross. Nylon straps, instead of nails, locked him down. Larson twisted his head left and right, first toward the warden, who was a waiting for a call of reprieve, then to the viewing gallery with friends, family, and lawyers.

Larson's eyes fixed on the intravenous tubing connected to his arm. It snaked across the room through holes in the wall, into the control room next door. Two death-watch guards fussed with the automated equipment designed to deliver the fatal dose of barbiturate when the warden flipped the power switch. The execution team was running through a checklist, hoping to prevent a foul up—the kind that plagued a Missouri prisoner when equipment failed to deliver the lethal drug cocktail. Instead of a quiet death made possible by the injection of a sedation drug before the lethal injection, the prisoner suffered a violent end—jerking, bucking, and choking as the killing process continued for two hours. If you could believe news reports. The grisly events traumatized prison staff and viewers. Anti-death penalty advocates screamed for justice, using the example as evidence of their argument of cruel and unusual punishment.

Mark Larson heard the faint sound of a phone ringing in the next room. He saw the warden hang up, look at the guards, and shake his head. Larson would get no reprieve.

Mark screamed, "No, no, no."

Thick glass windows muffled his pleas for mercy. He looked at those in the gallery for support and saw two friends wagging their fingers. Panicked, he turned toward the warden again. The warden's face had morphed into a scowling woman. It was Helen Williams, his ex-girlfriend. She would be his executioner. The prison guards weren't anonymous people. They were his best friends, Kim Jansen and Jim Briggs.

Mark had let down Helen, had done nothing to help her in her moment of greatest need. He failed to recognize her grief for a husband killed in a freak accident and trauma of the gang-rape she suffered a few weeks later at the hands of a group of homeless men. He failed to support her or help her find justice. Now he was paying the price for his incompetence as a detective.

A moment later, as his eyes locked onto Helen's in a plea for mercy, she made a show of flipping the switch that started the flow of the lethal drug. A satanic smile erupted.

Larson knew he would get no Propofol to sedate him and eliminate his pain. He would suffer the worst possible death—and deserved it. Looking at his three friends, he mouthed, "I'm sorry," tears streaming down his face. Fifteen seconds later, his mind was screaming for oxygen, as if someone had sliced his brain with a razor blade into a thousand pieces. The last words he heard were Helen's. "Welcome to Hell. I'm your worst nightmare."

2

Mark Larson woke up shaking. His eyes were wide open, bugging out, as if he had seen a ghost. And he had seen a ghost—the ghost of former girlfriend Helen Williams whom he witnessed killing herself a year earlier. Endless therapy had not stopped the nightmares—or the guilt for not doing more to help her.

A call from Night Owl yanked him out of his Death Row dream. Night Owl was the ringtone for Rick Carrigan, founder and CEO of Paragon Security, his boss. Carrigan was on duty 24-7.

"Hey boss," Larson said, answering the phone. "What's up?" The words came out in a stutter, his throat dry as cotton. Like so many times before, the nightmare had literally scared the pee out of him. The waterproof mattress pad caught most of it. Sweat covered the top sheet. A few nights, usually after a stressful day, he even wore adult diapers in anticipation of the execution dream.

"Are you okay, Larson?"

"Fine," he said, forcing his voice to sound neutral despite the mess he had made of his bed.

"What's up is that a thief broke into the John Wilson Room at the Central Library, wounded a guard who discovered the break in, and got away."

"Shit," Larson thought. "How could that happen? Security was supposed to be foolproof."

"What time is it?" he asked.

"Larson, it's midnight—it's time to get your butt up and over to the library to see how we screwed up on security." Carrigan could be the Marine drill sergeant he had been 20 years before. Other times, he was a marshmallow. Larson never took Carrigan's rants personally. He understood there was more going on than Paragon's failure to keep the library secure. Carrigan had a personal stake. He was a voracious reader, loved the library, served on the library board of directors, and had donated $50,000 to adult literacy programs. He also had offered Paragon Security services at half the going rate.

"Are the cops on the scene?" Larson asked.

"It's secure," Carrigan said. "The guard, a guy named Elliot Delaney, is in surgery at the hospital with a severe neck wound. Portland Police Bureau Detective Kim Jansen is on the scene."

"I'll be there in 30 minutes," said Larson. He got up, rolled up the wet bedding, and put it in the washer. He took a quick shower, scrubbing off the sweat and urine until his skin was raw. Closing his eyes, he let the water run over his head, down his face, and into his mouth. He wanted to wash out his mouth. And his brain, along with washing away the horror of witnessing Helen's death. And the memory of arriving too late to stop it. Looking through double-paned windows at Jim Briggs' weekend home, Helen held up a cardboard sign—like the homeless looking for handouts. The sign was an apology. A veterinarian like Briggs, she had killed five homeless men who had raped her in a city park and stuffed her mangled body inside a garden equipment shed. Larson tried to talk her down. But Helen knew she would be going to jail for life without the possibility of parole or be executed.

As penance, Larson had quit the police force, turning in his shield after only six months on the job.

Following his resignation, Larson took a month off, then applied for a position at Paragon Security. A year after taking his new job, Carrigan promoted him to a regional commander position at $150,000 a year—twice his Portland Police Bureau detective salary—supervising operations in Oregon and Washington.

Larson turned off the shower, dried himself, threw on a pair of black slacks, a black tee shirt and a black jacket with a Paragon logo on the breast pocket.

3

Larson parked near the Central Library and walked up the front steps, where a Portland cop stood guard at a line of crime scene tape. "Hey Sarge, good to see you," said Officer Jeff Maddox. "Been a long time."

"Good to see you, too, Jeff."

They bumped fists.

"You're working for Paragon, right? A top-notch organization, I hear."

"They're first rate."

"Ever miss the streets?"

Larson, who helped train Maddox after he graduated from the police academy, nodded.

"I'm here to see Jansen," Larson said, leaving out the fact that Paragon was the library's security provider. The break-in and attack on the guard wasn't a testimonial for Paragon's services.

Maddox called Detective Jansen on his radio and got the okay for Larson to enter.

"Good seeing you, Sarge," said Maddox, using Larson's rank before he had been promoted to detective.

"Same here," said Larson, as he disappeared inside the building.

When Larson reached the crime scene, he put on gloves and shoe covers and walked up the short staircase to the John Wilson Room.

He walked in and was face-to-face with Detective Jansen.

"Great job on security, Larson," Jansen snapped.

"I love you, too," said Larson, who leaned in and whispered, "Fuck you."

Jansen smiled.

"Love you, too, man," she said. She and Larson were best friends, police patrol partners for six years, and each had saved the other's life. They had a reputation on the streets as cops respectful to all (the homeless included). They loved happy hours at Portland brewpubs.

They also looked like fraternal twins. When they came to roll call late one day, their sergeant, Bull Harrison—as punishment—dressed them down of front of their peers and gave them a nickname: Wooden Shoe Blues. The wooden shoe reference was related to their white-blond hair and ice-blue eyes. Harrison assumed both were Dutch. Larson thought it was funny. Jansen had bristled at the stereotype.

Jansen and Larson were alike. And not. Ying and yang. Larson was cool, Jansen quick to blow up. Larson was quiet. Jansen liked to draw attention and say things that jolted people. Larson had a sense of humor. Jansen didn't get most jokes. And laughed rarely.

So far, none of the other detectives had called them Wooden Shoe Blues— to their face.

After jousting with Jansen, Larson spotted Bill Bowman. Larson had worked with Bowman to set up security for the rare book room. "Sorry about this, Bill," said Larson. "We'll figure it out. I'm going to work on the security breach while Detective Jansen handles the attack and theft. We will solve the case. I promise." Jansen shot him a look, letting him know he shouldn't make promises. He ignored her.

"Thanks, Mark," said Bowman. "I'm heartbroken. I hope Mr. Delaney pulls through and we get the books back."

"Is the camera over the entrance real?" asked Jansen.

"Yes," said Larson. "We set it up to save a year's worth of activities. Every tour group is recorded and stored on servers in multiple locations. I will start reviewing the video when I get back to the office," said Larson. "We have remote access."

Larson walked over to the Wilson Room entrance door and examined the lock. No evidence of damage. He stuck his head back in and asked Bowman to come over. He asked him if he could have left the door unlocked. Or if the burglar could have hidden inside the room. Larson knew there were no hiding places. He had inspected every inch of the room—every cabinet or cubby-hole where a person could stow away.

Bill shook his head. "I follow a procedure every evening. I walk the room, return materials to their proper places, check cabinets, and test the entrance door as I walk out. I also look for stragglers. But as you can see, there aren't many empty spaces to hide out."

Bowman offered another possibility. "They could've hidden in the stacks, although the guards have been trained to look for people wandering around after close. The homeless love to find remote areas of the library to sleep, maybe stay overnight."

"Isn't there a classroom downstairs?" Larson asked. Bowman nodded. "We keep it locked when not in use."

When Bowman stepped away, Jansen leaned in and said, "Larson, remember, this is a crime scene. Check out the classroom. Look, but don't touch. We don't need the investigation fucked up because you broke the custody of evidence chain."

"Got it, boss," said Larson.

"I appreciate you putting your eyes on the situation," Jansen said. "If you need a tech to grab something, I'll send them down."

Larson walked down the stairs, turned left toward the classroom, and peered in. He put on a pair of gloves, turned the knob, and found it was unlocked. "Bingo," he thought. He walked in, scanned the room, and looked at a space under a long table beneath the window, which would not be visible to a guard standing outside, looking in. Several chairs were pulled out and pushed aside. He got down on his knees and found an empty jellybean bag. Larson did not touch it. This is where the perp hid out before the break in. Unless the guard had opened the door and entered the classroom, he wouldn't have seen someone hiding. The intruder knew what he was doing. Larson wondered if the perp was an ex-cop.

Larson locked up the classroom and walked back up the stairs to the Wilson Room. He alerted Jansen to the candy bag in the classroom.

"Is it okay if I check out this lock?" Larson asked Jansen.

He pulled out his master key, which he inserted into the door. The key slipped in easily. No apparent damage. It took a skilled individual to insert the bump key and hit it with the right force to make the tumblers fall into place, unlocking the door. "I'm guessing a bump key was used," he called out to Jansen.

He found a step stool inside the Wilson Room, pulled it to the doorway. He stepped up, reached up above the door opening to the camera, and rubbed his finger across the lens. A greasy substance came off on his finger. He smelled it. Petroleum jelly. A perfect choice to blur the lens so you could not identify the burglar. That was assuming they took other steps to disguise their identity. A ski mask worn inside an oversized hoodie would prevent a camera from seeing a face.

"Find anything, Larson?" Jansen asked.

"The perpetrator is a pro," said Larson. "The guy not only used a bump key to open the lock, but he also smeared petroleum jelly on the lens over the camera to obscure their identity. Our job just got a little harder."

"So, what else is new?" said Jansen.

"Jansen, I'm going to stay here, set up my laptop to review the recordings for the past month and report back this evening or tomorrow." He explained his boss's connection to the library and said, "Carrigan will want answers. Any problem with me telling him about the lock and camera or the classroom hideout?"

"That's fine," said Jansen. "Make sure he keeps the information confidential. I don't want my case blown before it gets off the ground."

"Larson, I've got a thermos of coffee," said Jansen. "Let's review the digital recording together." Jansen didn't want to pull an all-nighter but had seen little of Larson and was eager to catch up.

"Bill, you can take off," said Jansen. "We'll talk in the morning."

Bowman's head appeared to spin as he looked around the room at the rare book collection. He seemed frantic, rechecking the locks on every cabinet in the room before leaving.

"Don't worry," she said, noting Bowman's hesitancy to leave them alone with his precious collections. "We won't take anything."

"Sorry, detective. Nearly everything here is extremely rare, which means very little of it could be replaced if damaged or stolen. I didn't mean to imply that you might steal."

"That's good to know," said Jansen, smiling. Bowman smiled back.

"Okay, I leave you to it," he said. "I trust you'll lock up when you leave." Jansen nodded.

Bowman put on his jacket, his head hanging, as if he had just lost his best friend.

"Let's kick this case in the butt," said Larson. "We'll find out who the perp is, track them down, get the books back, and bathe in the glory."

"And keep your boss from kicking your ass, Larson," said Jansen.

"That, too," he admitted. He wondered if it was time for another job change. After 10 years as a patrolman, he had barely 6 months under his belt as a detective before Helen killed herself and he turned in his badge. While he had moved up the ranks quickly at Paragon, security wasn't his cup of tea. He enjoyed being a cop.

After reviewing the video, Larson and Jansen finally found what they were looking for. A man entered the frame, looked around the room to make sure it was empty, prying open a locked cabinet before pulling out the Curtis books and placing them on a table.

"He knows his stuff," said Larson. "His clothes are all black, with nothing distinctive—not even the shoes."

"Damn, Larson, this isn't a good start," said Jansen.

"I agree," he said. "I need to call my boss. He won't be happy. He'll be pissed he didn't follow staff recommendations to install cameras inside the room. He figured a single camera, the remoteness of the John Wilson room, and security guards, would be enough to protect the collection."

"I better get to the station and start assembling the case file. Let's catch up tomorrow."

Jansen had noticed something odd as they reviewed the security footage. The thief didn't randomly grab books and pile them on a nearby table. He looked first and ran his fingers over the volumes, then pulled the first book from the middle of the shelf. What was that about?

CHAPTER 14

1

Meghan McQuillan stood at the front window of McQuillan's bookstore, looking out at passing traffic. A dozen customers who had entered the store when it opened were browsing. She knew from experience they might not reappear from the labyrinth of books for an hour, then buy a used paperback for 50 cents. Or they would spend an hour reading back issues of vintage magazines and walk out empty-handed.

Did they confuse the bookstore with the public library? Had people been trained to look rather than buy. They could buy a single cup of coffee and sit for hours. She had learned from her dad that you should keep such thoughts to yourself. Smile, and thank them for stopping in, no matter how long they browsed and how little they bought. That was the nature of the business. The comfort of a friendly, cozy place pays off in positive reviews, drawing in more customers. And more cash—one cup or one used book at a time. Given the meager cash coming in, barely enough to pay the rent, a tougher policy might be in order, she thought.

Meghan loved her job as CEO of McQuillan's, even if it wasn't the library position she envisioned when she graduated from the University of Washington. After 10 years as a librarian and library branch manager, she was two days away from becoming deputy director of the Multnomah County library system—a dream come true—before it all came crashing down.

Her dream died when a heart attack nearly killed her dad, Bruce McQuillan. She resigned the library position she had accepted to assume the day-to-day operations of McQuillan's, Portland's oldest bookstore, which her grandfather founded in the late 1930s. Sadly, McQuillan's was hanging on by a thread, beaten down by Amazon and other online booksellers. Meghan knew when she took over the bookstore operations that the lofty title of CEO was a joke—captain of the Titanic was closer to the truth. What choice did she have? The founder's dream was to provide secure jobs for generations of McQuillans. Great idea in the 1930s during the Great Depression. Now, not so much.

A few months after taking over as CEO, she had the website rebuilt, reached out to the many book groups she had worked with at the public library, and hired a student to build an eBay presence to advertise McQuillan's rare books. Sales had ticked up.

In the meantime, her social life had evaporated, along with her spare time and energy. Her boyfriend Marc Stanfield, Bill Bowman's predecessor, disappeared shortly after losing his job. He had done nothing wrong, but when the library's copy of James Audubon's four-book masterpiece *Birds of America* went missing, the library board needed a fall guy. After all, you need to blame someone after books worth $10 million go missing. Stanfield also disappeared shortly after *Birds of America* was stolen. He never responded to another one of her texts, phone calls, or emails. He had apparently abandoned his apartment and all his possessions. He ghosted her. Despite her 24/7 work schedule, she was lonely without him.

Meghan looked at her reflection in the window. She was a 32-year-old woman, too thin from eating too little and working too much—despite her love for beer and pie. She dressed in jeans, flannel shirts you would wear camping, and vests, with no make-up. Her hair was pulled back in a scrunchie, with a long ponytail flowing down her back. Not much to attract a man, she thought.

In the middle of her daydream, a man near her age walked in. She was momentarily speechless. It was as if she had imagined her ideal companion, and here he was.

2

Meghan stared at the man for what seemed like minutes. She scanned him: white-blonde hair, ice-blue eyes, 6-feet-2, solid. He could easily have been the fraternal twin of her girlfriend, Kim Jansen. He was clearly a man who worked out and took care of himself. Realizing that the man had smiled at her when he entered the store and walked past her to the front counter, she turned to greet him. She saw him look around, then call out, "Bruce, are you there?" He was looking for her dad, who had often left the front counter for long periods to stock shelves. He never worried about people stealing books or breaking into the cash register. People would leave money at the front counter to pay for their used books and magazines. They had a few shoplifters. No doubt they were tourists popping in for a quick look at one of Portland iconic bookstores. McQuillan's was nearly as popular as Powell's Books.

"Good morning," she said. "Welcome to McQuillan's. May I help you?" Mark Larson turned around and looked at her.

"Do you work here?" he asked, no doubt noticing that her clothes weren't appropriate for working in a retail store.

"I'm Meghan McQuillan, Bruce's daughter," she said. "I'm running the place now."

Larson studied her for a moment and said, "I'm Mark Larson. Have we met? You look very familiar."

"I'm not sure," said Meghan. "Aren't you a Portland cop?"

"I was," he said. "I left the department and took a job at a security firm. I recall Bruce mentioning he had a daughter in college."

"That's me. I've been out of college for a long time. When I was in college, I spent most of my summers here. Dad kept me in the stacks, helping customers find books, and managing the book inventory."

"It has been a couple of years since I was here last," Larson confessed.

"I won't hold that against you."

"I came by to alert Bruce to the possibility of a call from a man offering to sell several stolen rare books," Larson explained. "Last night, there was a break-in at the John Wilson Special Collections in the Central Library. Taken were several books from *The North American Indian*. During the burglary, a guard walked in on the thief. A fight followed. The burglar severely injured the guard. We have little more to go on."

"That's terrible," said Meg, who explained her association with the library. "I feel so bad for Elliot. He's a sweetheart with a lovely wife. I hope he recovers."

"Me, too," said Larson.

"I know Bruce would love to talk to you, but he is in semi-retirement," said Meghan. "He had a heart attack and is slowly recuperating. I'm filling in for him."

"Sorry to hear about your dad. Please give him my best."

"I will," she said.

Larson didn't need to tell her that McQuillan's might be the first place a thief would come to sell the books for quick cash.

"I'll alert you if I get an inquiry about buying the Curtis books," said Meghan.

"Better yet, give Kim Jansen a call," said Larson. "It's her case. She is the lead investigator. I'm assisting."

"I have her number," said Meghan. "She and I are pals. We regularly have girls-nights-out."

"Good to know," said Larson. "I'll have to join you."

"Perhaps you missed the word 'girls' in girls-night-out." Sassy, bold Meghan had suddenly replaced sullen, mousy Meghan. When Larson frowned, she knew she had blown it.

"I guess that's why I'm lonely," she thought.

"Just putting you on, detective. You could join Kim and me for an evening out any time you like."

"Are you asking me out for a date?" Larson said, his face blank, his attempt to tease her. Meghan blushed.

"A group date," she said. The words came out in a squeak. She had forgotten how to act around men. Larson raised his eyebrows, waiting for her to say more about dating or going out. Instead, she changed the subject. "Dad schooled me on how to value rare books, what to look for in terms of condition, how different editions change the value. He also warned me about scammers trying to palm off books as rare first editions. Or stolen rare books they want to pawn."

"I'll contact Kim if anyone with Curtis books calls and offers them for sale."

"It was nice meeting you, Meghan. I look forward to our date," he said, holding her gaze and smiling.

"There might be hope for me yet," Meghan whispered to herself after Larson left.

3

"Hi, this is McQuillan's Books."

"May I please speak to the book buyer?" Val said.

"That's me. I'm Meghan McQuillan. CEO, book buyer, and chief bottle washer." Meghan wasn't sure why she felt the need to detail her role at McQuillan's.

"This is Robert Hill," Val said, using his alias. "I've inherited several books from my grandfather, who was part of the Edward Curtis expedition. He was a photography assistant for Curtis and helped create several volumes of *The North American Indian*. I want to sell them."

Was this the man who stole the books and injured the guard? Meghan wondered. He was polite and soft-spoken, not how she pictured the thief who attacked Elliot. Couldn't the Curtis books belong to his family? He could be the books' owner. Still, it was an enormous coincidence that police would alert her to the theft the same day a man calls with Curtis books to sell.

"If you bring a book by, we'll be happy to have our expert value them," said Meghan, who tried to tamp down her fear. She was gripping the phone so hard her fingers turned white. She fought to keep his voice low and calm. "After we authenticate it, we can discuss a price," Megan said. "We maintain relationships with a long list of collectors. It's not unusual to get multiple competing offers for a rare book."

"That's good news," said Val. "I think they are original first-run prints. I can drop by at 10 a.m. tomorrow."

After Hill hung up, Meghan wanted to pick up the phone and call Kim Jansen, as she had promised Mark Larson. If this wasn't the guy police were looking for, brokering the deal would provide badly needed cash. The proceeds could pay rent on the store for at least six months.

An alarm went off in Meghan's head. A bookstore, even one that sells rare books, would not be the first choice for anyone interested in making money from the sale. They would go to an auction house. It sounded suspicious. Or the seller could be one of those people who finds a dirty, odd-looking thing in the attic, Googles Antiques Roadshow and snags a few minutes with an expert. Most of the time they come home disappointed. A few hit the jackpot.

The man on the phone showed good manners when he said, 'May I please speak to the book buyer.' Doesn't sound like a criminal," Meghan thought. How dangerous would it be for her to meet the guy, get hold of the book, and wait to call police until she could verify its authenticity?

CHAPTER 15

1

Jim Briggs was locked inside *Have Paws—Will Travel*, his mobile dog care van. Tied down on a seven-foot-long metal table used for canine medical procedures. He could not move except to swivel his head. He looked down at his body. It was petite, less than 100 pounds, and five feet tall. Couldn't be. He knew he was six-feet-six and 225 pounds. Standing over him was a giant woman. In her hand was an enormous syringe with a thick, eight-inch-long needle. She was pushing the air bubbles out of the tip, flicking drops of a clear fluid onto the floor.

"Hi there, little man," a raspy voice croaked. "Remember me? I am your old friend, Maxine Dorothy Reid."

"Wait a minute," said Briggs. "You're dead. I euthanized you."

"Yes, you did, and I was thankful for it. Then again, just because I was a miserable, used up, homeless meth addict didn't give you the right to kill me."

Briggs twisted his head violently left and right and yelled, "No!"

"Goodbye, little man," said Maxine, as she slipped the needle into his vein. "You'll only feel a pinch. Well, maybe a little more."

"Wait," he yelled. "You forgot the Propofol." Propofol was a drug commonly used in human surgeries to sedate a patient. Briggs used it when putting down a dog to protect them from pain created when the heart-arresting barbiturate flooded their organs.

"Well, maybe you killed me too soon, Little Man. Who appointed you judge, jury, and executioner?" A moment later, the drug ripped through Briggs' body like a tree limb fed into a wood chipper. His insides exploded with pain. He bucked, twisted, and gasped for air.

2

"Briggs, wake up!"

Briggs' eyes flew open. Looking down on him was Kim Jansen.

"Where am I?"

"You're home, in bed, with me. You're alive and safe."

He took a big gulp of air and let it out slowly. His blood pressure was returning to normal, his muscles relaxing. Jansen reached down, slipped her hand into his boxers, and did her best to create a distraction from the recurring nightmare about Maxine Dorothy Reid. She had been one of over 50 homeless people for whom he provided free care to their dogs. In a drug-induced mental meltdown one day she had begged, "God, please take me." After failing to find a home for the woman, he granted her wish, ending her suffering with heart-arresting canine euthanasia drugs. She hadn't resisted. She seemed relieved at the prospect of escaping homelessness. Still, Briggs was conflicted over what he did. He was not a medical doctor with an M.D. with the right to prescribe suicide pills, only a doctor for animals. He had no right to administer the death penalty to Maxine. Maxine's death resulted from an ongoing struggle he had with a dark inner voice. He gave the voice a name—Devil in My Ear. DIME, for short. DIME countered his positive, happy self. DIME's negative voice was like his mother, who never praised him when he was a kid. No matter what he accomplished, she said he could do better. After he killed Maxine, the DIME voice disappeared. Briggs wished his haunting nightmare with Maxine as his executioner would also go away.

Jansen's approach to calming down Briggs worked every time. When they finished making love, Jansen climbed out of bed. "Briggs, I need to get to the office. Capt. Melrose will be all over my ass to solve the library case. Are you okay?"

"Better than okay," he said. "I'll join you in the shower. I need to get on the road, too."

3

When Jansen arrived at the Portland Police Bureau headquarters in Downtown Portland a little before 8 a.m., she took the elevator to the detective division. Her boss was already at his desk. Rather than wait for Mike Melrose to yell for her to get her butt into his office, she grabbed a cup of coffee, walked through Melrose's doorway, and plopped down in front of his desk.

"Hi, chief. I thought I'd give an update on last night's break-in and assault at the library."

For the next 15 minutes, Jansen filled in Melrose on the attack, Larson's evaluation of the security breach, and the condition of the guard—he was in grave condition with a fifty-fifty chance of survival. Melrose's head snapped up when she told him the value of the stolen books and their historical significance.

"It's not a homicide yet, but could be," Melrose offered. "The very least, it is a Class C felony, 10 years in prison, and a $125,000 fine. If the guard dies, the perp is looking at life in prison or Death Row."

"I expect to have more leads in the case today," she explained. "I plan to call Meghan McQuillan, who's running McQuillan's Books since her dad's heart attack, to see if anyone has tried to sell them to her. Bill Bowman, curator of the rare book collection at the library, is expected to drop off a copy of the visitor log. He says everyone is required to sign in."

"I guess you better get busy," said Melrose.

Jansen refilled her coffee cup and walked back to her desk. Other detectives were filing in, among them Alice Munson, a 10-year veteran detective.

"How convenient," said Jansen. "You look fine to me, Munson. Playing hooky?"

"Jansen, quit busting my balls. Had a case of the runs. Couldn't get off the toilet all night."

"That's the shits," said Jansen, proud of her comeback.

"Hilarious," said Munson.

Jansen gave Munson an overview of the case.

"Hell, I'll trade," said Munson. "I've got an interesting missing person case."

"Nice try, Munson."

Jansen's cell phone rang. The caller ID showed it came from the Multnomah County Library. "Jansen," she answered.

"Hi, Detective Jansen. It's Bill Bowman. I got the okay to drop off the visitor's log. I'll walk it over to you or email a copy."

"Email is fine, Bill."

"You asked me to call if I had any information that might help with your case. I noticed last night that you focused on a hiking stick. I heard you say it might be the weapon used in the attack on Elliot Delaney. In the past two weeks, I've had two visitors using canes," explained Bowman. "One was the history professor I mentioned, Bryan Byrne. He is on sabbatical from Canyon College near Tucson. The other was a last-minute sign up for a tour." Jansen thought it was too much of a coincidence for two men with canes to visit the library's rare book room in the same week.

"Could you tell why they were using canes?" Jansen asked.

"The history professor said he has a bad hip and is waiting for surgery. Coincidentally, he claimed to be the great-grandson of William Bryan Byrne, a photography assistant to Edward Curtis." Jansen made a note, "Bryan Byrne connected to books. Walks with cane."

"You sound doubtful," said Jansen.

"I wasn't when we met, but with the disappearance of the books, I have been rethinking our interaction," said Bowman. "Honestly, detective, I don't see it. I even shared a document with him which confirmed his great-grandfather's role on the Curtis expeditions. What motive would he have?"

"You tell me," Jansen said.

"None," said Bowman. "He would want to preserve them at all costs. This is sacred stuff to historians."

The need for cash was motive enough for the professor to steal, Jansen knew. A teacher at a small college in Arizona might earn $70,000, the national average, she had learned from googling national teacher pay. Maybe he has a big mortgage or was still paying off a huge student loan. Jansen didn't share her thoughts with Bowman, who suddenly felt he needed to reinforce his argument for Professor Byrne's innocence. "Academics," he said, "are all about preserving history. Above all else, they would like every important historical document to be in the public domain rather than in the hands of rich collectors. They would do nothing to damage or harm a history collection."

"Do you have time to come to the station, bring a copy of the visitor logs, and give me a description of the second man?"

"Sure," said Bowman. "I can be there in an hour."

4

When Jansen got off the phone with Bowman, she called the detective bureau's research assistant, Kelly O'Connor. O'Connor was a twenty-something social media whiz with a master's degree in library science. She could find anything on the Web lightning fast.

"I need everything you can find on a Bryan Byrne, a professor at Canyon College in Tucson—age, description, recent photos, driver's license, public financial records—anything and everything. We just had a theft from a rare book collection and an assault during the commission of the crime. Byrne is a person of interest. I also need information on a Robert Hill, no other known information."

A half hour later, Bill Bowman arrived, and Jansen settled him in a conference room. She sat opposite him as she reviewed the visitor log he brought.

"Bill, you said only part of the Curtis collection was stolen," said Jansen. "Do you have any theories why they didn't take all of it?"

"The value is in the entire set," said Bowman. "I have no idea."

"What can you tell me about Professor Byrne's grandfather?"

"I know he worked for Edward Curtis from 1924 to 1930."

"Bill, don't you think it is more than a coincidence the stolen books match the years Byrne worked for Curtis?" She wasn't going to tell Bowman about the video recording that showed the thief selecting books from the 20-set volume.

"You have a point," said Bowman. "Still, I can't believe Professor Byrne was involved."

"Tell me about the second individual with a cane who was part of the tour group that visited the library," Jansen said.

"He signed in as Robert Hill," said Bowman. "Part of my presentation was showing the pictures of Native Americans in the first volume of the Curtis *North American Indian* set. Afterwards, Hill hung around for a while, asked lots of questions about our rare books, and was complimentary about the tour."

"Was he out of your sight at any point?"

Bowman thought back to the tour. "You know, I took a quick bathroom break. I was gone for less than five minutes. When I returned, Hill was sitting right where I left him. It appeared he hadn't moved. He said he needed to sit down and rest because of an old injury. Arthritis had stiffened his leg, requiring the cane, he said. Otherwise, Hill looked healthy. He was fit, tall, over six feet, and well dressed. Professor Byrne is slightly overweight, mid-to-late 30s, I would guess. One more thing: Professor Byrne has jet black hair and deep blue eyes. The hair color and eyes are identifying traits for Black Irish." Jansen made a note.

"Anything else you can remember, Bill?"

"Professor Byrne said his father owns a vineyard in Newberg." Newberg was in the heart of Oregon Willamette Valley wine country. Compared with California, Oregon's wine output was miniscule. Oregon's pinot noir, however, won more than its share of wine competitions against Napa Valley vintners. Jansen knew it well. She and Briggs had made a point of visiting wineries in the Willamette Valley and the Columbia River Gorge where they owned a weekend getaway.

"Bill, you've been a great help. I will make a copy of your visitor log and get it back to you. Don't worry. We will find your books. And we'll get the man who hurt the guard."

"I hope so," said Bowman, frowning. He looked down at the table, closed his eyes, began rubbing his face. He wiped tears out of his eyes. "If we don't get the books back, I'll probably lose my job. With the president of our security company on the library board of directors, the board will be looking for a scapegoat, rather than blame a board member for the security breech."

Jansen walked Bowman to the elevator and urged him to call if he remembered anything else that could help the case. She sensed he knew more than he was saying. She would give him another day to grieve over the loss of the Curtis books, then cycle back and question him again.

5

Two hours after she had asked Kelly O'Connor to compile a report on Professor Byrne, an email alert appeared in her email with an attached file. She opened it and began reading. It confirmed that Byrne was a tenured professor at Canyon College. He was born to Colin and Angela Byrne in Walnut Creek, California on April 19, 1978. The report included classes he taught, and a three-page list of academic publications attributed to him. At the end of the report was contact information for the professor.

Jansen dialed Byrne's office number and got a recording telling callers the professor was on sabbatical with a referring number to Stanley Watkins, dean of the college. She called the number and got the dean's secretary, Maggie Montes.

"This is Detective Kim Jansen with the Portland Police Bureau in Oregon. I'm calling about one of your professors. I'd like to speak with Dean Watkins."

"The dean has a busy afternoon," Maggie said. "I could schedule an appointment next week." Of course, it was her job to throw a wall around her boss. Still, Jansen had no patience for the run-around.

"Maggie, that's your name, right?"

"Yes, it is." The answer was curt. Jansen could almost see the woman through the phone, her back up, chin out, fists balled, ready for battle.

"Well Maggie, I 'm a police detective and your professor, Mr. Bryan Byrne, is a person of interest in our investigation."

"Oh my God," said Maggie. "Is the professor dead?" Maggie had read too many detective novels, Jansen thought.

"As far as I know, Maggie, Professor Byrne is very much alive. However, I need to talk to him. And his phone voicemail recording says he is on sabbatical and gives this referring number."

A moment later, a man came on the phone. "Is Professor Byrne wanted for murder?" The words poured out of Dean Watkins' mouth.

"Is this Dean Watkins?"

"Yes. My secretary said a detective was on the line about a case and said you were after Bryan Byrne."

"I'm afraid Maggie is overexcited," said Jansen. "We had a break-in at the Portland Public Library. The thief escaped with rare books and injured a guard who caught the thief in the act."

"How is Professor Byrne involved?" Watkins interrupted. He offered no "sorry" for the guard's injuries. More important was the impact on the school's reputation and fund-raising efforts.

"A few days before the theft, the professor made an appointment with the curator of the rare book room," said Jansen. "They discussed Edward Curtis'

North American Indian. Now seven Curtis books are gone. Do you think the professor could be involved?"

The phone went silent. "Normally," Watkins stuttered, "I would expect Professor Byrne to visit history libraries and museums on his sabbaticals. He has always used his time off to gather information for his western history classes. He feels the knowledge he gains from fieldwork makes him a better teacher. Based on his student rating, he's right. His multi-media presentations are the envy of every faculty member."

"Then you must have a copy of his itinerary," said Jansen. "I assume you discussed the trip and Professor Byrne's goals for his time off—and his curriculum."

"Actually, we didn't discuss it. There were extenuating circumstances," said Watkins.

"What do you mean?" asked Jansen.

"Normally, I wouldn't discuss personnel matters with an outsider. I believe you should know that I forced him to take time off. He was involved in a theft at a local drugstore." Watkins hesitated for a moment.

"See, detective, Professor Byrne has a bad hip. He has put off hip replacement for over two years because he didn't want to be away from classes. Then he got hooked on painkillers. A few weeks ago, I got a call from a local pharmacy telling me Professor Byrne had walked behind the counter while the pharmacist was helping other customers and grabbed a bottle of pain pills. When the pharmacist spotted him and asked him what he was doing in the prescription-filling area, he said his doctor had called in a prescription. He said he was in a hurry. Since the druggist was busy with a line of customers, he thought he would help himself."

"Was Professor Byrne arrested?" asked Jansen.

"No, he got lucky," said Watkins. "The pharmacist who caught him is my friend. He was mad as hell, but he knew the arrest of the professor could do a lot of harm to the school's reputation, jeopardizing my job. He called me instead. I thanked him profusely and promised him two bottles of Rombauer Chardonnay — $50 a bottle — that he and I could share. He accepted my offer but also said I needed to get Byrne under control—get him help or next time he would have to involve the police. I told Byrne to get his hip fixed, kick his drug habit, and then he could come back to work."

"He didn't tell you where he was going?" asked Jansen.

"No, he didn't. However, he sent a text saying he had moved up the date of his hip surgery and was working on his problem. That was three or four days ago. I can give you his cell phone number and you can call him. When you find out, please let me know. I am especially interested to learn if he was involved in the incident in Portland."

Jansen assured Watkins she would keep in touch. She hung up and called Bryan Byrne's mobile number. A voicemail recording said, "The Professor is in the field, probably out of cell phone range. He may not have access to this voicemail for weeks. Leave a message and he will return the call when he is back on the grid." Jansen thought the voice was probably Byrne's, speaking in the third person, as if the answering machine was his personal assistant.

She also knew she couldn't wait weeks for a return call. If Bill Bowman was correct about how quickly the global black market swallowed rare books, Jansen needed to find Byrne and find him fast. Byrne may already have pawned them. He was clearly on the run, addicted, and suffering from a bad hip that required a cane—possibly the cane used to attack the library guard.

CHAPTER 16

1

Jim Briggs parked his *Have Paws—Will Travel* mobile dog clinic on 6th Avenue across from the train station and closed his eyes. After a busy night caring for wealthy paying clients, he needed a catnap before opening for the inevitable long line of homeless whose dogs he doctored for free.

"Hey, Doc, you asleep?" a woman's raspy voice penetrated his quiet space.

Briggs' eyes flew open. He looked over and saw the face of Ginger Portman, a 50-year-old homeless client. Her hands grabbed the top of the partially rolled-down window on the passenger side. She offered a big grin, minus two front teeth. Her mousy brown hair was chopped off just below her ears. Ginger's breath, which smelled of cigarettes and garlic, pushed into Briggs' space. He pressed his lips together and put his hand up to his mouth to stifle a gag. He made it appear as if he was yawning.

"Hi, Ginger. I was just snoozing. I was up late last night with a dying dog."

"Sorry to hear about that," she said. "When are you opening for business, Doc? Me and Bunny need patching up." Bunny was her fluffy poodle mix.

Usually, twenty to thirty homeless lined up with their dogs within minutes after Briggs pulled to the curb. He told Ginger to grab a place in line. No nap today, he thought. He had just climbed out of his van when a man with striking jet-black hair and blue eyes appeared with a dog. The man walked to the head of the line, causing those waiting to grumble. "Cheater!" a voice screamed.

"I'm Bryan Byrne," he said, reaching out to shake Briggs' hand, ignoring the protests.

Byrne backed away to take in Briggs' full height.

"I'm six-feet-six if you were wondering," said Briggs. "A common question. By the way, I'm Jim Briggs. I'm a veterinarian."

"That's why I stopped," said Byrne. "I'm staying around the corner at a hotel and took Dino out for a walk. He's limping. I think his feet got beat up in a desert canyon where I let him run. I should have gotten him a pair of hiking booties."

Briggs looked up at the anxious faces who saw the man walk up to the head of the line. "Don't worry, folks. I have an injury that needs urgent care. I'll only be a few minutes. Every one of you will get help today." He turned back to Byrne.

"What brings you to Portland?" Briggs asked, while he got down on one knee and cozied up to Dino. The border collie didn't resist. Briggs scratched his ears, then gently lifted and examined each paw.

"You're right, his paw pads have road rash," said Briggs, avoiding medical jargon with clients. "They're very raw."

"Can you help him?" asked Byrne.

"I'll apply antibacterial ointment, cover the wounds with soft pads and booties. I want you to apply the ointment twice a day. Keep the booties on for a week. After that Dino should be fine."

"To answer your question, I'm a college professor," said Byrne. "I teach courses focusing on historic treks, including the westward movement on the Oregon Trail. I'm in Portland doing research for the course."

"Shouldn't you be in class this time of year?" Briggs asked, scrutinizing the man as if Briggs were a principal talking to a wayward student.

"I'm on sabbatical. I got time off to get my bad hip fixed," Byrne said, holding up his cane. "I need hip replacement surgery, which is scheduled at the end of next month. Thankfully, my doctor just moved the surgery up because of a cancellation. In the meantime, I'm collecting class material and trying my best to deal with the pain."

"Wish I could help with the pain," said Briggs, anticipating a request for drugs. His homeless addict clients often used lines like 'can you help my dog,' to get pain pills. "Pain management is not my field of expertise."

"Got plenty of pills," said Byrne, sensing Briggs' thought he was looking for a fix.

After patching up Dino, Byrne said, "What do I owe you, Doc?"

"If you let me give Dino a collar with a tracking chip, which I will provide for free, then there is no cost."

"You've got a deal. I've been meaning to get a new collar to replace the one he lost. I have to admit, I kept the collar too loose."

Briggs strapped on a collar with a PupFinder GPS tracker. "The GPS tracker will allow me to find you for a follow-up visit to see how Dino's paws are healing."

"Not sure how long we'll be in town, but it won't hurt to have the collar if Dino and I get separated."

"Here's my cell phone number in case that happens." Briggs handed Byrne his business card with his mobile number and Byrne texted his number to Briggs.

PupFinder, an app on Briggs' phone and tablet, made it possible for him to keep track of about 50 dogs of his regular homeless clients. He couldn't count on those with cell phones to keep them charged. Since many were nomadic, constantly moving in search of food, shelter, and handouts, follow-up care for their dogs would be otherwise impossible. He had tried to establish several free clinics around town, but he still was only reaching a fraction of the unhoused population.

"The homeless are getting restless," said Briggs. "I better get moving. I've got a busy day ahead of me."

"Thanks for patching up Dino," said Byrne. Briggs watched as the man limped away, leaning heavily on his cane to relieve the pressure and pain on his leg.

CHAPTER 17

1

Blogger Chuck Grayson read the online police report about the library break-in and called Detective Jansen for details.

"Detective Bureau, Jansen."

"Detective, this is Chuck Grayson," he said, his voice gravelly from a lifelong smoking habit. "Reporter for Urban Street PDX." He liked using the word "reporter," as if it had weight. It made her smile.

There was no need for the formality. Jansen had known Grayson for several years. He was a straight shooter. They often spoke about police investigations off the record—when she was a patrol officer and as an investigator. He had never violated her trust or revealed her as a source.

"Chuck, how are you?" Unlike most cops, who rarely welcomed reporter inquiries, Jansen liked Grayson. "Nice to hear your voice."

"Kim," he said softer. "Nice to hear yours. Been awhile. How are you?"

"I'm really okay. You might think the stabbing and loss of my baby would make me lose my love for the job—and my nerve in the field. It hasn't. I feel stronger than ever. Don't know why. Therapy with the department psychologist may have helped. Or good genes."

"How about you, Chuck?"

"Much better," he said. "We haven't seen each other in a while. I've gained weight, getting regular haircuts, drinking less, and exercising more."

"What brought on the change?" asked Jansen.

"It might surprise you, but I've found a woman who I really care about. We've been together for about a year."

"Good news," she said, recalling that shortly after retirement, Chuck's wife had died of cancer. The aftermath was ugly. He began wasting away physically, drunk most nights, with his wife's dog his only comfort.

At heart, he was a good guy, Jansen felt. She would never forget the compassion he showed her when he found out that Jim Briggs, the husband-to-be and father of her unborn child, had euthanized Maxine Reid. She wasn't sure how he found out. Mark Larson may have let it slip or leaked it. Any other reporter would have broadcast the story across the world. Chuck buried it. He pitied Maxine and had witnessed her suffering. Because of his mercy, Briggs escaped a jail sentence, or worse. That Briggs' dad and Grayson were reporters at the same newspaper and best friends may have saved Briggs' life.

The decision must have been painful for Grayson, whose life and mental health were hanging by a thread, along with his identity as a reporter. Once he retired, he found it harder to get information for his blog. It was not the same as working for a big newspaper. And a big story, like Briggs's part in a woman's death, would have put him on top again. He must have wrestled with his ethics.

"Chuck, I never thanked you for how you handled the homeless murders and Jim's involvement." Grayson had revealed how Briggs' veterinary colleague Helen Williams euthanized five homeless men who had gang-raped her. He left out the fact that Briggs knew about William's revenge campaign and said nothing. He clearly was an accessory to the crime. Even worse, he knew she burned up the bodies in his pet crematory and said nothing.

"No need to thank me," said Grayson, who choked up. "I did what I thought was right."

"You also saved Jim's life and prevented me from having a life of pain without him. All I could think of was raising a child alone, explaining to her why her father was in prison."

"You're welcome," he offered quietly.

Jansen didn't want to make Grayson any more uncomfortable, so she moved on.

"How can I help you today?

"Tell me about your case."

"You know the drill. First off, this is not for attribution. Fuzz it up however you like. Just make sure it doesn't sound like it came from me. Is that fair?"

"Fair enough," said Grayson. "I agree to your terms." He always clarified that they had an understanding and that he would not violate it. She filled in Grayson on the theft details.

"What we don't know is why only seven of the Curtis books were stolen," she said. "So far, there is no evidence that the number of books taken means anything other than the burglar intended to get all of them, then panicked when confronted by the guard," She held back the clue that connected Professor Bryan Byrne and his great grandfather to the books.

"We found a cane at the scene which appeared to have blood and skin on it," she added. "Likely the weapon used in the attack. Not sure if it is the guard's blood or possibly from the suspect. We have ordered a Rapid DNA test. I expect results in the next 24 to 48 hours. I will text you what we find."

"Anything more, Kim?"

It surprised Jansen he used her first name. Like cops, he almost always referred to people by their last names.

"Not so far. I am hoping Bill Bowman, the curator of the rare book collection at the library, might have more information to share once he gets over the shock of the missing books."

"Thanks. Keep me in the loop."

"I will. You'll be first to know if anything important comes up."

"Chuck, you won't forget to call me if you find out anything that might help my case," said Jansen.

He agreed, and Jansen hung up. She knew that Chuck Grayson, like her, would hold back information as a bargaining chip. It was part of their game. She gets his help. He gets the exclusive at the end of the case.

2

**Priceless Books Stolen from Multnomah
County Library, Guard Wounded**

*By Charles "Chuck" Grayson,
Editor, Urban Street PDX*

A security guard was severely injured last night at the Central Branch of the Multnomah County Library when he tried to prevent the theft of books from the library's rare book room, according to the Portland Police Bureau incident report.

Library security guard Elliot Mark Delaney, 67, is in the critical care unit at Providence St. Vincent Medical Center in Northwest Portland with a deep neck wound. His condition is listed as "grave." A member of his medical team not authorized to comment on the case suggested they might need to induce a coma to allow Mr. Delaney's brain to recover from the massive blood loss. He was unconscious and struggling to breathe when paramedics arrived. The wounded man was discovered by a second guard who could not raise Delaney on his radio. Delaney had been making routine security rounds at the library when the incident occurred.

Police sources report that Delaney, father of four and grandfather of ten, apparently caught the burglar in the act and attempted to prevent the theft of an unspecified number of books in the Edward S. Curtis North American Indian series. A complete set recently auctioned for nearly $3 million.

Curtis was famous as a photographer and a man passionate about creating a record of Native American cultures he believed were headed for extinction. Besides photos of native Americans, Curtis and dozens of assistants made recordings of tribal languages and documented their customs. Curtis published his first book in 1907. Volume 20 came out in 1930.

"They are priceless," said William Bowman, curator of the John Wilson Collections of rare books at the central branch of the Multnomah County Library. "Losing even one volume is catastrophic. Losing seven is incalculable in terms of lost scholarship, as well as a major library asset."

Said Bowman, "Before the theft we owned a complete set of Edward Curtis's The North American Indian—20 original volumes of text, plus 20 volumes of large folio prints. These were acquired by the library directly through an exclusive subscription when they were published. Funds were supplied by a large group of prominent Portlanders who were acknowledged in volume one."

Considering that Curtis could only get 250 subscribers for each set of his complete works makes the Portland Central Library especially valuable, Bowman noted. Theodore Roosevelt wrote the introduction to The North American Indian. Along with the funds from subscriptions, J.P. Morgan provided most of the financing.

Why would a thief only take seven of the twenty volumes when the value was in possessing all 20? That is a question concerning police. One source suggested the burglar wanted all 20 but grabbed what they could and ran after his confrontation with Mr. Delaney.

Homicide Detective Kim Jansen, who has been assigned to the case, said it was too early in the investigation to make any conclusions. She was not willing to share any theories police may have developed. Stay tuned. I'll have regular updates as the case unfolds.

Leave comments below.

CHAPTER 18

1

Nino Parducci saw Detective Jansen approaching the front door of his restaurant. She was moving quickly, her jacket swinging open, revealing her badge and gun. Parducci grabbed the door and yanked it open, as if Jansen might crash through the glass like super woman. "The man you are looking for is in the back," said Parducci.

"Thanks," she said, moving around the counter and into the dining area.

"Don't get up," she admonished, pushing the man back into his seat. Nearby diners appeared startled at the appearance of an armed Portland Police Bureau detective issuing a warning. To their shock, she grabbed the man behind the head and pulled him into a kiss.

"I love you, Briggs," she said, following with a hug. He hugged her back. She looked around and told other diners that he was her husband. There was a collective sigh of relief.

"I'm Detective Kim Jansen," she announced. "This is Jim Briggs, the best veterinarian in the city. No doubt you've seen his mobile dog clinic, Have Paws—Will Travel." Briggs flushed bright red as all eyes focused on him. After Jansen finished, other diners returned to their meals.

"I wish you wouldn't do that," Briggs protested. "It's embarrassing."

Jansen smiled. "Got to support my husband," she said, finally settling into the chair opposite Briggs. "Sorry I'm late."

Their townhome was five blocks away from Via Pancetta, their favorite Italian restaurant. Jansen often walked there on her days off. She would tie her blonde hair back with a scrunchie, throw on her sweats, and head for the restaurant when Briggs left for work—or when he was sleeping in after a night of urgent client calls with sick pets. When she was a sergeant working in patrol, in her police uniform, Jansen and Nino often pretended she was coming to make an arrest when she was there to meet Briggs, like today.

"I'm starving," she said to Nino, who suddenly appeared table side.

"I've got your favorite, detective. Spaghetti and meatballs. The sauce is made of sauteed baby spinach, plum tomatoes, and marinara." He had described the menu item as if Jansen hadn't ordered it a dozen times before.

"Perfect," said Jansen. "Don't forget the beet salad." Nino smiled and nodded.

"I'll have your beet salad," said Briggs, who could easily eat half the lunch items on the menu at one sitting and still be hungry. And not gain an ounce. Even Briggs' steady diet of junk food didn't add extra weight.

"Excuse him, Nino. He's on a diet." Nino shook his head, frowned at Briggs, and said, "You need to eat more." Briggs couldn't help thinking that was Nino's Italian mother speaking.

Briggs smiled and shook his head. "You're incorrigible, Jansen. I've been living on donuts, lemon drops, and popping licorice pieces like popcorn. I need roughage."

The food arrived as Jansen was describing her day and developments in her theft case.

"Any leads?" Briggs asked.

"The likely weapon was a hiking pole used as a cane," she said. "Our forensic team found something on the tip, which was extremely sharp. Most likely it's from the guard's neck wound. Lindsay Fell, one of our forensic team leaders and an avid backpacker, says she has a hiking pole just like the one we found. The spike digs into rocks, she says, adding stability on narrow trails. The crime scene samples are at the lab for DNA analysis. Nothing to report yet."

"What's odd," Jansen added, "is that two men with canes visited the John Wilson rare book collection in the same week. One was part of a tour, which included showing off a volume of Edward Curtis' *North American Indian*. The other guy was a professor who teaches courses on Western U.S. History. He was on sabbatical and spent a lot of time looking at the Curtis books and discussing them with Bowman. We have a second visitor's name, but no contact information."

"Kimmy," Briggs said, moving in closer in a bedroom whisper, "If I have information that helps you with your case, will there be a reward?"

She knew his reward was a morning in bed, enjoying his favorite positions. "What could you possibly tell me that would motivate me to give you more than a smack on the butt?"

"I know the professor you're looking for and I know how to contact him," said Briggs, a smirk on his face.

"Quit dicking around, Briggs. I need to eat lunch and get back to work," she said, suddenly annoyed by his ridiculous assertion.

"I met the professor this morning," said Briggs.

"What are you talking about, Briggs?"

"What I'm talking about is information to help you solve your case. My help doesn't come cheap," he continued. "I want a reward."

"I give in, Jimmy, I'll do whatever you want," she said, leaning in and whispering in his ear. "Now, give me the information or I'll arrest your ass for obstructing justice."

"Okay," said Briggs. "When I was setting up for my homeless clients down at Portland Union Station this morning, a man came by with his dog. Both were limping. The man introduced himself as Bryan Byrne and his dog, Dino, a border collie. Byrne said Dino had injured his paws on rough terrain during a hike in the Arizona desert on his way out to Oregon. He mentioned going to the library downtown and over to Oregon Historical Society. He said he is related to a photographer on the Edward Curtis treks in the early 20th century."

"Bryan Byrne is the name of the visiting history professor, according to Bowman," said Jansen.

"I tagged his dog with a PupFinder GPS collar and got Byrne's mobile number to provide follow-up care for Dino's feet," Briggs explained.

"I already have his number, but he doesn't answer," said Jansen. "Help me track him down and you'll get a double reward." She jumped up and started out the door. "Let's get your laptop and find this guy."

"Relax, Jansen. Sit back down and enjoy your lunch. After lunch, I will log onto PupFinder and tell you exactly where to find Professor Byrne."

"Give it to me now," Jansen commanded, standing up straight, hands on her hips. Diners stopped eating to witness the unfolding drama.

"No, your husband is ordering you sit down and eat, then you can race off," he said. "You're awful!" said Jansen, surrendering. "And I guess you're the best too, Briggs." When Jansen plopped back into her chair, the tension went out of the room and the lunchtime chatter resumed. Briggs and Jansen changed the subject to the sexy details of a romantic getaway they had been planning for months. Nino was back at the table offering dessert just as Jansen took her last bite of spaghetti.

"Not today," said Jansen. "I'm on the trail of a suspect. Gotta go."

Nino smiled. He loved to hear her talk about cases, as if she was letting him in on a secret.

2

After walking back to their townhouse, Briggs launched PupFinder to locate Bryan Byrne. Jansen looked over his shoulder, waiting for Byrne's location to appear on the computer screen. Oregon law prohibited tracking an individual without their permission. No such rules applied to dogs. Technically, Briggs was tracking Byrne's dog, Dino, not Byrne. It was a slippery slope, open to ethical considerations. Still, it allowed Briggs to provide free care to the dogs of the city's nomadic homeless. Jansen never challenged him on it.

"It appears Dino is near the Oregon Historical Society," said Briggs. "He may be locked in the car. Byrne is likely in the society's research library. Or he and Dino could be out for a walk."

"I'm not sure this bit of information is worth a reward," said Jansen, who gave Briggs a neutral look.

Briggs moaned.

"Just kidding, sweetie pie." She leaned over to kiss him. "You'll get your reward. I'll give Byrnes another call. I better get going. Bowman says the longer the Curtis books are missing, the more likely they'll end up on the black market and sold to a wealthy rare book collector halfway across the world. This afternoon, I'm going over to McQuillan's to see Meghan. She or her dad, Bruce, may have been contacted as potential buyers for the stolen books."

Jansen walked back to her car, radioed that she was back on the clock, and called Bryan Byrne. The call went straight to voicemail, like before.

Jansen left a message, briefly describing again who she was and asking him to call her as soon as possible. Thirty minutes later, he returned her call.

"Jansen," she answered.

"This is Bryan Byrne. I just listened to your message. I was in the library and wasn't allowed to use my cell phone. Did you say my name has come up in an investigation?"

"Professor Byrne, I didn't expect a call back for 24 to 48 hours. I guess you are a busy man."

Byrne got the gibe. "I do that so students who think they have a problem learn to use their growing brains to help themselves. Most of the time, students are lonely or feel like a minor issue deserves a 9-1-1 response. I often play babysitter for insecure, lonely kids. Detective, I love my students, but you need to draw the line, or they will be in bed with you like a kid afraid of the dark who runs to their parents' room every time they hear a bump in the night."

"They want to sleep with you?" Jansen taunted, still peeved about the voicemail on Byrne's phone.

"Hilarious, Detective," said Bryan. "How did my name come up in an investigation?"

"I prefer to talk to you in person. Can you come by and chat with me for a few minutes? I'm sure it is nothing," she said.

Jansen tried to make her request for a visit to the police station appear routine.

Byrne got the address and confirmed that he was inside the Oregon Historical Society research library. He was only about six blocks from the Portland Police Bureau main office. If his hip wasn't in such terrible shape, he could walk. Instead, he hobbled a half block to a parking space for the handicapped and drove over to the police bureau.

CHAPTER 19

1

When Bryan Byrne arrived at the police station, a patrol officer took him to a conference room. On a side table was a pot of coffee, scones, and fresh fruit. Detective Jansen allowed Byrne to settle for 10 minutes, then walked in. She didn't want to make him nervous or uncomfortable. When Jansen walked into the room, she apologized for being late, claiming she had been in an urgent meeting with her boss. Byrne didn't seem to mind, pushing the last crumbs of scone into his mouth, avoiding the fresh fruit. "The scone was great," said Byrne, acting as though he was unconcerned about being summoned to the police station.

"They're maple-walnut," Jansen said, "My favorite. I'll join you." It was her we-are-just-friends-having-coffee routine.

"Do you have any idea why I asked you here today?"

"I assume it involves police business?" said Byrne, who was breaking off chunks of a second scone and washing it down with gulps of coffee, like a man who hadn't eaten in weeks. A sign of nervousness, Jansen thought. She also noticed him squirming in his seat. Each movement produced a grimace. Was he in pain? She would make a note of it and ask him about it later.

"Did you hear about the break-in at rare book room at the Multnomah County main branch library?" asked Jansen. The perpetrator attacked a guard and got away with seven of twenty volumes that make up a collection of Native American portraits called *The North American Indian?*"

"What are you talking about?" Byrne said, his eyes wide. He sat up and pushed away from his food as if it were poison, while still gripping a scone so tightly it crumbled between his fingers and dropped onto the floor. "I just saw Bill Bowman yesterday, and we had a long conversation about Curtis. Everything was fine." Bryan leaned forward again, picked up a fresh scone and began eating. "I get it. You're joking to get a rise out of me."

"This happened in the last 12 hours," said Jansen. "The intruder critically wounded the guard, who interrupted the theft."

Byrne dropped the last bite of scone on a paper plate, hung his head, and slumped in his chair. He had closed his eyes and was eerily quiet for a minute before speaking, as if trying to make up a story.

"This is devastating, Detective Jansen. Why would anyone steal the Curtis books?"

"We are trying to find the answer to that question."

"Am I a suspect?" Byrne said, suddenly realizing why Jansen had asked him to come down for a conversation rather than answering her questions on the phone.

"No fucking way," said Byrne, shaking his head. "Never, never, ever. I'm a historian. I would never do anything to damage a precious collection like the one Bill Bowman has."

Jansen ignored his rant.

"Do you own a cane?" Jansen asked.

"Yes. I've got a hip problem."

"Where is your cane?"

Byrne looked around the room. "It must be in the car. I guess I ran off without it. Which is kind of a joke, detective, since I can't run. I took pain medication before coming. When the pain is gone, I can walk short distances without the cane."

"What brings you to Portland, Professor Byrne?"

"I'm rounding up bits of history to feed graduate students in my pioneer trail class," he said. "I'm collecting oral histories, photos, and video of the Oregon Trail for the next semester. I made my mark as a teacher and won tenure five years earlier than most professor..." Bryan stopped talking. He took in a gulp of air, let it out like a deflating balloon, and began his confession. "I'm lying."

2

Jansen relished the coming confession. She would arrest Byrne, walk him to the jail to get his photo and fingerprints, then write her final report. She and Briggs could take off for a few days, she thought, smiling to herself.

Jansen put down her pen, sat up straight, and looked the man directly in the eyes. "Go ahead, make your confession," she said, getting his permission first to record the interview. She realized she sounded more like a priest than a cop. She wouldn't be giving him absolution or a penance. Unfortunately, what was often in her head often came out her mouth. She could be too honest. Lucky for her, none of her colleagues heard it and Byrne was too distracted to notice. She waited a moment more, and the professor began talking.

"I'm a drug addict, hooked on pain pills. I've got a hip that needs replacement. I waited too long to get it repaired and have been suffering excruciating pain for months while waiting to get the surgery. I got caught trying to snatch pain medication from a local pharmacy in Arizona. Luckily for me, the druggist-owner was friends with my boss, Dean Stanley Watkins. They let me off, but Watkins told me to leave school until I got my hip fixed and kicked the drug habit."

Was he in pain, or was it an act? Jansen wondered.

"Do you really use a cane, professor?"

"Of course. I can't do without it."

"I'm looking around the room and I don't see it," said Jansen.

"I told you. I must have left it in the car."

"If you need it, why would you leave it in the car?"

"I was nervous about coming here," he said?

"Do you have a reason to be nervous, Professor Byrne?"

"Isn't everyone nervous when the police summon them for no apparent reason?" he shot back. "I just didn't. Guess I got an adrenalin spurt that pushed me through the pain. And like I said, I took a pain pill an hour ago. That helped."

Jansen wasn't buying the explanation, but let it sit. She could pursue it later. She knew all about Byrne's so-called sabbatical. Byrne's story matched what Jansen had learned from Dean Watkins. Still, she needed to double check the details of the professor's story.

"Why is my cane so important?"

"Because a walking stick or cane was used to fend off the guard who caught the thief in the act moments after he broke into the rare book room. The burglar used the cane as a weapon, slashing the guard's throat."

"Oh no," said Byrne, grimacing at Jansen's description of the attack.

"What brand is your cane?"

"I don't even know. It's second-hand from an outdoor gear store. It was a wilderness hiking stick before my hip problem. Now it's a cane." Jansen shifted to a new line of questioning. She opened a folder in front of her and pulled out a sketch of a man created from Bill Bowman's description of a visitor to his library.

"The man in this sketch, who also walked with a cane, was the other person—besides you—who visited the library rare book room in the past week and showed interest in the Curtis books."

Byrne studied the rendering and said, "It looks like Val James."

"Who is Val James?" said Jansen, sitting up tall, on high alert.

"He's a friend of my father. They were roommates in college."

Jansen was puzzled. Two suspects who apparently knew each other visited the John Wilson Collections in the past week and carried canes—each unaware of the other's visit. Were the canes planned disguises? Was it a coincidence? She didn't believe in coincidences.

"Why would Val James be interested in the Curtis books?" She asked.

"You'll have to ask Val or my dad."

"Who is your father?" asked Jansen.

"Colin Byrne, owner and founder of Byrne Vineyards. We had dinner earlier this week. He told me Val had visited him the day before and that he was down on his luck, a bookie after him for a big gambling debt, and had lost his house and family. Dad offered Val a job and money to help get him back on his feet."

"You think Val would steal the Curtis books?"

"I know he worked for a big security firm at one point. He no doubt has the skills to pull it off. Dad says he's got a gambling problem. But honestly, I can't imagine Val would steal rare books."

Jansen could. A man with a gambling addiction was a man possessed—a desperate man with a never-ending thirst for cash, with endless dreams of cashing in big.

"Bill Bowman says you're related to Edward Curtis."

"No, that's not right. My dad's grandfather was William Bryan Byrne. He helped gather information for the 20 books that make up *The North American Indian* and may have taken photos attributed to Curtis."

"Is that all?" asked Jansen.

"What do you mean?" he shot back, now angry.

"What would you think if a suspect looks at a drawing of another man and immediately recognizes him as a family friend? Are you sure he isn't an accomplice?"

"That ridiculous," said Byrne. "Val has a distinctive look. Age hasn't diminished him. I would recognize him anywhere—even in a rough sketch."

Jansen looked at Byrne for a few minutes more and decided he got what she needed from the interview. She took down Colin's Byrne's contact information, thanked Bryan for coming in, and asked him to put her in his contact list. "I may need to talk with you again," she said, then asked an officer to show him out.

"Next, you're going to tell me not to leave town."

"You can leave town," she said. "Just answer your phone when I call."

She wasn't ruling out Professor Byrne as a suspect or a co-conspirator. A more likely target now was Val James. The puzzle pieces were falling into place. Jansen's next stop: a discussion with Colin Byrne.

CHAPTER 20

1

After questioning Professor Byrne, Jansen headed back to her desk, logged onto her computer, and entered her new suspect's name in the search field. In seconds, hundreds of news items on a Valentine "Val" Robert James appeared. Most of the news centered on his athletic heroics in college. And his crippling football career-ending injury as he made the winning catch on the goal line. Despite the injury, his post college career took off. He was a paid commentator for his college football team and a sportscaster on the local CBS affiliate. Local advertisers fought for his product endorsements. Before she immersed herself in James' history, Jansen emailed department research assistant Kelly O'Connor, who was looking into Robert Hill, the name listed on the rare book room's visitor log. That Val's middle name was Robert suggested the possibility the last name, Hill, was an alias for Val James.

How did Val James go from scoring the go-ahead touchdown that sealed his team's first championship in decades to loser hooked on gambling? Jansen sent 50 pages of news articles to the department's high-speed printer and moved onto public and law enforcement databases. Her search turned up a divorce decree that detailed how Val had emptied the family bank accounts, including his daughter's college tuition fund, and mortgaged his home to the hilt. He eventually lost the house and moved the family into an apartment. All the gory details were splashed on the front of local newspapers. The adverse publicity humiliated his wife and daughter and killed his jobs as a sports commentator. Most businesses dropped him as their advertising pitch man. His career went from 200 miles per hour to zero, like a race car that blows an engine in the middle of a NASCAR race. A hell of a thing for a middle-aged man to fall off a cliff of his own making.

Jansen got an impression of the man from the articles, which included photos. James was a talented man. Nice hair. Beautiful eyes. Tall. A stud. Mr. Popular, the boy who married the prom queen and was living the good life before his downfall.

A year later, after the news media had moved on, James got a license to work for a west coast security firm as a consultant. When Jansen checked on the status of his security license, she found it had lapsed. She made a note to call the firm and determine his employment status and get contact information.

If he was unemployed and broke, would he call old friend Colin Byrne for help? Or appeal to his bookie, who was taking illegal bets? Val may have thought his only option was to hit it big—the dream of every gambling addict. Pay off his debts and win back his family. With that in mind, Jansen would contact the FBI about Val James' possible connection to organized crime. Her effort to pin down James' current location was a dead end. If not for Professor Byrne's report of a recent meeting with Colin Byrne at the Byrne Vineyard, Val James would be a ghost.

That James had a crushing knee injury playing football supported the idea that he might have bought a hiking stick to use as a cane. But why wouldn't he have taken it with him after attacking the guard? Even in a panic, he would have grabbed it for support to help get away with the Curtis books, especially down the steep stairs that led to the library's rare book room. Was it a disguise?

Jansen wouldn't know if James was the likely perpetrator until the DNA report came back. She hoped it might match DNA already in one of the law enforcement databases. Since Bill Bowman had given her copies of the sign-in sheets for visitors, she might connect Val James by comparing the log signatures with his signature on his driver's or security officer's license. In the meantime, she called Colin Byrne and left a message.

She was just about to pick up the phone to call local outdoor gear stores, to pin down recent sales of hiking poles, when she recognized a return call coming in from Byrne Vineyards.

2

"Detective Jansen, this is Colin Byrne. I'm the owner of Byrne Vineyards in Newberg. You left a message. I don't understand why a Portland Police Bureau detective would call me." The voice was confident, with no sign of stress.

"I'm investigating the theft of rare books from the Portland Public Library main branch and the injury of a guard who caught the perpetrator in the act."

"I read about that. What a shame. How is the guard?"

Colin spoke the right words rapid fire. The flat tone of his voice revealed that he didn't have a drop of interest in the guard or his welfare.

"Fighting for his life," Jansen answered. "He a 67-year-old man with grandchildren, who loved libraries and became a guard to early extra money for post-retirement vacations."

"Tell his family everyone is praying for him," said Colin. Jansen again sensed he was feigning interest and compassion for a man he didn't know. Colin confirmed his lack of genuine interest, moving to the bottom line. "Do you have any leads in the case?" he asked. All very business-like, Jansen thought. Was that because he was a busy man who was needed elsewhere at the winery—a CEO with a passion for efficiency? Or was he involved in the theft? Jansen didn't couldn't think of any motive that would put a suspect target on Colin's back.

"We are exploring several leads," said Jansen. "I would prefer to come out to visit you and speak in private. Would 1 p.m. this afternoon work for you?"

"I have a busy day with wine buyers and a late afternoon staff meeting," Byrne said. "I can fit in a brief meeting. Are you sure I couldn't answer all your questions on this call?"

"It's a little more complicated. I want to share a picture of a suspect and other information."

"I'll see you after lunch then," he said. Jansen noticed a slight waver in his voice.

3

Jansen bought a Thai wrap for lunch from a food cart a half mile from the police station near the Portland Art Museum, then drove 20 miles southwest to Byrne

Estate Vineyard, meandering along Highway 99W rather than battle traffic on Interstate 5.

Driving through the countryside, Jansen's mind returned to Briggs' question about whether she still wanted to have children after the loss of her newborn daughter. Although motherhood was never on her radar as she moved up the police ranks, from patrol rookie to detective, her pregnancy, and the reality that she was carrying soon-to-be-born Lily Kimberly Briggs, gave her a feeling of contentment that soon faded.

Maybe she wasn't meant to be a mother. Lily had been an unintended pregnancy. Although Jansen wasn't opposed to abortion, Briggs' excitement about being a father erased any thought of terminating the pregnancy. This time, she would make a choice to have another child.

Before the stabbing, she was fearless in the field. Now, she wondered if another pregnancy might create a sense of vulnerability, making her more likely to get her or another officer injured or killed. It was a tremendous burden. She pushed aside the thought as she began winding through the Willamette Valley, home to 700 of Oregon's 900 plus wineries.

After stopping to take a few pictures along the way—a hobby she had developed over the past few years—she arrived at the entrance to the Byrne Estate. Jansen drove up the long road to the tasting room. Pulling into the parking area, she noticed she wasn't the only visitor. Not surprising. It was summer and tourists would be wine tasting. At the top of the steps leading into the building, Jansen stopped and looked across the vineyards and rolling hills. With the money Briggs had inherited, they could sell their weekend home overlooking the Columbia River and buy one in the Willamette Valley. She could have a baby, then while away the days dreaming—and drinking the wine and serenity—far from urban Portland, its failed city government, wishy-washy mayor, and endless abuse from the homeless. Thoughts of more sex and excellent wine temporarily erased any thought of nursing babies or endless diaper changing.

4

Jansen snapped herself out of her daydream, pulled into a parking space in front of the tasting room, and turned off the engine. Before she could open the door, a woman appeared on the front porch. Jansen stepped out of the car and smiled at the woman.

"Ready for a tasting?" the woman asked.

"I wish," said Jansen. "The chief of detectives would not be too pleased if I got a DUII—or worse yet, I ran over someone after enjoying a flight of wines. I'm here on official business. I have an appointment with Colin Byrne. I'm Detective Kimberly Jansen with the Portland Police Bureau." The woman cocked her head, her lips puckered like she had been sucking on a lemon. The welcoming smile disappeared. "I'll Stella Mason, Mr. Byrne's estate manager. I don't see an appointment on his calendar, which I manage." She was obviously perturbed Byrne had left her out of the planned meeting. "Besides," she added, "He has a busy day." She said it as if she was going to cancel the meeting.

"As you might expect, I'm here to talk to Mr. Byrne about a crime. He might have some useful information to help solve the case." Mason came to her senses. She was supposed to facilitate Vineyard Estate activities, even those planned at the last minute. She pulled out a mobile phone and made a call. While talking, she was nervously pacing as if she were a suspect about to be found out. A moment later, Mason ended her call and returned.

"Colin says he can see you in about 15 minutes when he breaks from a V.I.P. luncheon he is hosting." Mason looked at her watch. He won't have much time to talk."

"I won't need much time," Jansen said. "I have just a few questions."

"You can wait on the terrace," Mason offered, pointing to a seating area overlooking the vineyard. It appeared she wasn't going to lead Jansen outside, a courtesy she would have extended to other visitors, especially VIPs coming for one of Colin's personal wine tastings. Mason seemed to regain her composure and said, "Follow me, detective. May I get you something to drink? We have water and sodas.

Jansen would have loved a big glass of red wine. Or two.

"Water will be fine," said Jansen, smiling to her suddenly friendly hostess. A minute later, Mason was back with the water.

Jansen had taken one sip of water when a voice from behind gave her a jolt.

"You call this work, Jansen?"

Her headed snapped around and there he was—her best friend, former patrol partner-detective, who gave up his gold shield for a security job with twice the pay.

"Larson, what are you doing here? How did you even know where I was? You must have talked to Jim. You can't be here. I'm here on official business."

"So am I," said Larson, sweeping back his jacket to reveal a detective shield. "I guess Chief Melrose forgot to tell you."

She waited to hear more.

"Melrose called and said he had an opening and that my badge number was still active," said Larson. "I couldn't stomach any more security work, as good as Paragon is. I need to be a real cop, doing actual work."

"Melrose left me a message a half hour ago, but I was driving and didn't listen," Jansen said. "I guess you are the message."

Jansen would have given Larson a hug, but figured a nod and a smile would get her message across that she was happy to have him. A moment later, Colin Byrne walked onto the terrace.

5

"You must be Detective Jansen," he said, then turned to Larson. "And you are?"

"I'm Mark Larson. Detective Jansen and I are seeking leads in the attack on a guard at the Multnomah County Library and the theft of rare books worth millions." Larson was exaggerating the value but figured it would take big numbers to get the attention of a wealthy man like Colin Byrne.

Byrne was a beautiful man, Jansen thought. Over six feet. Trim. Jet black hair with some gray flecks. Freckled skin. The bluest eyes. Eye, that is. One eye was covered with a patch. Extending below the patch was a deep scar. Jansen knew he was 58. He looked closer to 50.

"I'm Colin Byrne," he said. "Welcome to our little estate."

"How about cheese plates, detectives?" Colin asked, apparently concerned about offering what might look like a subtle bribe. "We provide them to all our guests."

"I ate before coming down," said Jansen.

"I didn't have time to eat lunch, so I'd welcome it," said Larson.

The day was perfect with a bright blue sky. Puffy white clouds danced with the sun in a game of celestial hide and seek.

Colin's little estate, as he called it, appeared to be worth a fortune—the more reason to rule him out as a suspect. Or even involvement in a theft. Jansen's mind began working overtime. Could the vineyard be in financial trouble? Maybe he was a rich guy looking for kicks. Maybe this and maybe that. Her mind batted around possibilities.

"Detective Jansen, are you sure you wouldn't like a latte or espresso since you've already eaten?"

"If I were here with my husband, Jim, I would gladly go for the wine. I've had your 1992 Byrne Vineyard Estate Pinot Noir several times. I love it. Since I'm working, I will take you up on a double espresso."

As if listening in on their conversation, Stella Mason appeared at the door. "One double espresso coming up," she said.

"Make that two," said Byrne.

"I guess we should get down to business," he said, the polite, warm manner suddenly turning cool. Again, business-like. "I have a staff meeting in an hour, so we won't have a long time to talk."

"Do you know a man named Valentine James?" Jansen asked.

"Of course. He was my college roommate."

"I understand he was here visiting you last week."

"He was. I called him to catch up. And found out he had just arrived in town as part of a longer road trip. He came by, we drank wine, talked about old times, and he left." Jansen thought it sounded like a business deal, once again, all emotion absent. Was Colin Byrne all business—a guy with no sense of humor or genuine feelings for others?

"He didn't tell you why he chose Portland as a destination?"

"I don't recall asking," said Byrne. "Detective, what does this have to do with the break in at the library?"

Jansen pulled out a manilla folder, opened it, and pulled out a picture. "Do you recognize this man?"

"It looks like Val. Why?"

"Because this is a drawing our artist made with the help of Bill Bowman, curator of the Wilson Special Collections, the rare book room at the Portland Central Library. The sketch is of a man who visited the Wilson Collections before the break in. He joined a tour group to view the rare books. He signed as Robert Hill."

"Hill is his mother's maiden name. Robert is his middle name," said Byrne.

"Why would he use an alias?" Jansen asked.

"I have no idea," he said. "Are you suggesting Val broke in and attacked the guard?"

"I am. A witness saw him with a cane or hiking stick, like the one used to slash the guard's throat. The perpetrator left the hiking pole behind with blood on it. We'll be looking for a DNA match." Byrne wiggled in his seat, as if trying to get comfortable or he had a sudden itch.

Jansen noticed Byrne's white skin flush. Was he shocked that his friend could have been involved? Or did he fear some plot he and Val had cooked up was about to be exposed? She was sure he was about to reveal his involvement in the case. She waited.

Byrne took a depth breath, closed his eyes, and sat back in his chair. He opened his eyes and looked at her, but said nothing.

"Public records show he lost everything, then divorced," said Jansen. "He disappeared for a year, then surfaced as a security consultant."

"You seem to know a lot about Val, detective."

"A web searched turned up hundreds of pages of news items and official documents detailing his life and losses."

"I know all about Val's personal and financial problems," said Byrne. The truth—a version of the truth—was in order.

"Did you help him?" she asked.

"Val has a gambling problem," said Byrne. "A bunch of hoods are after him to collect a big debt. He told me he was on the run. No doubt that is why he used Robert Hill as an alias. He asked me for help until he could get back on his feet. I offered him a job here at the vineyard to earn some money and said I would pay for an apartment for a year—if he would attend Gambling Anonymous meetings."

"Mr. Byrne, that's awfully generous," said Jansen.

Byrne's eyes narrowed and his face tightened. "I'm loaded. I can afford to be generous with my best friend."

"Why would Val visit the library's rare book room?" Larson asked.

"That's no mystery," said Byrne. "He asked about what sights he might want to see while in town. In college, he was a jock, buy also smart as hell. He was an English literature major. He loved reading Charles Dickens and wanted to see first editions at the library. I also reminded him of my grandfather's connection to Edward Curtis and told him he should check out *The North American Indian.*"

Jansen glanced at Larson, a silent code passing between them, saying that Byrne's answer was too convenient, contrived. Jansen made a note.

"Anything else you want to share with us about your interaction with Val James?" Larson asked.

Byrne looked away. He seemed to make a calculation about how much more to say, then looked back at Jansen and Larson.

"I gave him a debit card with $1,000 on it to get food and a hotel room. He wanted time to consider my offer. He has been homeless, living out of his car somewhere down by the Portland Train Depot or old Greyhound Bus Station. I couldn't, in good conscience, allow him to suffer the humiliation of homelessness."

Byrne stood up, looked toward the vineyard. Opening his hands like Moses parting the Red Sea, he said, "You see all this? I built this over 30 years. I have picked grapes, pruned vines, worked the bottle filling line, and managed the construction of every building, and helped clear and plant every field. Because of hard work, I sell thousands of cases of wine each year."

"Impressive," Jansen said.

"Detective, I am very successful. Not to be crass, but I'm loaded. In my world, a thousand bucks is dinner for four with a few bottles of wine. I would do anything to help Val."

"Did Val steal the Curtis books?"

"Why would he do that, detective?"

"As a favor to you?" Larson said.

"You need to explain, Detective Larson."

"Your son, Bryan, said your grandfather was part of the Curtis expedition and may have taken some photos in the books," said Jansen.

"Yes, Grandfather William Byrne helped Curtis capture pictures of indigenous people for his books. Why were you in contact with my son?"

"He is also a person of interest in our case."

"I don't understand what you're saying, Detective Jansen. How could Bryan be involved?" Colin didn't wait for the answer. "You are both way off target. And what does any of this have to do with me?"

Neither Larson nor Jansen answered.

"Do you know where we can find Val?" asked Jansen.

"He promised to call in a day or two to let me know about whether he would take the job."

"Val is a sports guy, not a winemaker, right?" Jansen asked.

"During college, Val and I worked each summer at a different winery for the sake of variety to make extra money for school. We both had scholarships, but they didn't cover all our expenses. Val used every extra dime he earned, plus money he borrowed from friends, to satisfy his gambling addiction. He had a pretty good win record, but like most gamblers, he lost more than he made."

"Are you telling us that Val likely broke into the library to get books to sell to pay off his bookie?" Larson asked.

"You're putting words in my mouth," said Byrne, a flash of anger in his raised voice.

Byrne was clearly on the defensive. Jansen knew he was hiding something, so she changed direction.

"Is it possible your son, Bryan, and Val cooked up a deal to steal the books?"

"You've got to be kidding, Detective Jansen. Bryan is a historian. He would do nothing to destroy or damage a precious collection of rare history books, like Curtis'. Is he a suspect?"

"He and Val James are the only two men with canes who visited the Wilson Collection the past two weeks. Both canes were hiking poles that were similar to the one left at the scene of the attack on the guard. Bryan came in for an interview without his cane, despite his hip pain. Since we found a hiking pole at the scene of the theft with the guard's blood on it, we made the connection. Bryan denied his involvement and said he had left his cane in the car. Did you know your son is addicted to pain pills? He is essentially a drug addict who needs cash to buy extra pills can't get from his doctors. And James is desperate for money to pay off his bookie."

"Bryan is in a world of hurt, I have to admit," said Byrne. "No doubt, he's addicted to pain pills. But I have arranged for his surgery to be moved up and

I've found a Portland pain specialist who is working to wean him off hydrocodone."

Jansen wondered if Byrne was throwing his son under the bus to direct the blame away from Val James.

Byrne began fidgeting, running his hands through his hair, and opening and closing his hands. He was taking rapid breaths, clearly stressed by the questioning. He sighed and said, "I need to finish up with the VIP lunch I'm hosting in the other room. I think you are way off track. You need to look harder at the evidence. Bryan and Val aren't criminals."

"A motive for stealing the books could be to protect a little piece of family history involving your grandfather," Larson said.

"No way," said Colin.

"Isn't it possible Val, as a gift for your support, stole the books for you?"

Jansen did not know it, but she was dangerously close to the truth.

"What would I do with the books? I could always go see them in the library."

"Do you have Val's phone number?" said Jansen. "We would like to talk to him."

"He may be desperate for money, but he's not stupid. Val is not your man. I'll give you his mobile number. Why don't you call and ask him these questions? His involvement is a ridiculous idea." Byrnes gave Jansen the number, which she wrote in her notebook.

"Good luck with your investigation, detectives," he said. "Stella will see you out." Jansen turned around and saw Stella smiling at her.

"This way, detectives," she said.

Jansen had a feeling there was a connection between the break-in and Colin's grandfather's association with Edward Curtis. But how? The events took place 100 years apart. None of it made sense.

"Thank you for your time," said Jansen. "Here's my card. If Val gets in touch, please call us ASAP."

Byrne nodded, gave a one-hand wave, and left the terrace, walked across the lobby to double doors and entered. Jansen and Larson could see a group inside, already well on their way to a wine-soaked lunch.

"Call and make an appointment next time or you can talk to him on the phone," Stella admonished.

"Will do," said Jansen. She noted that questions about Edward S. Curtis and his grandfather set Byrne on edge.

When Jansen and Larson got to their cars, Jansen said, "We still need a motive."

"It's got to be money," said Larson. "Val James and the Professor both need money."

"I agree," said Jansen. "Something isn't right. And I think Colin Byrne may provide the missing link. There's something he's not telling us."

CHAPTER 21

1

Val wasn't ready to face Colin's wrath. Colin wasn't violent, but he could be scary when he was mad. Val pulled into the parking garage at Providence-St., Vincent Hospital. He opened the window for his beagle, Mac, and walked to the information desk, just inside the front door. A volunteer directed him to a set of elevators down the hall where he could go up to the intensive care unit. When the door opened, he walked to the nurses' station, where he showed his fake identification card to one of two nurses who stood up to greet him.

"I'm Robert Hill," Val said. "I'm a close friend of Elliot Delaney. We work in security together."

"Sorry, Mr. Hill. We have strict orders not to allow any visitors in his room. No one but family."

"I'm family," Val whispered. "Elliot and I always joked how we were brothers from a different mother. He is like an older brother." His protest did no good.

"All I can give you is his condition. He's critical. You really shouldn't be here."

"I understand," Val said, defeated. He just wanted to look in, hold the comatose man's hand, and beg him for forgiveness. Val closed his eyes. His entire body was about to collapse and melt into the floor. The nurse must have noticed Val's distress and said, "Mr. Delaney's wife is in his room. I could ask her if you can visit. I'll have her come out and talk to you."

Val backpedaled. "Don't bother her. She has too much on her mind. Having his family around him is what is most important for him right now. I just thought if no one was there, I could talk to him—give him words of support. Besides, I only met his wife briefly at a staff party years ago. She won't remember me."

"I'll tell her a friend from work came by to wish the best for Mr. Delaney's recovery," the nurse said. "Will that be okay?"

"Thank you," said Val, who turned and walked to the elevators.

2

When Val got back to the parking garage, he picked up Colin's third frantic voicemail. "The cops have a sketch of a suspect. It's a dead ringer for you. And I confirmed to police our dinner, my job offer, and that a bookie is after you."

"Fuck," said Val, punching off the phone. Why would Colin give the police any information? Val would now be a police target and on the news. His bookie's enforcers would be all over him once they discovered his location.

"I know what to do next," Val said to no one. "I've got to get rid of the Curtis books." Until he figured out a solution, he would hide them in the wheel-well of his Subaru Outback station wagon. For a moment, he considered tossing them in a dumpster, crushing his phone, and leaving town. Then he remembered what was at stake—paying off his debt, overcoming his gambling addiction, and winning back his family. No way he was giving Colin the books until he got the money. It was Val's only leverage to make the deal quickly and get away before police closed in. Val was packing up when another call came from Colin. This time, he answered Colin's call.

"About time you picked up the phone. Where have you been?"

"Colin, it was an accident," said Val.

"How do you accidentally cut a man's throat?"

"It wasn't supposed to happen," said Val.

"We've got big trouble because of what you did," said Colin.

Val explained his planning, hiding until after the library closed, disabling the camera, and opening the door to the rare book room with no problem.

"I had the books on a table and was putting them in my backpack when a guard came in," said Val. "He wasn't supposed to start his walkthrough for another 10 minutes. I had everything carefully planned. When he saw me, I tried to talk my way out of it, but he wasn't buying it. How could he? I was wearing a black hood, night vision googles, and a mask. When he picked up the radio for backup, I grabbed my hiking stick and swung at the radio to knock it away. Suddenly, he was on the floor, holding his neck. Blood was gushing. I panicked. I grabbed the books and ran."

"You left the hiking stick behind, according to Detective Jansen. She says she sent blood found at the scene to a lab for DNA analysis." One more nail in his coffin: he had cut his hand at the scene and left blood everywhere. No doubt he had left enough blood trail for police to connect to him. The guard's blood was on some pages. Val may also have smeared his own blood on the books.

"Where are the books?" There was silence on the phone.

"Val, where are my books?"

"I've got them. But if you don't give me the money you promised—and pay off the debt to my bookie immediately—I'm going to toss them in a dumpster or, better yet, the river, and get the hell out of town."

"You're talking to your best friend. How can you threaten to destroy my family's heritage?"

"Yes, you're my best friend," said Val. "Or you were. You got your best friend in a mess. Things are worse than when I came by for dinner. A best friend, especially a rich one like you, would've offered to pay off my debt and allowed me to work it off with no pressure to commit a crime. You could have bought these books. There must have been another way."

"Be reasonable, Val. Bring the books out to my place," said Colin. "I'll send the money to pay your debt. We can hide the books on my estate—put them in one of my wine caves. You can come work for me. No one will know we were involved."

"It can't be that simple," said Val. "I'll wire the information you need to pay my debt."

"I can't just pull that amount of cash out of my ass," Colin protested, his voice rising. "I need time to get the money together. Give me a couple of days."

"Colin, I don't need the details of where you hide your mounds of treasure. Get the money and you'll get the books."

"Val, we've been friends for a long time. Let's settle down and think clearly. We can work this out. The guard will be fine, and you'll be in the clear."

"They wouldn't let me see the guard when I went to the hospital," Val said. "I think his wife is on death watch."

"You went to the hospital? I thought you were smarter than that. Are you an idiot? You nearly kill a man, steal priceless books, and the police have your picture. Then you show up at the hospital to check on the man's condition. What were you thinking?"

"You're being a jerk, Colin. I wanted to see if the man was still alive. I wanted to offer him an apology. Unfortunately, his wife was there with him, and no one was allowed in."

"I can't believe what you're telling me. You slash a guard's throat in the commission of a burglary and want him and his wife to forgive you?"

"I think the man is dead," said Val. "Police are keeping the information secret. I'm going to be arrested for murder and aggravated assault. If I get caught, I'm going to Oregon Death Row."

"Don't talk like that, Val," said Colin in a quiet, comforting voice. "I know you're upset. I'm sorry for getting you into this mess."

"Two messes—the guard's injuries and the book theft," said Val.

"Yes, two messes," Colin agreed. "I'll get us both out of it."

"Yes, you will. You will pay off my bookie and give me the cash you promised to get me back on my feet. The rest is your problem. You can keep your job. I'm getting out of the country."

"When do I get books?"

"You'll get them when I get the money."

Val hung up. He no longer trusted his friend—no longer had any friends. No wife. A daughter who despised him. No job or money—nothing.

He sat in his car and cried. Mac jumped in this lap and licked his face. Val responded by hugging his dog. "I love you, too, Mac. You're my only friend now. What would I do without you?" The hound listened, then licked away Val's tears.

CHAPTER 22

1

Val James looked at the gas gauge as he pulled to the curb under the Broadway Avenue overpass next to the Portland Train Depot. The tank was nearly empty—like him. He felt like he had been running forever—from poor decisions, his gambling obsession, and now a murder charge. He knew he could use the debit card Colin had given him to get a room and buy gas, but he feared the police would be tracking his purchases.

Val had run out of options on this dead-end street next to a line of tents filled with homeless people. He got out of his car, put Mac on a leash, and began walking. He didn't get far. A wave of mental and physical exhaustion washed over him. He walked across the street to an island of green—a mini park—between the train station and visitor parking lot.

When Val entered the park, it appeared empty. Now a fugitive, he gave a furtive glance to see if anyone was nearby, fearful he would be captured any moment. Even though he appeared to be safe, his chest tightened, his heart raced; a tingling in the back of his neck told him eyes were everywhere, screaming "killer on the loose" and pointing to Val. A paranoid thought, he knew, but he couldn't help it.

Val plopped down on a wood and metal bench with a thud, like a sack of potatoes hitting the floor. Mac jumped up beside him and put his head on his lap. Val closed his eyes and listened to a freight train announce its departure with a horn blast. As the horn sound faded and the clacking of the train wheels against the tracks receded, he heard a steady drumbeat. The voice of a man chanting, in a language foreign to Val's ears, filled the tiny space. The chant and drumbeat were synchronized.

Ho HE LOW He LO HO O HAY Ho HE LOW He LO HO O HAY

HA HAY LA-A HA A HA

Hi HI HI HI AY LA-A HA-A

HOO-HOO-OOO-HO HAY LA-A HA-A HAY YA HAY

At first, Val could not identify the sound's source. It was close-by, but he did not see anyone else in the park. The spot was an oasis lined with palmetto trees. A dozen benches positioned to allow some privacy had been built around a semicircular walkway just 25 yards from the train station entrance. No doubt the park was created as a respite for nervous or road-weary train passengers, a place to relax and breathe fresh Pacific Northwest air while waiting to catch the next Amtrak train to Seattle, San Francisco, or Los Angeles.

Just as he closed his eyes, a second wave of chanting floated on the light breeze.

Ho HE LOW He LO HO O HAY Ho HE LOW He LO HO O HAY

HA HAY LA-A HA A HA

Hi HI HI HI AY LA-A HA-A

HOO-HOO-OOO-HO HAY LA-A HA-A HAY YA HAY

Val stood up and walked a few yards to the park's center and looked around the corner. Sitting on the ground was a man singing.

As Val got closer, Mac ran over to the man's dog, a jet-black mongrel. The dogs circled each other, sniffing, their tails wagging. The man appeared to be in another world. Even Mac's intrusive sniffing did not faze the man, who sat cross-legged, back straight, head and face upturned toward the sun. He was shirtless, his back covered with tattoos, words rather than pictures. Val moved closer. The tattoos were an admonition. The words Never Forget stretched across heavily muscled shoulders. Below the words were a list of the Pacific Northwest Native American and Canadian Indian Tribes.

The man's shiny black hair was pulled back in a long ponytail. A feather earring with a stone hung from one ear. The source of the drums was a boombox.

Val opened Google Translate on his iPhone.

"SIRI, identify the music," he commanded.

"There is no English translation," SIRI reported, much too loud, jolting the man from his meditative state. His eyelids flew open, his eyes bulging, as if he had seen an evil spirit. A second later, the eyes relaxed and focused on Val.

"Sorry," said Val, "I was sitting at the other end of the park when I heard your singing."

"Who are you?" the man asked, his voice soft, without urgency.

"I'm Val James. This is my dog, Mac. We are living in a car across the street, pointing to a line of nearby tents and aging cars along the roadway entrance to the train station. What were you singing?"

"I wasn't singing," said the man. "I was praying. I am a member of the Coastal Salish. I was reciting Chief Dan George's prayer song. It is our anthem. There are no English words to convey the meaning. It is meditative music.

"I'm Billy," he said, but did not offer his hand, which rested in his lap.

"What's your last name?"

"Salishman—a man from the Salish—like our people."

"Beautiful tatts," said Val, making small talk.

"A native brother gave them to me in prison."

Val didn't ask why Billy had been in prison. He felt he had found a kindred spirit with a troubled past who might empathize with Val's predicament.

Val's dog walked over to Billy, who extended his hand. Mac sniffed, moved to Billy's side, and sat down. Just like that, he had become Billy's best friend— one more blow to Val's self-worth, further sapping what mental energy remained. How could he blame Mac, who caught the scent of death on Val, and chose life over another day with a desperate loser?

"Tell me about the Salish," Val said.

Billy explained Salish was not a single tribe, but a common language among coastal Indians in the Pacific Northwest. After listening to Billy talk about his people, Val decided. He didn't care if he was caught. The police would get him, eventually. What harm could come from sharing his predicament with Billy. He would appreciate the books' value and their contribution to history. It would be Val's last act before going to jail.

"I have something I believe you'll like," Val said. "I have inherited books with images of Native Americans. My grandfather helped capture the photos, which might include members of your tribe."

"I would like to see them," said Billy, showing slight interest. He imagined they were photos of Indians at treaty signings getting peace medals from the Great White Father, or some other bullshit depiction of indigenous people.

"Come by at eight tonight," said Val. "I'm in the beat-up green Subaru Outback across the street. I can offer you a beer."

"I'll see you this evening," said Billy, who immersed himself again in his prayers, the boombox sending out the drumbeat as Billy sang the words of Chief George.

2

The sun was long down when Billy Salishman entered Val's lantern light. "Hello," said Billy. Val jumped at the sound and hurried away from the backpacking stove he had been using to heat soup for his dinner. Once his eyes adjusted to the darkness, he saw the face of the man who had been chanting in the park earlier in the day.

"Am I disturbing you?" said Billy.

"You caught me by surprise, is all. Looking into my stove's flames brings back comforting memories of my nights alone, sitting around a campfire in the wilderness. I love to backpack. My form of prayer and meditation. Have had little chance because of work and family obligations the past few years."

Billy was wearing a thin cotton shirt with hand-stitched Native American symbols. They covered his tattoos. He was 5-feet-7, Val guessed. But wiry. Strong. The lack of body fat made his muscles stand out. No doubt the result of endless hours of exercise to help pass the time in prison.

"Would you like some coffee," asked Val. "Or would you like to join me in the beer I promised?" Billy opted for the coffee. Val pulled out a cup from a plastic container where he kept all his kitchen supplies. He emptied an instant coffee packet into the cup, filled it with hot water, and handed it to Billy.

"I've come to see the Indian photos you mentioned," said Billy, who took a sip.

"Are you sure you wouldn't like beer?"

"No, thank you," said Billy. "Booze got me busted once for a year. After too many shots of tequila, I got into a fight, stabbed the other guy. Lucky for me, the man survived. I claimed self-defense. The white jury ignored the evidence and found me guilty. Only been out of jail for two months. I'm living in a tent with my dog."

"We're both homeless," Val said as he opened the wheel well cover and pulled out a Curtis book.

"Here it is," said Val. "This is one of seven books I have. Tell me what you think."

Billy opened the book cover, read the printing and trademark information in the front, felt the paper, and looked up. "This is a rare book, one from a set that comprises *The North American Indian*," said Billy. "Very few were published. They are priceless."

"How come you know so much about Curtis and the books?" Val said.

"I learned about the Curtis books when I was in prison. I worked in the library. I read three or four books a week. Among them was *Short Nights of the Shadow Catcher*. It's a story about Curtis, his triumphs, and the problems he faced during his 30-year project to—in his words—save Native American culture. Publication of the last book in 1930 was the culmination of his life's work."

"I know nothing about him," said Val. Which was not true, since Val had done his own research before the break-in. He wanted to hear Billy's take on Curtis.

"His critics say he had some of my native brothers and sisters dress up in costumes to make the pictures more authentic," said Billy. "In one case, he doctored a photo with a clock that would not have existed during the period Curtis was trying to depict. He also wasn't very nice to his brother, Asahel, who had taken many of the photos for which Edward Curtis claimed credit. When

Asahel confronted him, Edward said he paid for his brother's work. He said it was his project, and no one deserved credit more than him. He said he was the one risking everything. He gave his brother no extra money or credit. Asahel promptly quit the business, leaving an enormous gap in Edward's book production capabilities. They never spoke again. I heard other assistants were treated similarly when they asked for extra pay and credit. From what I can tell from Indian lore, he could be mean as an angry snake."

"Where did you get these books?" Billy asked.

Val looked around. No one was nearby or listening.

"I stole them," Val admitted, slurring his words. He had finished three 16-ounce cans of PBR, $2 a can. He knew he had nothing left to lose. "I'm a gambling addict with a bookie chasing me. A friend said he would pay my debt and help me reunite with my family if I stole them from the public library."

"Why does he want them?"

"I trust he had a good reason," said Val. "We have been friends since college, so I didn't ask." Val didn't explain the Byrne family connection.

"Why didn't your friend steal them?"

"I guess because he is rich, owns a winery, and didn't want to take a chance. Besides, he is a bit of a coward. I came to his rescue many times when one bully or another threatened him when we were kids and in high school."

"What are you going to do with the books?" Billy asked.

"If my friend comes through with the cash I need, I'll give them to him. Otherwise, I'll try to sell them to a book dealer, like McQuillan's downtown. In fact, I've got an appointment there tomorrow at 10."

Billy looked at the Curtis portraits. None were of Salish. They must have been included in earlier volumes of *The North American Indian*. Val tried to show interest but began nodding off after finishing two more beers, finally passing out.

CHAPTER 23

1

After Val James passed out, Billy climbed inside Val's car and pulled the limp man inside, covered him with a blanket, and called his dog. Mac jumped in. Billy shoved the Curtis books into Val's large backpack and easily shouldered the 70 pounds. To help with the weight distribution, he tightened the body straps to bring the pack close to his body. He locked the car door with Val and Mac inside, then walked back to his tent, in a nearby homeless camp, a fenced area a block away. He had never told Val where he lived, so he felt safe Val would not burst into his tent and confront him.

He had stolen and sold a few rare books himself, two Charles Dickens' first editions several years before, to Bruce McQuillan, owner of McQuillan's books. McQuillan asked no questions. He took one look and paid Billy $5,000 cash. Billy knew the payment was a tenth of the books' value but took the money and ran. Although Billy was a suspect in the case, there was no physical evidence to prove either he or Bruce McQuillan ever had possession. Presumably, McQuillan sold them to a collector overseas. McQuillan, who was known as an ethical business executive who had cooperated with police in other book theft cases, said Billy offered him a legitimate story about how he came to possess the books. What McQuillan didn't say was that the bookstore was struggling, and he needed a quick infusion of cash to keep the lights on. In Portland's understaffed detective division, the case quickly was relegated to cold case status.

2

Billy stayed up all night paging through the books, looking at images of Native people. He found a dozen photographs of tribesmen and women he recognized from other history books, none of them from the Salish Tribes. What a treasure, he thought, despite Curtis' less-than-perfect portrayal of indigenous culture. Then he saw the rusty brown stain on the cover and pages of one book. Blood, he thought. In prison, Billy had seen dried blood many times. It's a distinctive color.

Billy's first instinct was to return the books to the library anonymously to reunite them with the other 13 volumes, completing *The North American Indian* set. His need for money to keep his life on track after getting out of prison overcame his moment of sentimentality. He would keep Val's appointment at McQuillan's, hoping to make a quick sale. Val's cover story that he had inherited the books would work well for Billy, who could claim they were a gift from his great-grandfather. He wondered if Bruce McQuillan would be interested, given the trouble that resulted from their previous transaction.

Billy knew the books would go to a collector who would cherish them—and have money to restore the blood-stained book. In the meantime, he needed to find a hiding place until he could show up for the appointment Val had set at McQuillan's. It was 6 a.m. when he walked into the Portland Train Depot. The ticket counter had just opened, and no one was waiting.

Billy stepped up to the window and bought a one-way ticket to Seattle for $36. It was the cheapest ticket he could buy with his limited cash, and he had many relatives there who would give him a place to stay once he arrived. With the ticket in hand, he walked to the baggage holding area and checked in the backpack, minus the book he would take to McQuillan's. The baggage handler grunted when he lifted the backpack. "Is this filled with bricks?" he asked.

"No, just large print books for my grandfather whose eyesight isn't so good," said Billy. The handler nodded, satisfied with the answer. He grabbed the bag with both hands, carried it into the back room holding area, and returned with a claim check.

3

Billy was standing outside McQuillan's Books when it opened. A young woman welcomed him.

"I'm looking for Bruce McQuillan," he said.

"He's semi-retired, comes in two days a week," said Meghan McQuillan. "Today is his day off." Billy was confused. He had called and talked to a woman who confirmed the appointment to show the Curtis book. He assumed she was a secretary or clerk, but his meeting would be with Bruce McQuillan.

"I'm Billy Salishman," he said. "I called and confirmed an appointment this morning to show a Curtis book I inherited from my great-grandfather."

"You talked to me," she said. "I'm Meghan McQuillan, Bruce's daughter. I took over the business after dad had a heart attack last year."

"Is Bruce okay?" asked Billy. "He and I have done business in the past."

Meghan remembered a different name given for the appointment. The voice was unfamiliar, too. Of course, mobile phones can distort a voice, so she was not surprised.

"I was expecting a man named Robert Hill," said Meghan.

"Bob... Robert Hill is my cousin," Billy said, the lie pouring out of his mouth before he could think about it.

Meghan accepted the explanation and moved on. "Let's see what you have," she said.

Meghan knew instantly from the book cover and binding it was the real thing as she examined it from all angles before opening the front cover. The spine was imprinted with Volume 14 and *The North American Indian*. She read the printing date in the front and felt the paper.

"It's the real thing," Meghan confirmed. "This is a valuable book." Although she found it odd Billy claimed to only have a partial set, she kept her thoughts to herself. "If you trust me with the book, I will show it to Bruce. He knows the likely buyers and can help me come up with a price. I could talk to him late this afternoon or evening and have an answer for you tomorrow."

"Your father is a good man," said Billy. "No doubt you are a dutiful daughter. I will trust you."

"If you would like to call or come by tomorrow at 2 p.m., I can have an answer for you, and you can bring the other books. I believe Dad will want us to make a deal."

"See you then," said Billy.

After Billy left, Meghan picked up the phone and called her girlfriend, Detective Kim Jansen. It went to voicemail. "Kim, it's Meg. Detective Larson came by yesterday to talk about the library book theft. He said you were the lead detective on the case, and I should call you if I heard from anyone trying to sell

Edward Curtis volumes. Well, a guy came in here and left a Curtis book and said he had several more he inherited from his grandfather. It appears to be the real thing. He's coming back tomorrow afternoon to pick up this one or make a deal to sell them all. Call me."

CHAPTER 24

1

The bright morning light stabbed at Val James' eyes. His head pounded. His mouth was dry as cotton. Before he could lift his head off the pillow, Mac was in his face, sniffing his breath. It must be terrible, Val thought, because his beagle loved the odor.

What the hell had he been drinking? Then he remembered: PBR, formerly known as Pabst Blue Ribbon. Five 16-ounce "tall boys"—nearly three quarts in all. About seven shots of whiskey. No wonder he felt dizzy. He needed air. Opening the hatchback, he scooted to the tailgate and sat up. A wave of nausea hit. "I need water," he said to Mac, reaching out and petting him. He picked up a nearby bottle and began guzzling water like a dying man in the desert. The water would help relieve his dizziness. As he looked around outside, he recalled he was homeless, living in his car, just one step away from being a permanent urban tent dweller, like his neighbors.

A memory came rushing back. Val had been drinking with an Indian. A guy named Billy Salishman. He had shown the books to Billy and confessed how he got them and the accident involving the library guard. He stood up, pulled off the blankets covering the floor of his Subaru, and pulled up the cover of the wheel well. "Shit," he said. His backpack and the Curtis books were gone. "Oh no," he groaned. "What more in hell can happen to me. This is a disaster." A neighbor who had stepped out of a tent glanced at him and moved on. No doubt the man was used to fellow homeless talking to themselves, swearing, and bemoaning their fate.

Val knew he needed to find the books. Otherwise, his leverage over Colin Byrne would evaporate. Now he would have to lie to force his friend's hand. He picked up his phone and called Colin, which went straight to voicemail. "Thanks for calling. Looking forward to talking. I will call you back as soon as possible. Have a great day." Val pulled out his phone and logged into his anemic bank account, $150 remaining, to see if there were any new deposits. Of course, he still had the $1,000 debit card Colin had given him. He would keep that for emergencies, rather than blow it on a hotel room at $200 a night.

Annoyed by Colin's sunny message, Val called back and left a terse reply: "Colin, I checked my bank account. I see no evidence you have come through with the promised money. If I don't hear from you in the next four hours, I'm dumping the books in the river and leaving town. I'm not kidding. You owe me—big time. This mess is your fault, and you need to fix it."

Val hung up and sat back down on the tailgate of his car, drinking more water, while trying to remember where Billy was staying. He realized Billy never said. Val rubbed his eyes and called Mac to his side. "It looks like it's just you and me, buddy. We gotta stick together. You won't abandon me, will you?" Mac stood up on Val's lap and licked him.

"We've got to find Billy," he said to Mac. Val could ask around to see if anyone knew how he could find an Indian with tattoos but figured no one would help. The homeless were a tight community that closed ranks on outsiders. They would never betray their own.

Val's panic receded, the water clearing his head and lubricating his mouth. He grabbed a bottle of acetaminophen and took five 500 milligram caplets— more than the recommended dose—to ease the pain in his head. With his mind clearing, a light went on. He would clean up at the train station, then wait until the sun broke through the clouds before returning to the tiny park where he first met Billy. Val had a feeling Billy was a creature of habit, his prayer chants essential to his being. Billy would appear when the sun came out. Val would let Billy chant, then confront him. He was certain either Billy stole the books or knew where they were.

Could Billy have already sold them and skipped town. Could his life get any worse, Val thought, tears leaving a trail on his dirty face.

CHAPTER 25

1

Bill Bowman was still in shock.

The vision of the guard's blood that had soaked into the carpet of his beloved rare book room, filled with book treasures he treated like his children, gave him the shivers. The theft of the Curtis books had drained his energy and left his stomach burning. He could not think of a motive for stealing from a public library. Wasn't the library a sanctuary for people of all stripes?

Adding to his stress was the knowledge that the Curtis book theft was like a major library loss a year before—the disappearance of James Audubon's *Birds of America*. The Audubon masterpiece was a collection of four books containing 435 hand-colored, life-size prints of North American Birds made from engraved plates; each page measures 39 inches by 26 inches. A first edition sold at auction in 2018 for nearly $10 million. The Portland Public Library had been the proud owner of one of only 120 known copies. Insurance paid two-thirds of the value. A pittance, Bowman thought, for a priceless book.

Despite what police termed a "thorough investigation," they never turned up a credible clue to the whereabouts of the Audubon Book. Bowman felt certain it went onto the black market and ended up in a collector's private library, never to resurface.

Rare book experts tracking such things confirmed 10 copies of *Birds of America* were in private hands, the others in university libraries and museums. The missing books were no doubt in private hands. But whose hands? Bowman's predecessor, Marc Stanfield, was fired after the Audubon theft. Behind closed doors, the library board determined Stanfield was negligent, with each side signing a confidentiality agreement. Despite the magnitude of the loss, Bowman felt the penalty was harsh. Stanfield had been a respected university librarian and museum art curator with an impeccable reputation before accepting the position of managing the John Wilson Collections in Portland. After Stanfield left, Bozeman had heard gossip about some irregularities involving two Charles Dickens first editions that went missing during Stanfield's tenure. The estimated value: $100,000. Shortly after Stanfield left, he disappeared without a trace. It was conjecture, but Bowman had a wild thought that someone paid off Stanfield to assist with the theft, then got rid of him to tie up loose ends.

When Bowman took over, he worked with the Multnomah County Library Board of Directors to strengthen security procedures. Paragon Systems, whose CEO was a big contributor to the library, had assured him and the Board its strategy to protect the rare book collection would deter future thefts.

"I'm a failure," Bowman thought. "They entrusted me with the Curtis masterpiece, one of our library's most precious works, and I could not keep it safe. I'll be lucky to work in another library—even as a volunteer."

As negative thoughts roiled his normally calm demeanor, he ate in silence, tearing off chunks of a peanut butter sandwich and swallowing them whole. He washed down the dry sandwich and side of potato chips with a diet cola.

While he ate lunch, he picked up the journal left by Professor Bryan Byrne. The journal described Byrne's great-grandfather's interactions with Edward S. Curtis. Byrne had promised to let Bowman read the other six journals that Byrne's father, Colin, had given him.

As Bowman turned the pages, he got an idea: seven journals covered each of the seven years Great-grandfather William Byrne spent with Curtis. Which aligns with the years the seven missing books were published. What was the connection? Bowman didn't know. He needed to call Detective Jansen and share the connection between William Byrne and the theft.

Bowman picked up his phone to call Jansen, then put it down. "Will she think it's a silly idea?" he asked himself. He put the phone down, thought about it for a moment more, and decided he had to call. Detective Jansen had said every sliver of information could help solve the case.

2

"Detective Jansen. Can I help you?"

"This is Bill Bowman, the curator for the John Wilson Collections at the Portland Public Library. We met last night."

"Bill, of course I know who you are. How can I help you?"

He explained his theory connecting the journals and the stolen volumes. And he recounted the dispute between Edward Curtis and his brother, Asahel. Asahel wanted credit for photos he had taken. Edward Curtis refused. "The brothers never spoke again," said Bowman. "William Bryan Byrne kept detailed notes about photography sessions. Apparently, like Asahel Curtis, he filled in on photo shoots when Edward Curtis was sick or stressed."

"Does Curtis give Great-grandad Byrne credit in his book?" Jansen asked.

"No, he doesn't," said Bowman. "Stealing the books may have been retribution for the lack of recognition for William Byrne."

"Bill, you're stretching one fact, a feud between brothers a 100 years ago, into a motive for theft a hundred years later."

"When you put it that way, it sounds crazy," he said.

In his defense, Bowman added, "You told me to call if I thought of anything that might help."

"I'm sorry, Bill, you're right," said Jansen. "Just because we haven't found a connection doesn't mean there isn't one. Could you bring by the journal?"

"I need to check with Professor Byrne first. It belongs to him."

"Sure, call him," said Jansen. "Ask him if we can see all the journals. Tell him I will guard them with my life. I'll return them in a few days. Don't wait too long to talk to the Professor. Like you said, the longer it takes to catch the perpetrator, the more likely the books will be overseas, into the hands of a private collector."

The idea of a greedy, rich collector buying books stolen from a public library made Bowman's stomach churn. A wave of nausea passed over him. He took a deep breath and had a sudden change of heart.

"Detective, I'll bring the journal. I am confident Professor Byrne would want to help. I like and trust Professor Byrne. He is a historian with a genuine concern about the missing books. It's a gut feeling, but he isn't someone who would steal history books from a public library."

Jansen wasn't so sure. The professor's addiction to pain killers, and the constant need to get more, was incentive enough to turn valuable books into cash for drugs. The evidence, including the cane found at the scene of the crime—and the fact that Byrne showed up at his interview without his cane, despite his alleged hip pain—made him the prime suspect.

Jansen had already made the connection between the seven missing books and the years William Byrne worked for Curtis. Was Bowman's theory about someone stealing the books to get back at Edward Curtis, far-fetched? Had there been a Hatfield-McCoy feud between Byrne and Curtis descendants, with the library theft the latest battle in a war dating back a hundred years?

Unlikely, Jansen thought.

CHAPTER 26

1

After talking with Bill Bowman about motives for the library break-in, Detective Jansen spent the next two hours looking at the department's online databases for each of the Byrnes: William, Curtis' assistant in the 1920s, son Peter, grandson Colin, and great-grandson Bryan. Besides driver's licenses for Colin and Bryan, Jansen found a speeding ticket from three years before, for Colin. She had figured online records didn't go back far enough to capture any criminal activity in earlier generations. She was right. She found nothing on William or Peter Byrne, so she sent another request to O'Connor, her researcher.

An hour later, Jansen got an email from O'Connor who discovered several crime reports for Peter Byrne, among them two drunk driving charges, and a conviction for assault with a deadly weapon—a beer bottle. Peter had pleaded guilty and had been sentenced to three months in a county jail for smashing another drunk patron over the head. The victim had suffered a concussion and needed 50 stitches to close the head wound. The report also confirmed that he had a young son named Colin, and wife, Mary.

After reading O'Connor's report, Jansen sent a follow-up email. "Kelly, great work. Can you see what more you can find about Colin Byrne. He owns a vineyard in Newberg, Oregon." Jansen had another idea. Jim Briggs might help. She speed-dialed Briggs.

"Briggs, how are you, sweetheart?"

"Fine, Kimmy. How's my honey bunny?"

"Briggs, you know I hate cutesy names," she said.

"How about QBU?"

"I give up. What's QBU?"

"Queen Bitch of the Universe—a line from the sci-fi horror film, The Abyss. It's the captain's name for his ex-wife."

"You keep up with these silly names and you might have an ex-wife," she said.

"You're hilarious, Jansen," said Briggs.

"So, Detective Jansen, how can I help you?"

"I need a favor."

"Your wish is my command," said Briggs.

"Bill Bowman, the curator at the library's rare book collection, thinks the theft of the books relates to events that happened when Bryan Byrne's great-grandfather was working as a photography assistant to Edward S. Curtis. They worked together from 1924 to 1930, which corresponds to the years the missing books were printed. I don't know if it has any significance. Could you do your genealogy thing and see if you can build a family profile? I'll text their legal names and dates of birth. Remember that Bryan Byrne is a suspect. You can take it from there."

"I am on my way to an urgent client call to care for a sick Frenchie. Afterwards, I'll head to the library. I hope Chuck Grayson is there. I want to thank him for what he did for us. I used to see him there all the time, researching his family line. I haven't seen him in a long time. I don't know whether he's lost interest in his family genealogy, or if he's been busy with his new girlfriend."

"Good idea, Briggs. I thanked him when we talked about this case, but he needs to hear it from you. If you see him, tell him hello, and let him know I haven't forgotten our deal to share leads in the library theft. Whatever you find, keep it to yourself until I have time to review it. However, you can tell him you're looking for a family link."

CHAPTER 27

1

Jim Briggs drew stares everywhere he went because of his 6-foot-6 height. Tight spaces in restaurants and bars accentuated his size. The Portland Public Library main branch downtown was an exception. The 27-foot ceilings and huge open spaces dwarfed him, allowing him to walk freely without drawing attention to himself. He climbed the stairs to the second-floor genealogy research area, sat down at a computer, and logged into an ancestry database. Briggs could access online services anywhere from his laptop. At the library, he had access to great reference librarians who helped with searches.

Briggs was considering online search terms to build a Byrne Family genealogy when Chuck Grayson appeared.

"Dr. Briggs. How are you?"

Briggs' head swiveled toward the familiar voice. He quickly stood up and wrapped his arms around Chuck, engulfing the tinier man. "Nice to see you."

"Easy, Briggs, let's not get all teary-eyed. You're making a scene."

Briggs smiled, nodded, and stepped away.

"What are you working on, Briggs?" Grayson asked.

Briggs lowered his voice and looked around. "Kim asked me to build a family profile of the Byrne family as part of her library theft case."

"How's that going to help?" Grayson asked.

"Is this for background only? Not for publication?"

"On background only," Grayson confirmed.

"Kim thinks there could be a connection between Bryan Byrne, who recently visited the Wilson Room, and his great-grandfather, William Byrne. She said she didn't have time to explain how the information will fit. Or if she had a hunch about a connection."

"How could events from 100 years ago relate to the burglary and assault?" Chuck muttered, as he looked over Briggs' shoulder at the computer screen.

"I'm trying to help Kim answer that question," said Briggs.

"Sounds like a stretch to me," said Grayson. "I'll let you get back to it. I've got my own family tree to build. Take care, Briggs. And let's have a beer together sometime."

"I'd like that," said Briggs, smiling. Chuck and his dad worked at the same paper and often went for drinks after deadline. They were best friends. When his dad died, Briggs was only 12. Memories of his father were few. Chuck filled in more of the picture each time they met over drinks. The drinks seemed to loosen up Chuck, make him more willing to share facts about Briggs' dad—many stories less than flattering. No doubt the association of sitting on the bar stools— the same ones Grayson and Jim Briggs Sr. sat on— triggered memories.

Over the next several hours, Briggs built a picture of the Byrne Family from public census information, and birth, death, and cemetery records.

In the 1910 Census, William Byrne was five years old. By 1920, at age 15, he lived in a rooming house in Seattle. Under "occupation," he was listed as a photography apprentice. In 1930, he was still in Seattle, but married with his own son, Peter. Their address was registered as "unknown, living on the street." Must have been victims of the Great Depression, Briggs thought.

Next, Briggs turned to newspapers.com, which offered digital copies of papers going back to the 1700s. Following a person's life through newspapers often revealed their social status. They were filled with detailed stories about local school events, birthday parties, club activities, and crimes.

In his search of Seattle newspapers, a headline dated August 5, 1973, on page 12, screamed, "Father Dies Hours After Nearly Beating Son to Death." The story was long, 16 column inches. The father was Peter Byrne. The son was Colin Byrne, 10.

Briggs used the Newspaper.com clipping feature to grab a copy of the article. He immediately forwarded it to Jansen in an email with a note: "Kim, this may be of interest. Tells you something about your suspect's father and grandfather.

Not sure how it all fits together. I'll finish up the family tree and get that over to you shortly.

As Briggs was about to leave, he walked over to the computer station where Grayson was busy with his family tree. "Chuck, thank you for everything you did for me. You'll never know how much it means to me."

"I think I do," said Chuck, glancing at Briggs for just a moment before looking back at his screen.

"Dad would also be grateful if he were around," Briggs added.

"See you later, Briggs," said Grayson. Briggs nodded. Nothing more needed to be said.

2

While Jim Briggs was at the library gathering information on the Byrne family, Detective Jansen returned the call to Meghan McQuillan. Jansen's call went straight to voicemail. She wasn't surprised. She knew Meghan's mobile phone got poor reception when she was deep in the bookstore's stacks.

Since the police bureau was less than three-fourths of a mile from McQuillan's, Jansen walked. It was a beautiful day: 68 degrees, with blue skies and just a hint of a breeze. The air was filled with the scent of pine forest, no doubt coming from Portland's Forest Park, at 5,000 acres, one of America's largest urban wilderness areas.

Jansen arrived at McQuillan's where she found Meghan at the register checking out a customer who had filled two grocery bags with used paperbacks. When Meghan finished, she looked up, saw Jansen, and rushed over.

"Hey girlfriend, how are you?" she said, hugging Jansen.

"Been too long," said Jansen. "Married life and my new job have kept me on the run."

"You've been through Hell and back," Meghan said. Jansen nodded.

"I've been buried in the details of running a business," said Meghan. "I spent thousands of hours here as a kid, then summers during college semesters and none of it prepared me for the blizzard of paperwork that goes with running a business, much less a place like this with a million book titles. Don't know how Dad managed it by himself all these years."

"How is Bruce?" Jansen asked.

"Old. Tired." said Meghan, who shook her head and frowned. "Not well at all. Dad is only 67 years old, but all those years of smoking have caught up with him. Emphysema has left him weak, breathless, and depressed. He rarely goes out. I tell people he is semi-retired and comes in a couple of days a week. That makes dad's fans feel better. They don't need to hear the gory details."

"Sorry to hear that," said Jansen. "The reason I'm here is that you called and left a message yesterday. Sorry to be so slow to respond. I got interrupted by an emergency call to assist another detective."

"That's okay, I understand," said McQuillan. "I'm just so happy to see you."

"The day is too nice to stay in the office, so I thought I would walk over and catch up in person," said Jansen.

"I'm not sure if this is connected to your case," said Meghan. "But a guy came in here yesterday with an original copy of Volume 14 of *The North American Indian*. He claimed he had several more, which he said he had inherited. He wanted to talk to Dad, who had bought books from him in the past. I told him Dad had retired but that I would get his opinion about potential buyers. The man left the volume."

"Bingo," yelled Jansen. "Your book seller must be the guy we are looking for."

Meghan explained that the man's family could have owned one of the few copies of the Edward Curtis books known to be held in private hands. Jansen didn't think so.

"What did he look like?" Jansen asked as she pulled out her notebook and began jotting details.

"I believe he was Native American. His belt, moccasins, and woven necklace were handmade in the style of Northwest Tribes," said Meghan. "He has deep, liquid brown eyes and smooth, black hair pulled back into a ponytail that touched the middle of his back. The other striking thing them about him: it was a cool day, and he came in without a shirt. His chest and back were filled with tattoos. On his back were words, in large letters, Never Forget, followed by a list of northwestern native tribes." Jansen pulled out her notebook and recorded the description. "Let me get the book," said Meghan. "I locked it in the office safe."

Meghan returned with a box and led Jansen to a small table, where she spread a clean, soft pad. She lifted off the box top, pulled out the book and laid it on the table.

"He said his name was Billy Salishman," said Meghan. "He may very well have some personal connection to the books because of Salish ancestors that Curtis photographed. But I checked and Salish tribes were included in Volumes 7 and 9," said Meghan. "None is shown in the missing volumes."

"I suspect that even if the missing books included Salish portraits, Salishman might try to sell them," said Jansen. "Money can trump family ties. You hear about families having bitter fights over inheritances. It all comes down to who gets what. When is Salishman due to return?"

"I told him to come at 2 p.m. today." Meghan said. Jansen looked at her watch. It was 11 a.m., three hours until contact with Salishman.

"If it's okay with you, Meghan, I'll return with another officer before 2 p.m. We'll pretend to browse. We need to hear his story. The man might be telling the truth. However, his possession of an identical book to one of those stolen would be a cosmic coincidence."

"If he's your guy, at least you'll know they haven't hit the black market," said Meghan.

Jansen and Meghan discussed the details of the upcoming transaction: McQuillan's unnamed client would offer $5,000 a book or $35,000 for all seven, well below their value.

"Meghan, I want you to cut the deal but insist on keeping at least one book to show your buyer, who you can say wants to see and verify its authenticity," Jansen instructed. "If you can get him to leave all of them, even better. Tell him it will take 24 hours to confirm the buyer's interest and secure funds. I'll try to get some cash to give him as a hook. Would $2,000 be enough?"

"I think $2,000 cash would be a nice incentive to complete the deal," said Meghan.

"When he returns with the other books for the sale, we can grab him and the books," said Jansen. "We also will try to follow him after he leaves your store. He might lead us to his home and the other six books."

"Sounds like a good plan," said Meghan, who then changed the subject.

"Kim, let's have a girls' night out when the case is over."

"I would love that," said Jansen.

They hugged one more time, then Jansen walked through the open front door and stood on the sidewalk, looking at the blue sky and smelling the fresh air.

"One more thing I should mention," Meghan called out. "Salishman was the second inquiry I've had in two days about Curtis' books." Jansen turned around and walked back into the store.

"What are you talking about?"

"Two days ago, I got a call from a different man," Meghan said. "The other guy identified himself as Robert Hill. He agreed to come by with a sample book. He never showed. But Billy Salishman did." Jansen took a note. "When I questioned Billy, he claimed he was representing his cousin, Robert, who was sick."

"Robert Hill?" said Jansen, "That's Val James. Hill is his alias."

"You think two people are involved?" asked Meghan.

"Looks like it. See you, girlfriend. I need to get back to the station and get another officer here with me this afternoon. See you later."

3

Jansen double-timed back to the police bureau. No time to savor the sunshine. It appeared she had finally gotten a break in her case. When she arrived at the office, she found an envelope in the middle of her desk. She opened it and read the contents. It was her DNA from the library theft case. Two samples had been analyzed— one from the cane tip and another from broken glass on a cabinet. The DNA sample on the broken glass was identified as belonging to Valentine James, Colin Byrne's friend. "The guy with the gambling problem," Jansen thought. "I've got Valentine James, Colin Byrne, Bryan Byrne, and Robert Hill, four suspects." She called her boss, Chief Melrose, to arrange an undercover officer to meet at McQuillan's for Salishman's 2 p.m. visit. By the end of the day, she hoped the case would be wrapped up.

4

Detective Jansen and Sgt. Melanie Midwell, an undercover officer in the narcotics division, arrived at McQuillan's 30 minutes ahead of Salishman's planned arrival. Both held bags filled with books Meghan supplied and wore jeans, trying to fit in with other book buyers and browsers. An hour later, Jansen pulled Meghan off to the side. "Did you hear anything from Salishman?"

"Not a word," said Meghan. "Which is a surprise given the size of this deal. I can't see him pulling out of it." Jansen and Midwell hung out for another hour before calling it quits. They knew their suspect was a no-show.

"If Salishman calls and gives you a new time, please call or text me ASAP," said Jansen. "I'll be ready to intercept him, day or night."

"Of course," she said. "Wish it had panned out."

"Not your fault, Meg," said Jansen. "Don't worry. And you can count on me calling you in the next week or two for a girls' night out." They hugged, and Jansen and Midwell headed back to the station.

After Jansen left, the idea of dating Mark Larson popped into Meghan's head. She pulled his business card from her back pocket and turned it over and over in her hand. "To call or not to call, that is the question," she said out loud. She had been an independent woman who felt she would never need a man or any other person to fulfill her hopes and dreams. However, she had been alone for so long, she was excited about the possibility of male companionship. Larson was the first guy in a long time she found attractive. Most bookstore patrons were nice enough, but most were quiet book nerds. Like her. None of them was as interesting as Mark Larson.

CHAPTER 28

1

Two hours later, as his lunch for wine buyers was winding down, Colin Byrne saw a silenced call light up his phone. It was from Val. He had called Val to tell him that his DNA has been found at the library crime scene.

Byrne walked next door to his private office and took the call.

"Where's the money you promised?" said Val, cold as ice. Colin ignored the question.

"Val, the police have confirmed finding your blood at the library. Detective Jansen said the injured guard is in grave condition. You said you had a plan to get in and get out quickly. No one was supposed to get hurt. How could you screw up such a simple job?"

"Up yours," said Val. "Remember, this was your hare-brained idea. You put me in a corner when I was desperate. You even pledged to take the hit if we got caught. Now, you're blaming me for your insane scheme and breaking your promise to pay off my bookie."

"For the second time, where is the money? When will it hit my bank account?"

"I'm working on it?"

"Work faster," said Val.

"Settle down," said Byrne, who realized telling an angry person to settle down was like snapping a red cape in a bull's face.

"You fucking settle down," Val shot back. "My ass is on the line. I'm already looking at decades of jail time for grand theft and assault with a deadly weapon during the commission of a crime. If the guard dies, I'll be on Death Row before the year is out."

"Sorry, Val. You're right. I dragged you into this over a grudge with Edward Curtis for the way he treated my grandfather."

"Yes, you did. I have the books and I want you to pay off my debt, as promised," Val said. "You need to transfer the money to my bank account today. You hired me to do your dirty work because you're a coward. I never understood why you were so timid, so afraid of any fight or conflict. Now I don't care. I want my money."

"Where are the books?" Colin pushed back. "I want the books before you get the money."

"Nice try," said Val. "The price of getting the books back has gone up because of the complications. I need enough to pay off my bookie and get out of the country. That number is $100,000. If I don't get the money, I'll sell them to a black-market book dealer I have contacted and just disappear."

"You've got to be kidding, Val," said Colin. "How do you expect me to come up with that much money by the end of the day? I will need at least 24 hours."

"Colin, don't screw around. I'll give you 12 hours, but then you must come through for me. My life is quickly imploding. If I don't pay off my bookie, he'll have me killed. If I get caught, I'm going to jail and may die there, at the hands of some angry prisoner or by lethal injection." Val hung up.

"What have I done?" thought Colin, tears coming down his face. "I've put a target on my son's back, pushed my best friend to commit a crime, and my entire career and business are in jeopardy." After a few more minutes, he stepped into the private bathroom in his office, washed his face with cold water, dried off and put his patch back on.

He was about to make another call to Val, but figured it was no use. Val wasn't interested in excuses or apologies. He wanted money and wanted it now.

Colin closed his phone and headed back to his VIP group.

"This will not end well for Val or me," he thought.

CHAPTER 29

1

Jansen and Larson were discussing the article Briggs found about the 10-year-old Colin Byrne being severely beaten and the boy's father dying when a call came in from Chuck Grayson.

"Hey, Chuck, how are you?"

"Kim, I'm well. Thanks for asking." Grayson quickly shifted to the Curtis book theft.

"I'm calling to get an update on the library case—more fodder for my column. I just saw Jim at the library, and he said he was building a genealogy of a suspect family."

"Like I promised, I'll give you all the details," said Jansen. "But you need to promise me, like we agreed, that you will not reveal me as your source, and you'll withhold information that, if made public, would jeopardize the investigation." Despite their agreement, she wasn't ready to give Grayson the information that would tie Colin Byrne to the case.

"I agree with your stipulations, Detective Jansen," said Grayson.

Jansen told Grayson about the DNA evidence and the name of the suspect, her interview with Colin Byrne, the involvement of Byrne's son, Professor Bryan Byrne, and noted that Mark Larson had rejoined the detective ranks. And that he was on the case with her. She also told Grayson about a second suspect who was trying to find a buyer for several volumes of *The North American Indian.*

"I'll mention the DNA and that police have identified a suspect, but I will withhold the name—for now. That sound good to you, detective?"

"Perfect," said Kim. "Like I said, I'll keep you in the loop. If we make an arrest, you'll be first to get the story."

Portland Police Identify Possible
Suspects in Portland Library Break-in, Attack on Guard

By Charles "Chuck" Grayson
Editor, Urban Street PDX

PORTLAND, OREGON—Police have identified a suspect they believe broke into the Multnomah County Library three days ago, attacked and gravely injured a security guard, and absconded with priceless books of Native American photographs taken by Edward S. Curtis in the 1920s. The books as a complete set are valued at nearly $3 million.

The theft is a devastating loss for the Central Library's John Wilson Special Collections, according to its curator, William "Bill" Bowman. Bowman said the Curtis work was insured but there is virtually no chance of replacing the missing volumes.

"Without all the original volumes, our set is not worthless but damaged and worth a fraction of its original value," he said, adding, "Historians and history teachers, as well as Native American cultures, will suffer from the loss." Bowman choked up while talking about it.

The injured guard, Elliot Harold Delaney, 67, father and grandfather, is still in critical condition at Providence-St. Vincent Medical Center. A hospital spokesperson reported his condition as grave.

A family spokesperson said Delaney is in an induced coma to help him recover from a potential brain injury. He suffered massive blood loss and lack of oxygen after the library intruder slashed his throat during the library theft.

The weapon used to attack the guard was a steel-tipped pole, the kind hikers and backpackers often use on narrow, rocky trails, and for stream crossings. According to my sources, police have identified the individual whose blood and DNA were found at the scene along with the guard's blood.

Police also have a second suspect in the case, a man who offered to sell several Curtis books to a local book dealer. A witness has identified the seller as a man of Native American descent. Police are keeping other distinctive details secret until they have determined if two suspects are involved or how they might be linked. Sources also say there is no guarantee that the Curtis volumes offered to a Portland book dealer are the same as those stolen. However, given the rarity of the books, they are likely the ones taken, my source theorizes.

The detectives on the case, Kim Jansen and Mark Larson, each gave me a "no comment" when I spoke to them about details of the case.

There is still no answer to why the thief took only seven of the 20 volumes. One source suggested the thief—caught in the act—didn't have time to get all the books and fled with what he could carry.

A rare book buyer put the value of the missing books at $5,000 to $10,000 each. Since so few first editions were hand printed 100 years ago, museums and collectors would say they are priceless. As Bill Bowman notes, the library's goal is to help preserve history and educate future generations. "Value is secondary," he said.

I will provide updates on the library theft as they develop.

Like all good journalists, I like to separate news from opinion. I must admit the following is not necessarily an informed opinion, but I'll share it none the less.

Is it a good idea for our public libraries to own rare book collections worth millions of dollars—collections tightly controlled, with limited public access, when so many of our libraries are under-funded, and are struggling to stay on budget with a legion of volunteers needed to keep doors open? I'm undecided.

Still, it is a question worth considering. The library regularly opens the John Wilson Collections to the public for tours, allowing them to get up close and personal with priceless works of literature. That's the upside. And, as Bill Bowman points out, all the books were donated or purchased by private citizens without a dime of public funding.

Historians, teachers, and other researchers also have access. However, the past two years the collection has been under attack by thieves, and under scrutiny for lapses in security. All this drives up insurance costs, further draining scarce library financial resources.

I recognize that any institution with important works of art and literature faces similar threats. Here is more about the rare book collection, taken verbatim from the library's website:

"The Central Library's John Wilson Special Collections houses the rare book and other special collections of Multnomah County Library in a controlled environment for the preservation of rare and historically significant materials. The original focus was a gift of the private collection of John Wilson, an avid book collector with broad interests. Wilson, born in Ireland, arrived in Oregon in 1849. In subsequent years, other gifts and materials culled from the library's collections have widened the scope and depth of the John Wilson Special Collections' holdings to more than 10,000 volumes.

No doubt many of you are amazed to learn that our own local public library maintains such an incredible collection. I have toured the collection and encourage others to do so.

If you have comments about this story, or other stories in my blog, please leave your comments below.

As a historian and lover of all things in print, I commend the Portland Police Bureau and Detective Jansen for closing in on suspects in the case. Hopefully, it will lead to an arrest and a quick end to the case."—K. Kingston, history professor, Portland State University.

Chuck Grayson texted a link from his latest blog post to Detective Jansen. She read it and responded with a thumbs-up emoji.

2

While Jansen loved the comment at the end of Chuck's column commending police, she felt her case was falling apart. Professor Byrne, despite his need for cash and drugs, looked less and less like a suspect. Given his family ties to Edward Curtis and his status as a historian, Jansen couldn't see him destroying any part of the Curtis legacy. Val James was her primary target, but no one knew where he was. And then there was the Native American who brought in the Curtis volume to McQuillan's but never returned to seal the deal to sell it and other volumes he claimed to have.

Jansen picked up her phone and texted Mark Larson, her new partner: "Need to meet. Got to find Val James ASAP." Her next call was to Bryan Byne. She left a message telling him that they had confirmed Val's DNA at the scene. And that he needed to call her ASAP if he knew where to find Val.

CHAPTER 30

1

Bryan Byrne was reeling after listening to Detective Jansen's call confirming Val James, his father's best friend—someone Bryan grew up thinking of as an uncle—was a suspect in the Curtis book theft. Despite DNA evidence connecting Val to the break-in, Bryan found it hard to believe. The last time Bryan had seen Val, he had a successful career in security, which followed years as an ad pitch man that had sealed his legacy as a local sports legend. Although his dad claimed ignorance and surprise that Val could have attacked a guard and stolen priceless history books, he told Bryan that Val was down and out, nearly broke, and might accept a job at Byrne Vineyard.

Where was Val, and what was he up to? Bryan intended to find out. If he was living out of his car near the railroad station, as his dad suggested, he might surprise him. If he had stolen the books and injured the guard, Val might panic at the sight of Bryan and run. He had an idea.

Twenty minutes later, Bryan was walking his dog along the street in front of the Portland Train Station. With sunglasses and his cap, Val wouldn't recognize him. They hadn't seen each other in years. While his dog pooped, Bryan fiddled with a plastic bag to clean up the mess. When he looked up and focused on a group of homeless people across the street, he spotted Val. After depositing the poop bag in a trash can, he casually walked across the street toward Val, his cane clicking on the roadway.

"Val," Bryan called out.

Val's head jerked up, his eyes wide, darting right and left, as if looking for a quick exit.

"It's Bryan Byrne," he said, removing his sunglasses and hat. "This is my dog, Dino." Val's dog ran out to meet them. The two sniffed each other wildly, spinning around, then took off running—fast friends. Val relaxed when he recognized Bryan.

"Bryan, how the hell are you? Let me look at you. Except for that cane, you seem fit. You look so much like your dad. If you pulled a patch over your eye, you could have easily fooled me—at least from a distance."

"Thanks, Val, but I'm 20 pounds heavier than the last time you saw me. It's been at least 10 years. I'm living the fat and happy life of a history professor at a college in the Southwest. At least I was." Bryan had a sudden surge of candor. There was no sense in making up a story about how glorious life was. Maintaining a lie was exhausting.

"Val, I won't BS you. My boss put me on probation and suspended me from teaching because of an opioid addiction resulting from a bum hip that needs replacing. I came to Oregon on my forced sabbatical to see Dad, collect more photos and material for a new history course I plan to teach in the fall, and to see Curtis' *North American Indian*. I visited the rare book room a few days ago to check out the books first-hand. A day later, there was a break-in, and seven volumes were stolen."

Val looked down and began shuffling his feet.

"I read about that," Val said, suddenly sullen.

The lie made Bryan's face turn red, his fists opening and closing, his body supercharged with adrenalin. He wanted nothing more than to knock Val on his ass.

"Apparently, you did more than that. Look at me, Val. Tell me you didn't break into the library, attack a guard, and steal the books."

Val looked up, tears in his eyes.

"It was you," said Bryan. "For God's sake, Val, what were you thinking? Why would you do that?

"Bryan, I was desperate. I've had a gambling addiction for a long time. And, like most gamblers, I'm a loser. Lost many more times than I ever won. It's an addiction I've had since college, when I spent my weekends betting on ponies at local tracks. I've got a bookie who has sent two thugs to collect the money I owe him. They have told me to pay up or else. 'Or else' means they will kill me."

"I didn't realize the jeopardy you're in," said Bryan.

"I have been living in my car for the past two weeks," said Val. "I've been hiding while trying to figure out what to do next. With my security background, I figured it would be easy to break in undetected, steal the books, and quickly find a buyer. It all fell apart when the guard walked in. I tried to talk my way out of it. The guard would have none of it and picked up his radio to call for backup. I picked up the cane I was using as a disguise and swung at the radio to knock it out of his hand. Instead, I missed the radio, and the tip of the cane slashed his throat. There was blood everywhere. I spilled the books onto the floor. One or two landed in the guard's blood."

"Blood covered the Curtis books?" Bryan's eyes got big, his mouth twitched, and his jaw clenched. A moment later, when the horror show in his mind ended, Bryan urged, "Val, you've got to give yourself up. You can tell them it was an accident, return the books, and plead for mercy."

"No way I am going to prison for life," said Val. "And I need the money to pay my gambling debt. Hopefully, I'll have enough left over to pay my daughter's college tuition. I've been a shitty husband and father. I know they will never talk to me again, but the least I can do is help them get back on their feet financially."

"Where are the books?" said Bryan.

"I lost the books," said Val.

"You what?"

"I got drunk. I was bragging about the books to this Indian guy who knew Curtis' work. He claimed he's a member of the Salish Tribe, and that his people were among those Curtis photographed. I passed out after too many beers, woke up hung over, and discovered the books were gone. I don't know if he took them. He was the only person I talked to about the books. He must have seen me take them out of the wheel well of the car."

"What is his name? Where is he?" Bryan was frantic, asking questions rapid fire.

Val's shoulders drooped. His plan to escape with the money that Colin had promised was falling apart. There was no way Bryan was going to allow the sale of the books, regardless of Val's plight. Still, his so-called best friend, Colin Byrne, could come through with the money without his son knowing. If nothing else, Val could go to work at the winery and work off his debt.

"The Native American's name is Billy Salishman," said Val. "Yesterday, I saw him sitting cross-legged, his eyes closed, looking toward the sky as he listened to chants of the Salish Anthem. When he finished chanting, we introduced ourselves and he said he rarely misses coming to the train plaza to his daily meditation.

Bryan looked at his watch. It was 45 minutes before noon and Billy had not appeared in his usual spot. "Have you eaten, Val?" Bryan asked.

"Not much," said Val. "I'm saving what little money I have for gas for my get-away."

"Let's go eat lunch at the train station cafe," said Bryan. "I'll buy. We need to calm down and create a plan to deal with Salishman if we find him. We need to talk about your future and the return of those books." They locked up the dogs together in the back of Val's Subaru Outback with the windows cracked. The Broadway Street overpass above shaded the car. "Bryan, there is one more thing you need to know. Salishman recently got out of prison. Tattoos cover his upper body. Most relate to never forgetting Native American tribes. But he also has gang tats on his neck. He could be dangerous."

"We will have to take our chances," said Bryan. "Let's eat before we confront him." The thought of food calmed Bryan and, for a moment, pushed away the thought of pursuing Salishman and the potential risks.

In the train station, Val and Bryan ordered sandwiches, chips, and cokes, then discussed how to approach Billy Salishman and what he might take in exchange for the books. "A guy like him will want one thing—cash," said Val. "I don't know about you, but I'm a little short in that department right now." He pulled out the lining of his front pockets to show they were empty.

"I have some savings I could dip into, maybe cash from my retirement plan," said Bryan. "Dad might front the money to protect the books and the pictures my great-grandfather took."

"Good luck with that," Val thought.

"Okay, it's nearly 12 p.m.," Val said, looking at his watch. "Time to look for Billy. We should walk out the far entrance and circle back around to the area where he chants."

Sure enough, as the clouds gave way to the sun, music from Billy's boombox, and the sound of his voice chanting the Salish Anthem, filled the air. As Val predicted, Billy was a creature of habit. Val and Bryan approached quietly until they were standing over the man. Billy pretended not to notice. The chanting continued for a few more minutes. When it ended, Billy opened his eyes, reached over to turn off his boombox, and looked up at Val and Bryan.

"Hey, Val, what's up?"

"I'll tell you what's up. You're a thieving, Indian bastard," Val said, his voice rising, his mouth forming a tight line. "You stole my books and I want them back."

Ignoring Val, Billy stood up, looked at Bryan, and said, "Who are you?"

"I'm Bryan Byrne, Val's friend. I'm also the great-grandson of William Byrne, the photography assistant to Edward Curtis who took a lot of the photos included."

Billy smiled. "Nice to meet you, Bryan. Your great-granddad may have photographed my great-grandfather."

"Let's say I have the books. What are they worth to you?" said Billy, scanning each man's face to see if an offer was forthcoming.

"Cat got your tongue, Val? Last night, you were full of ideas for trading the books for cash. You said you had even lined up a book dealer." He didn't mention he plan to sell them at McQuillan's.

"Billy, if you have those books, you need to give them back," Bryan interjected. "There will not be any negotiation for history books stolen from a public library. What you're going to get is a get-out-of-jail free card if you give them up. Otherwise, it's back to prison for you."

"Fuck you," said Billy, who rolled to his feet, shoved Bryan into the bushes, and knocked Val down with a single punch to the side of the head. As Val was pushing himself up, Billy turned and sprinted toward the bus station.

Bryan got up and chased the fleeing man. He ran about 20 feet before a lightning shock of pain shot through his leg and hip. He went down like a bull elephant shot with a high-caliber rifle. His leg smashed into a metal bench. "Val, get him," Bryan screamed between his yelps of agony.

"Are you okay?" Val asked, reaching for Bryan. "Let me help you up."

"Get Salishman," Bryan screamed. "Go."

Val took one more look at Bryan, figured there was nothing he could do.

He turned toward to station's main entrance just in time to see Billy throw open the door and disappear inside. Although Val had suffered an injury in college that ended his plans for an NFL or MLB career, years of rehab had restored his strength and speed. Age had taken its toll, but not enough to prevent him from running down Billy.

Catching Billy was Val's only way to escape the mess he created. Val ran for the train station door, entered, and saw Billy leap over benches, dodge passengers waiting for trains, then turn into a corridor that led to the café, restrooms, and passenger loading area. Despite the warnings not to exit onto the tracks, Billy burst through the doors, ignoring the "Authorized Personnel Only" sign. Val was gaining on Billy and saw him bolt out the backdoors onto the loading platform.

A train conductor at the other end of the station spotted him and yelled for Billy to stop but didn't chase him. Instead, he pulled out a walkie-talkie and made a call. When Val ran into the track area, the conductor, a big man with a gut hanging over his belt, drifted toward him, waving his hand. Val ignored him and raced after Billy, who sprinted around the end of a steel fence, across tracks in front of an oncoming Max, an intra-city train, and up Third Avenue. The area around the train station was a hub for trains, streetcars, and buses. The public transit traffic was heavy, a hazard for pedestrians. And for Billy.

"Billy, stop," yelled Val. "Let's talk."

Billy wasn't interested and continued his run. He looked over his shoulder at Val and then back to the street, but not before a Portland streetcar came around a blind curve.

"Billy, look out," Val warned. It was too late. The streetcar hit Billy and sent him flying. Moments after Billy's body slammed onto the pavement, Val caught up with him. Blood was coming from a wound on the side of Billy's head. The man was inert. The shaken streetcar driver appeared frozen in his seat, then picked up a radio and called for help. The impact of the train had knocked a paper folder out of Billy's back pocket and onto the street. Val picked it up and looked inside. It was a train ticket to Seattle with a claim check stapled to the top.

Then he figured it out. Billy had hidden the books in the baggage claim area. The ticket could be Val's escape, along with the books. Forget Seattle. He could drive there. Val had thought Mexico was the best place to hide. Montana would also make a good hideout, he thought. He took the ticket and claim check and tucked it into his pants just as the streetcar door opened and passengers flowed out and surrounded Billy. Val melted into the crowd, then turned and walked away.

Val walked back toward the park in front of the station. He could see Bryan had gotten off the pavement and had dragged himself onto a park bench. Bryan's face was a mask of pain as he pressed his hand against the injured hip.

Val didn't need to ask if Bryan was okay. The grimace on his face was the answer.

"Did you catch Billy?" Bryan said.

"I almost had him. Then he stepped in front of a streetcar and got hit. I think he's dead."

Bryan closed his eyes and shook his head as if trying to rid his mind of this continuing nightmare. He opened his eyes and said, "We've got to call the police."

"Will do," said Val, who had no intention of calling the police. "I'm going to go let the dogs out and bring them back over here. Don't go anywhere."

"Hilarious, Val. I'll be lucky to stand ever again."

When he returned with the dogs, Val said, "Bryan, let's get you to your car. I have a lead on the books and will call you if I find anything."

"I'll be okay. I swallowed a couple of pain pills. They should kick in a few minutes. I can go with you."

"No way," said Val. "You're in no shape to go anywhere. You need to go to the hospital and have your hip X-rayed." A shock of pain shook Bryan, who writhed in pain.

"You're right, Val. I need an X-ray," Bryan finally agreed.

After helping Bryan to his car, Val said there was no way Bryan could work the gas pedal and brake with his hip. "I'm calling an ambulance. I'll take Dino and look after him."

Bryan did not argue, again his pain overcoming any objections. Val took out his cell phone and dialed 9-1-1. After describing Bryan's injury, the dispatcher said an ambulance was on the way.

"Hang in there, help is on the way," said Val. Fifteen minutes later, a fire department paramedic unit arrived and transferred Bryan out of his car.

"Call me when you know more about your hip," he said, just as the paramedics closed the door to the ambulance. "I will let you know where I am and if I find any clues to where the books might be hidden."

Of course, it was a lie. Bryan had tried to stop the book sale. Having him out of the way would allow Val's deal with Colin to conclude. If Colin didn't come up with the money, Val could sell the books, get the cash, and make a run for Mexico.

CHAPTER 31

1

Val waited until the ambulance was out of sight. He locked Dino in the car with Mac, then hurried to the train station with Billy's claim check. In baggage claim, he spotted a "Push Button for Service" sign. He heard a buzzer coming out of the back room, followed a moment later by a station agent. They greeted each other and Val handed him the claim ticket. The agent soon reappeared with Val's backpack.

"Are you one of those long-distance hikers?" the agent asked. "This is awfully heavy. Hope you are not planning to go far."

"I've got a load of books for a friend of mine who hates to read eBooks," Val lied.

"That explains it," the agent said. "He must be a good friend to lug all this stuff for him."

"A her," said Val. "An old girlfriend I'm trying to get back with."

"Anything for love, right?" the agent said.

"Right," said Val, offering the same fake ultra-white smile that drove his successful career as a TV ad pitch man for local businesses.

Val thanked the agent, who wished Val a safe trip, then disappeared back into the baggage holding area. Val unzipped the backpack and examined the contents. Only six Curtis books. Panic rose in his chest as his mind raced to remember where the seventh book could be. The adrenalin rush he had experienced chasing Billy and the excitement of discovering the claim check drained away. His hangover was back in full force—cotton-dry mouth, nausea, and a pounding head.

"Could the day get much worse?" Val wondered. Then a clear-headed thought struck him. Could he have told Billy about his plan to approach a local book dealer to make a sale? Had he already sold it and pocketed the money? Then he remembered. "I am such an idiot," he said out loud. "I've got to get the book and get back in time to cash in the Seattle ticket for one to Mexico or Montana. Better yet, I'll go to Wyoming." He had heard Powell was a quiet little town. Who would think of looking there?

Val's alcohol-sotted brain suffered a momentary memory loss. What was the name of the book dealer he had contacted? Val pulled out his phone and searched for Portland's used books stores. The first up was McQuillan's Books. "That's it," said Val. He found a number for McQuillan's and called the number listed on the website.

"Hello, this is Meg McQuillan. If you have reached this recording, it means I'm in the stacks finding books for other customers. Your call is important to us. Please text me with your request, and I'll call you back shortly."

Val texted, "I left an Edward Curtis book for you to review for purchase. I wanted to see if you had a chance to authenticate it and were going to make an offer?" Ten minutes later, Meghan McQuillan returned Val's call.

"Is this Billy Salishman?" She asked.

"Uh-oh, thought Val. Billy left the book, and she is suspicious about my call. How could she tell I wasn't Billy?"

"No," Val quickly recovered. "Billy is a friend of mine, doing a favor for me. He said he had sold books to McQuillan's years ago, and he had contacts there, so I gave him the Curtis book to bring in."

"My expert is still evaluating its authenticity," said Meghan, stalling. She realized that Billy described Robert as his cousin, while Robert said Billy was a friend. That sent up a red flag. "My father, who started our bookstore 40 years ago, is an authority on rare books. Unfortunately, he recently had a heart attack and is recovering. He only has so much energy each day to work on book projects I give him." Meghan did her best to stall the caller. She knew Kim Jansen would want to talk to him.

"I don't mean to be insensitive to your father's illness, but I have other dealers interested and would like to show them the book," said Val. "Is there any way to speed the process. I'm just visiting Portland and won't be here much longer."

"What did you say your name was?"

"Robert Hill," said Val, using the alias he used when he signed in for the rare book room tour.

"Damn," Val thought, realizing he had left another clue for police to follow. He knew he should have picked a different alias. He could feel the walls closing in, about to squeeze the life out of him.

"Meghan," said Val, using her first name to create a personal connection. "A streetcar hit Billy earlier today. A paramedic ambulance took him to the hospital. He was unconscious the last time I saw him, so he couldn't give me the claim check."

Meghan thought the story sounded false, but let it go. It might also explain why he didn't show for the 2 p.m. meeting the day before. "Sorry to hear about your friend. I hope he is okay. But the lack of a claim check complicates things," she said. "We wouldn't return a rare book to someone who didn't have a claim check. It's a basic security measure. You seem to have enough information about the books and Billy to suggest we could waive that requirement. I think we can move ahead on a deal once my dad gives the okay."

Meghan then offered a carrot, a way to keep Hill on the hook until she could reach Detective Jansen. "One of our reliable buyers—a woman of means—said she would pay $5,000 for an individual book, but $10,000 a book for five or more. I think Billy said there were seven books. Is that right?"

"Yes, I've got six more besides the one you have. I can bring those by as a way of verifying my identity."

At the possibility of $70,000 cash for the books, Val's hangover receded. If Colin Byrne didn't come through with the $100,000 Val had demanded, he would make the deal with McQuillan's buyer and disappear out of the reach of police. He would let his former bookie swing in the wind, while Val was living in a tiny house and fishing out in Wyoming. Mexico would be cheaper and warmer. In either place, the proceeds from the sale of the books would carry him for years. There might even be enough to leave his daughter an inheritance. They would never talk to him again.

Val pushed for a better deal. "The books are worth a lot more," he said.

Meghan, after several years as McQuillan's CEO and decades watching her dad make deals, understood the fine points of negotiation. "I'm sure they are," she said. "I'm sure you also understand that in the end, they are only worth what someone will pay. If you have a better deal, take it. To be fair to you, I'll see if I can push the buyer a bit."

"That would great," Val said, thanking Meg.

Again, Val had gambled that he could get a better deal. He still might. More likely, his gamble would fail, his bet lost, like always—the forever loser. He knew time was running out with the police closing in. Meanwhile, he was getting antsy at Colin's slow response to his demand to send the money.

"I'll consider the offer," Val said, his voice weak — the sound of defeat.

"Come by tomorrow at 10 and we can agree on a price," said Meghan. "I expect my dad to approve the deal late this afternoon or early evening."

Val made one more attempt to recover the book McQuillan's was holding. He knew that if he had possession of all seven, he would have more negotiating power with a potential buyer—and with Colin.

"Could I pick up the book this afternoon and then return it if we make a deal?" Val asked.

"Of course," said Meghan. "It's your book. However, my buyer is ready to go, and she will want to see and hold one to make sure it's the real deal. The longer the process takes, the more time it will take to complete the deal and get money into your pocket."

"Could you take photos and show them to your buyer?" Val offered.

"That won't work for her," Meghan said.

"Okay, I'll come by tomorrow at 10. Please text me once your dad okays the sale and we have a deal?"

"I would be happy to," said Meghan. "I look forward to meeting you."

After hanging up, she called Kim Jansen.

CHAPTER 32

1

An hour after arriving at the hospital, a CT scan confirmed Bryan's claim of a bad hip.

The fall against the steel-legged bench at the train station shattered his hip ball joint, which was already severely deteriorated from arthritis. The doctor said he would need emergency surgery and gave him a hefty shot of morphine until the surgical staff could find a slot for him. "It feels so good to be pain free," Bryan told the nurse, sobbing at the sudden pain relief.

In a few hours, he would have a new hip. He hoped he could deal with the post-surgical pain without drugs. His next challenge—rehab for the opioid addiction.

His head finally clear from the pain, Bryan called Detective Jansen to report what had happened with Val and Billy. Jansen picked up on the first ring.

"Professor Byrne, how can I help you?" Jansen had added Byrne's phone number to her contacts, so it appeared in her caller I.D.

"I'm going to help you, Detective Jansen," said Bryan, his voice relaxed. Jansen could almost see him smiling through the phone.

"Are you on drugs?" Jansen asked.

"Yes, I'm happy to report. Just listen, detective," he said. "I just had a run in with Val James and Billy Salishman. I fell and shattered my hip when I tried to pursue Billy, who apparently stole the Edward Curtis books from Val.

"Hold on a minute," said Jansen. "Where are you?"

"I'm at Legacy Medical Center on Northwest 23rd Avenue. I'm waiting for an orthopedic surgery team to give me the new hip I've needed for the past two years. And I've had a massive shot of morphine. I'm pain free and clear-headed, and you need to hear what I have to say."

"Go on," said Jansen.

"Val admitted stealing the books and injuring the guard. He said he needs money to pay off a gambling debt. He figured the job would be easy. He had the books he wanted and was putting them into a backpack when the guard walked in. According to Val, he had watched the guards, knew their routines, and picked a time of entry to avoid the door check. Apparently, the guard changed up his routine. Val says the guard got on his radio to call for backup and Val swung his cane to knock the radio out of the guard's hand. Instead, he hit the man in the throat. He claims it was an accident."

"Where is Val now?" Jansen interrupted.

"Wait, detective, there's more," said Bryan. "Turns out Val showed the books to a homeless man named Billy Salishman. He is a Native American who recently got out of prison. Val got drunk, passed out, and the next morning the books were gone, along with his backpack."

"Where is Salishman?" Jansen asked

"I'm getting there. Be patient, detective. Val figured Billy had the books. We located Billy and confronted him. He ran. I tried to pursue him, along with Val. That's when I crashed onto a park bench and shattered my hip. Val returned a few minutes later and said that Billy had run in front of a streetcar during the pursuit and was likely killed."

"Where is Val?" Jansen repeated, her patience draining away.

"Val said he had an idea where he might find the books," said Bryan. "He took off and promised to call. I don't know where he is or where he's going."

"Do you have a theory about how your dad might be involved?"

"I can't be sure," Bryan offered. "When I visited Dad several days back and had dinner, he gave me a stack of journals written by his grandfather William Byrne, who helped Edward Curtis plan and create the portraits of the Native Americans featured in *The North American Indian*. Dad seemed angry at what he read. He didn't tell me what was in them. 'You're a historian,' Dad said. 'The journals tell an ugly story.' He wouldn't say more. I've got the journals, but I have only had time to skim three of them. Great-Granddad Byrne describes how he took at least a dozen of the pictures in Volume 14 — a dozen pictures Curtis took credit for."

"Bill Bowman told us about the journal you left for him to review and said he would loan it to us," said Jansen. "He thought you wouldn't mind, given the stakes in this case. He plans to bring it over here today."

"The rest of the journals are in my hotel room by the train station. You have my permission to pick them up. I'll call hotel security and give them the okay to let you into my room. Maybe there are some clues to tell us what all this is about."

Jansen thanked Bryan for the call and update. She said she would follow-up.

2

Detective Jansen wondered if her case could get any more convoluted. She called the patrol sergeant on duty and asked her to send an officer over to the hotel to pick up the journals, then walked over to Mark Larson's desk to fill him in.

"Bryan isn't completely off the suspect list," she told Larson, despite the appearance that he wanted to help recover the Curtis books. DNA evidence had nailed Val to the crime. Salishman had possession of the books before the streetcar hit him and was likely dead. Now, wealthy vintner Colin Byrne was connected. "Add it all up and I'd say we have a massive conspiracy that has turned into a SNAFU. I can't see how the professor couldn't be part of this mess."

"What's our next move," Larson asked, "given that we still haven't identified a motive other than money? There's got to be more than that." Jansen knew the answer to the motive question would solve the case. First, she and Larson needed to locate Billy Salishman.

Jansen called traffic patrol to get a copy of the man versus streetcar report, then dropped Salishman's name into the crime database. Larson looked over her shoulder as Jansen opened Salishman's rap sheet and saw that he had been out of prison only two months. Previously, he served five years for theft. But not just any theft. He had stolen a first edition of Charles Dickens' Christmas Carol, in fine leather binding by Bayntun Riviere, with a portrait of the author on the cover. Market value: $32,500. He fenced it for $7,500 to Bruce McQuillan of McQuillan's Books. McQuillan said he felt the books had been legally obtained.

McQuillan sold them to a collector overseas in a no-questions deal. He claimed he was only a middleman. On another deal, Salishman had been a suspect but got off when the stolen rare book in question apparently disappeared into an overseas black market. Prosecutors had nothing to pin on Salishman or McQuillan.

"Salishman knows the rare book business," Jansen said. While she was reading Salishman's file, which was full of burglary and theft convictions, she got a call from traffic patrol. "Salishman had major head trauma," the dispatcher said. "He's in an induced coma at Legacy Summit Hospital."

With Val James in the wind and Billy Salishman out of commission, Jansen and Larson decided to take another run at Colin Byrne. She was about to contact Colin Byrne for an appointment when a call came in from the traffic officer on the scene of the accident involving Salishman.

"Hey, Gelman, how are you?" said Jansen.

"I'm surprised a hotshot detective like you remembers the name of one of the lowly officers you used to hang with."

"Come on, Bob. Quit busting my chops. I love you guys. Not my fault I have a little ambition. And I'm a smart SOB. You need to get off your butt and start working for a living. It will keep you out of the donut shops. You might even lose a few pounds."

"That hurts, Jansen. I'll try not to take it personally. Anyway, witnesses at the pedestrian versus streetcar scene reported the victim was being pursued by an unidentified male when the victim failed to see the danger and stepped into the streetcar's path. Lucky for him, it was nearly stopped when it hit him. He still got a nasty head injury."

"Thanks, Gelman, you're a peach."

"I am a sweet guy. Remember that and be a little nicer next time we talk." Jansen hung up and called Salishman's parole officer. He offered little to help the case. He said Salishman was smart. He was a Native American who prided himself on his knowledge of western history, battles with Indians, and settling the west. He ran the prison library. Claims he read 100 books a year — mostly history.

Salishman's involvement in the theft was making sense. Rather than a random meeting with Val, he must have targeted him — or had been working with Val all along, and decided to cut him out of the deal. The chase at the train station, and Salishman's desperate attempt to get away, appeared to be a case of a deal gone bad.

Jansen picked up her phone and called Colin Byrne. When she got voicemail, she left a message explaining she and Detective Larson were on their way to the winery. And that they needed a meeting with him ASAP.

CHAPTER 33

1

An hour later, Jansen and Larson pulled into Byrne Estate and drove up the long road to the tasting room. This time, Jansen was not dreaming about drinking wine with her husband, whiling away the day, overlooking the rows of vines, or gazing at the puffy white clouds above.

"Kim, based on facts you've uncovered, I'd say Colin Byrne is guilty of something. My gut tells me he is involved in this theft," said Larson. "We need to push him."

"Damn right," said Jansen. "This case is only a week old and I'm already tiring of it. Let's squeeze this guy's nuts."

"You'd like that, wouldn't you?" said Larson, keeping a straight face.

Jansen gave him a dirty look. It took her a moment to realize he was kidding.

"I might," Jansen shot back, smiling.

"That's the sassy partner I know," Larson said.

Like their previous visit, Stella Mason, Byrne's executive assistant, greeted them before they could walk up three stairs leading to the tasting room.

"Follow me," she said, an edge in her voice, her face blank. "Colin isn't too happy about this meeting. I don't blame him. This seems like harassment."

"I smell a pile of shit—a mound of guilt a mile high," Larson whispered to Jansen.

Instead of taking them to the outdoor terrace with sweeping views and an offer of wine tasting and charcuterie, Mason led them to a windowless private suite.

"Sit down, detectives," said Byrne, who was waiting, his arms crossed tightly across his chest. He remained standing, looming over them while they settled into their chairs. "What is this all about?"

"You tell us, Mr. Byrne," said Larson.

"I thought I answered all your questions," said Byrne.

"Yes, you did," said Jansen. "The case has expanded, and we have more questions." They were double-teaming him, keeping him off balance, forcing him to look from one to the other. Jansen and Larson led Byrne through a series of facts in the case.

"I still don't see how that involves me," Byrne said.

"Let me help you, Mr. Byrne," said Larson. "Your son, Bryan, seems to think there is a connection between the theft and your grandfather. Any theories you might care to share with us?"

"Why don't you tell us what this is all about," said Jansen.

Byrne still said nothing, looking from Larson to Jansen and waiting for more.

"If you are part of a conspiracy to steal the Curtis books, now is the time to fess up," said Jansen. "We have a guard in the hospital who may not make it. A second man we think was Val's accomplice was hit by a streetcar while Val was chasing him. As you can see, there are a lot of loose ends. What is not a loose end is the fact that if either of these men die, someone is going to jail for a long time—someone may get the needle."

Byrne sighed. "Let me show you what this is about rather than explain." Jansen and Larson sat up straight on the edges of the chairs.

Byrne pulled off his patch, revealing what appeared to be a white marble in place of an eye. The effect was scary, reminding Jansen of videos she had seen of a Great White Shark moments before crushing their prey. Their eyes rolled back in their heads, as if trying to avoid seeing the carnage they were about to create. Byrne unbuttoned his shirt. Massive scars covered his arms, shoulders, and back.

"Oh my God," said Jansen, unable to maintain the coolness of an experienced cop with plenty of up-close views of victims of suicides and gruesome murders.

"Who did that to you?" said Larson.

Jansen thought of the report her assistant dug up about a Peter Byrne who died shortly after he nearly beat his 10-year-old son to death.

"I'll tell you who did that to me. It was Edward S. Curtis."

The detectives looked at each other, a puzzled look on their face.

"How is that possible?" Jansen asked.

"Have you ever heard of intergeneration violence, detectives?"

"It has something to do with violent behavior passed from one generation to the next," Larson offered.

"Correct, detective. I might as well tell you the entire story. I recently found my grandfather's journals, dated 1924 to 1930, when he served as a photography assistant to Edward Curtis. In them, Grandfather William Byrne details about 100 instances when he stepped in to take Native American portraits when Edward Curtis was sick, injured or too stressed from money and marital problems.

"Despite Granddad's contribution to the project, Curtis never gave him recognition beyond listing his name and title in the back of the books. Curtis offered no special tribute or thank you. He never put William's name on the photos he took. He was a selfish bastard.

"When my grandfather went to him at the beginning of the Great Depression for a loan or a bonus, in recognition of his photography assistance — so my grandfather could literally save the family farm—Curtis turned him down. 'You got paid fairly,' Curtis told him. 'I'm not giving you a penny more.' The result was that the Byrne family ended up homeless, their farm repossessed. Grandfather Byrne's anger spilled over into self-pity. He eventually drank himself to death after years of beating my father, Peter, and my grandmother. The beatings were about his own failure and had nothing to do with his family."

Byrne stopped and wiped away tears, then continued his story. "My dad, Peter, was a failure in life, and an alcoholic, like his dad. He regularly beat up me and my mother when he came home drunk. Whatever he was unhappy about, he took it out on us."

"On this one occasion, I told him I was going out to play with a friend. He said I was defying him, and no one was going to defy him. After slamming my mother into a wall hook that slashed open her head, he took off his belt and began beating me. I was trapped and couldn't get away. The huge buckle of his belt stabbed me in the eye, broke toes, a rib, and arm, and slashed me to pieces before my mother staggered into the living room and pulled dad off me. He drove to a local bar, passed out in some bushes after leaving, and died of alcohol poisoning and hypothermia. I spent a month in the hospital recuperating."

"I'm sorry," said Jansen. "That's terrible. Still, what does the theft of the books have to do with this?" She had read the newspaper story about the beating but hadn't connected it to her case.

"It has to do with my lifetime of pain, passed on through the generations: Edward Curtis' act of cruelty, allowing my great-grandfather to lose his farm and our family to end up homeless, was taken out on my father, and our mothers. Stealing the Curtis books was a way to grab public attention and gain recognition, if not money, for my grandfather's contribution to history and creation of *The North American Indian*. I figured no one should benefit from my grandfather's work when he had lost so much. I wanted reparations for my own life of pain and the generations before me." Colin stopped and let out a sigh of relief—a heavy burden finally lifted off him.

"I also wanted the public to understand the consequences of intergenerational violence. So, I pressured Val to steal the seven books containing granddad's photos and bring them to me. I'm not sure what I was going to do with them beyond using them as leverage to force a correction in the history books."

"I even had a fantasy of stealing the seven books with Granddad's photos from every other set of the *Native American Indian* I could get my hands on. Without all 20 volumes, the collection is worth a fraction of its value as a complete set. One book taken from each of 300 first edition sets would have rendered them incomplete, their historical value diminished."

"Do you expect us to believe this story—something that happened 100 years ago led to the theft and injury of the guard at the Central Library in Portland?" said Jansen.

"Believe it. When I read the journals and understood what led to my beating, I was enraged. All reason went out the door. If you knew how much I have suffered since the beating, reliving the pain through endless nightmares, you would understand."

"I understand his pain," thought Jansen, who continued to suffer her own gutted-fish nightmare despite seemingly endless therapy. Larson, who had told no one about his dreams reliving the suicide of his girlfriend, Helen Williams, was speechless. He knew exactly what drove Colin Byrne to risk everything to extract payback from Edward Curtis, even though Curtis had been dead for 70 years.

Byrne then explained the details of the deal he made with Val.

"Where is Val?" Larson asked.

"Val won't tell me. He called and sounded desperate and told me to wire the money we discussed to his bank account, or he would sell or destroy the books. He gave me 12 hours to get the money together. He is angry and scared."

"We have to arrest you, Mr. Byrne, for a long list of charges involving the book theft and aggravated assault," Jansen explained. She didn't bother to tell him about Billy Salishman's condition. His death could result in a manslaughter charge.

"First, let's find Val and get back the books," said Larson. "Please call him again."

Byrne pulled out his phone and rang Val.

"Do you have my money?" Val asked without saying hello.

"Be reasonable," said Byrne.

"No excuses, Colin. Get the money. You now have six hours."

"Val, where are you?" Val hung up.

Byrne looked at Larson and Jansen and said, "Val told me I have six more hours to deliver the money we discussed, then hung up."

"Mr. Byrne, I should handcuff you and march you out of her for everyone to see," said Jansen. "But given what you've been through, I'm going to give you a break. You face a long list of serious charges. A 20-year jail sentence wouldn't be unreasonable. The district attorney may feel a more lenient sentence would serve the state well if the books are returned and the two injured men recover. We won't arrest you now. You can come down to the station and we can do all this quietly."

"Thank you, Detective Jansen. I am sorry for how this got out of control. No one was supposed to get hurt. Val, who has a security background, said it would be a simple job. And, for the record, I used Val's dire financial condition and his bookie's threat to kill him as leverage to push Val into my scheme."

Byrne put his patch back on and buttoned his shirt, using the tip of his shirt to wipe a tear from the corner of his eye. "You need to know that the cycle of violence ended with me. I yelled at Bryan more than a few times, and even slammed my fist into a wall once. But I never laid a finger on him." Neither Jansen nor Larson responded. Both just nodded in sympathy as Byrne examined their faces for a reaction.

"I'll have Stella cancel my afternoon meetings. I'll tell her I'm going into the city to take care of business," said Byrne. "I'll explain the situation with Val, then drive down to the station in the next two hours and turn myself in. Is that okay?"

"That's fine," said Jansen. "No longer. We need your help to find Val and save the missing books."

When Jansen and Larson got outside, Jansen said, "Let me call Meghan and see if she can get Val to come to McQuillan's this afternoon to make a deal."

"Great idea," Larson said.

Before calling, she checked her texts and found one from Meghan that came in while she and Larson were interviewing Colin Byrne.

"We're in luck, Larson. Meghan left a message that she had an appointment with Robert Hill, alias Val, tomorrow afternoon."

Jansen returned Meghan's call and discussed the meeting and asked her to move it up to today. Meghan scrolled through her calls received and found a number from Hill. Hill immediately picked up and agreed to come in early. He said he needed to complete the sale as soon as possible and leave town for urgent business.

Jansen got a text message from Meghan confirming a 4 pm appointment with Val. Jansen explained that she, Larson, and one or two other officers would be in place to take him down. The moment Val entered the bookstore, units would move in to block his exit, she said.

A minute later, Meg called back rather than send another text.

"I just spoke to Hill. A minute or two after he okayed the meeting this afternoon in a text message, he called and said he needed to reschedule. I told him our buyer was ready to make a deal. He said something weird. He said he needed more time. He did not explain. He sounded jumpy. I think he either doesn't have the other books to sell or he smells a trap. He said he wants to keep tomorrow's appointment."

"Damn," said Jansen.

"Be patient, Jansen, we'll get him," Larson said.

And that's when they got a break.

2

Val hung up his phone. "It's a trap," he knew. A warning flashed red in his mind. As much as he needed to get the book back from McQuillan's so he could complete his deal with Colin, he had run out of time. If Colin failed to come through with the money, he might rethink the risk of getting caught by selling the lot to McQuillan's. In the meantime, he needed to hide. In the big homeless shelter under the Broadway Bridge, he would be one more loser, blending nicely with Portland's unsheltered masses.

CHAPTER 34

1

"Kim, it's Jerry Atwell. One of our patrol officers, Bob Merriman, just spotted your suspect below the north end of the Broadway Bridge on Naito Parkway. He is standing near that big homeless shelter that looks like a circus tent. And he is wearing a backpack."

"Have Merriman monitor him, but don't approach," said Jansen. "If our suspect leaves the area, have your guy radio the location and direction of movement. We're on our way. We believe he is carrying rare books stolen from the public library. He's threatened to toss them in the river. We can't let that happen."

"You got it, detective."

"You guys are the best," said Jansen. "I owe you one, Sarge."

Jansen knew exactly where Val was. She would keep her thoughts to herself about the clowns at city hall and their failed attempts to solve Portland's homeless crisis. The new River District Navigation, placed under the roadway a couple of hundred yards from the train station, was one of the better shelters. Yet, it could only accommodate 100 of the city's 4,000 homeless. A drop from a bucket of misery.

"Larson, I'm going to call Briggs and have him bring his *Have Paws—Will Travel* van. He and I will close in on Val without alarming him. You can come from the opposite direction to head him off if he tries to run. First, let's get in position and then I will call him and see if he will give himself up.

Five minutes later, Jansen checked in. Larson was in place. A minute later, Officer Merriman texted that Val was on the move, climbing the stairs toward to the Broadway Bridge roadway. Jansen pulled up Val's phone number Colin

Byrne had given her and called. Jansen was surprised when Val picked up on the first ring.

"Val, don't hang up. This is Detective Kim Jansen from the Portland Police Bureau. Your friend, Colin Byrne, has confessed about his plot to get the Edward Curtis books. He says he pressured you into the deal, taking advantage of your need to get free of your bookie and get money for your family."

Jansen could hear Val take a deep breath and let it out before answering.

"The money I was expecting from Colin won't be coming through, and now there is no way I can sell the books." Val was breathless. He had been walking up the stairway to the bridge, so she was not surprised. "Guess I'm out of options. Jumping off the bridge into the Willamette River sounds pretty inviting right now," said Val.

"Come on, Val," said Jansen. "You know that's not the solution. Yes, you'll have some jail time, but Colin's confession and your cooperation could shorten your sentence."

"After I killed two people—Billy Salishman and the library guard—the only place I'm going is to Hell. Before that, rotting in jail for 30 years."

"No one has died," Jansen tried to assure him. "The guard is out of the ICU and in a regular room. Doctors say he will make a full recovery. Billy has a nasty knock on the head and stitches." The doctor told her Billy probably would recover, but he couldn't predict the extent of lasting brain damage Billy might have suffered. "The doctor said Billy just needs a little rest and he'll be fine."

"I don't believe you," said Val. "This is a trap."

"Call Colin. He has agreed to turn himself in this afternoon," Jansen said.

"I can't believe anything Colin tells me. Gotta go."

"Wait, don't hang up," said Jansen. "We can work this out. No need to hurt yourself or damage the books."

"I'm not buying that cool, sweet ice cream cone of a story you're trying to feed me," said Val. "You would say anything to make me give up. You'll be able to close your case and feel warm and fuzzy knowing that, at a minimum, I'm going to jail for the rest of my life." With that, he hung up.

Officer Merriman, who had been observing from the street below, texted, "lost sight of the suspect after he climbed the stairs. He's on the bridge."

Jansen picked up her radio and called Larson. "Unit 1, suspect sounds desperate. May be a jumper. I'm with Jim Briggs in his mobile dog care unit. Hopefully, it's enough disguise to grab Val before he does something stupid."

"This is Unit 2," Larson said. "Roger that. I've got Val in sight. He just walked into the bridge, into traffic like he wants to die." Just then, Jansen heard tires screeching over Larson's phone.

"A car just swerved to miss Val," said Larson. "He appears hellbent on dying."

Jim Briggs drove past Val, who was now on the south side of the Bridge, peering into the water below. Briggs and Jansen moved the van 50 yards ahead. Briggs threw on the van's emergency taillight flashers. Bridge supports blocked Briggs and Jansen from Val's line of sight as they got out of the van and moved toward him.

As Jansen and Briggs closed in, they tried to keep the bridge's support beams between them and Val. They didn't want to spook him.

Val took off his backpack. He dropped it to the sidewalk and looked both ways to see if any pedestrian traffic was approaching. That's when he spotted Jansen, who had moved within 25 feet.

Without hesitation, Val reached down, picked up the books, and threw them into the river. He did it in one smooth motion, the entire action from start to finish, about one second—not enough time for Jansen to yell stop. They had been so close to grabbing Val and the books.

"Don't come any closer, detective, or I'll jump."

"Val, if you jump, you are going to die. If the impact doesn't kill you, the river will suck you under and drown you. It would be a horrible death."

"I can die today, or rot on Death Row for 20 years in isolation."

"Val, I told you. Billy and the guard are going to be okay. At most, you'll get 5 years for theft and aggravated assault. That Colin Byrne pressured you into it will work in your favor. A jury will understand the pressure you were under and the need to get money to save your life and rescue your family. It's all going to be okay."

Val ignored Jansen's plea, climbing up on the railing. He balanced himself like a man on a wire. He looked down at the water and glanced at Jansen, who had inched closer. He didn't see Briggs or Larson closing in.

"Tell my family I love them," said Val. "And tell Colin he owes me, and he owes my family. I expect him to pay up." With that, he looked out at Mt. Hood 60 miles distant, then at the city skyline on his right, and finally, down at the Willamette River racing toward its sister river, the nearby Columbia. He put his hands out at his side, his body forming a cross, closed his eyes, and bent slightly forward. His posture was not unlike an Olympic diver balancing on their toes before plunging into the water below.

Everything was happening in slow motion. Detective Larson was racing toward Val but knew he would not make it in time. Jansen was 10 feet away, too far to grab him. Val's body was accelerating, gravity grabbing and pulling him downward. He was perpendicular to the railing and only seconds away from dropping to his death. Just as it appeared Val's death dive was complete, giant hands reached over the railing and grabbed his ankle. Jim Briggs, at six-feet-six inches tall, hands the size of baseball mitts, and body weight tipping 225 pounds, braced himself as the weight of Val's body threatened to yank him over the side into the river. Just as Val's body slapped against the side of the bridge, his fall temporarily arrested, other hands came over the railing to help Briggs. Mark Larson got hold of a pant leg and pulled his foot until Jansen could grab it. The three of them hauled Val's body back over the railing like a gaffed marlin yanked into a boat.

Stunned, Val lay inert for about five seconds before he realized what happened and began kicking away the hands holding him. "Let me go, I want to die," he screamed. Val tried to squirm away, but Jansen cuffed him, finally getting him calmed down while Briggs straddled him.

When the weight of Briggs, Jansen and Larson prevented him from moving, he said, "I give up," and began sobbing.

Jansen looked over the rail to see if she could spot the backpack filled with the Curtis books. It was gone. If not on the bottom of the river, sitting like a soggy log, it would be racing toward the ocean on the current.

CHAPTER 35

1

The next morning, Officers Jim Elwood and Devon assembled their diving gear on the shore of the Willamette River as Detectives Jansen and Larson observed. Given the power of the river, Elwood and Mike Devon would be risking their lives to recover the books. They saw it as a day's work. They knew the books were critical to the case against Val. For Val's sake, Jansen thought, no one better get hurt in the recovery operation. Val and Colin already had plenty of blood on their hands.

Since Briggs, Larson and Jansen pulled Val from his death drive, he had shut down and refused to answer questions about what he had done or if the books had been in the backpack. The pack could hold rocks—a ruse to throw off police and protect them for future recovery. Jansen knew Val was a gambler. He could have made a bet with himself that if the cops couldn't find the books, he could avoid the theft charges. He could claim his DNA was all over his cane and books from his earlier visit.

Val had been taken to the hospital where he was sedated, his hands locked to the bed rail. Officially, he was on a 72-hour hold and suicide watch. An officer stood guard outside his door with an unobstructed view of Val in bed.

"I have to warn you, Detective Jansen," said Elwood. "I wouldn't hold out much hope of finding the backpack. More likely, it's 100 miles from here."

""I understand," said Jansen. "I know you'll do your best."

At 40-feet deep, the Willamette was the 13th largest river by volume in the U.S., flowing under Portland's 11 bridges, including the Broadway where Val James tossed the backpack.

The divers masked up, strapped on heavy weights to take them directly to the bottom with ropes tied to the shore to anchor them against the strong current. Once secure, they disappeared into the murky water. Fifteen minutes later, they emerged, unspooling a rope attached to something in the water. Together, Elwood and Devon pulled up an object until it was on shore. It was the backpack. Jansen spun around in delight. She couldn't believe her luck. She couldn't stop smiling.

"You guys are the best," Jansen offered.

"We got lucky," said Devon. "One of the backpack's straps caught on a tree snag. It was firmly lodged, despite being pounded by the current."

Jansen moved to open it.

"Whoa, partner, don't open that now," Elwood warned. "Open it now and you likely will further damage whatever is inside." Jansen backed away.

"I'll let forensics handle it," she said.

Jansen and Larson each took a side of the backpack and set it softly on a blanket in the trunk of their car.

Back at the station, Jansen summoned forensic team members, who moved the backpack to one of their work areas. They hefted it onto a table and began wiping off water. The excess water removed, a technician carefully unzipped it.

After looking in the bag, Jansen pulled out her phone and called Bill Bowman.

She got voicemail and left a message: "Bill, we've recovered the missing Curtis books from the Willamette River near where our chief suspect tossed them. Please come over and identify them." Jansen had already picked up the seventh book from Meghan McQuillan.

2

When Bill Bowman arrived at the Portland Police Bureau, he was stooped, like he was wearing a 100-pound weight around his waist. A frown covered his face.

"Hi, Bill," Jansen said brightly. "You look depressed. What's wrong?"

"When I heard the books ended up in the river, I figured I might as well come over and see what's left of one of our beloved treasures," he said.

"Follow me," she said.

They walked into a conference room and there on the table were seven books linked up, covering most of the table. Bowman picked up one. "They are in perfect condition," he said. "How can that be?"

"Well, maybe not," said Jansen. "Although Val James, our chief suspect, is not talking, we know he put the books in a dry sack, the kind rafters, canoers, and divers use to keep clothes and other valuables dry and safe. They were in the river, submerged 40 feet and locked inside the watertight bag all night. As far as we can tell, not a drop of water has touched them."

"How sweet it is," said Bowman, picking up a book and kissing its cover. He then hugged it, like he was cuddling a newborn.

"There is a minor problem with one of the books," she said.

Bowman's eyes got big. "What little problem?"

"During the theft and attack on the guard, one book fell on the floor and landed in the guard's blood. The back cover and some pages have blood stains," said Jansen, handing him the book with the bloody pages.

Bowman examined it carefully, surveying the damage. "I think we can fix this," he said. "It's going to cost a lot—maybe tens of thousands for restoration experts to remove the blood. I'm not sure the insurance will pay for it. Nor do I think there is enough money in the library budget to fund the work. Right now, I won't worry about it. Most important, we will now have a complete edition of Edward Curtis' *North American Indian*. Once restored, we will put it back on display it for the public's enjoyment."

"Thanks for your brilliant detective work," Bowman added, putting the book on the table and hugging Jansen. She hugged him back. "You're welcome." She didn't tell him it had been sitting at McQuillan's for the past few days. That would have worried him unnecessarily. And he would have wanted to race over to check it out.

"Bill, one more thing. We need to keep the books here for a while. They're evidence. I promise we'll protect them like they are gold bars at the Mint."

"Detective, I understand the need to keep them here for the prosecution, but couldn't you let me keep them locked up in the proper temperatures and humidity while the case is working its way through the courts? I will, of course, make them available to you or any other law enforcement officer as needed. I'll bring them to court."

Jansen thought about it for a minute, then said. "That makes sense. They have been photographed and checked for fingerprints. Sure, I'll let you keep them. I know you will protect them."

After Bowman left with the books, Larson walked into the conference room. "How did it go with Bowman?" Larson asked.

"Happier than the proverbial pig in shit. I let him take the books back to the library to keep them safe. Banging around in a box in our dank, cold evidence room wouldn't be good for them."

She mentioned the cost of restoration for the blood-stained book and said, "I have an idea how I can get the money to pay for the restoration. It won't cost the library a dime."

"You're a genius," said Larson when he heard the plan.

As promised, Detective Jansen called former crime reporter and UrbanStreetPDX.com blogger Chuck Grayson to give him the details. By the afternoon, Grayson had published a long story revealing the arrests, the motive for the break-in, and included extensive background on the men involved, their relationship, the recovery of the books, and fates of library guard Elliot Delaney and Billy Salishman. He also wrote a sidebar on the incidence and societal impact of intergenerational violence. He used the Byrne Family tragedy as his example.

Local newspapers, including the Oregonian, Portland's major daily, picked up Grayson's story in whole and gave him a byline. Two years after he was kicked off the paper because he refused to write for the online edition, he was back on top—the local media recognizing his talent, experience, and the quality of his work.

Shockwaves spread through the community when news that millionaire vintner and philanthropist Colin Byrne, founder of Byrne Estate Vineyards, had plotted the theft of priceless books from the Portland main branch library. The community was split over what punishment was fair, given the personal histories of Byrne and James.

CHAPTER 36

1

Three weeks after Colin Byrne and Val James were taken into custody, the Multnomah County District Attorney announced a plea deal. After consulting with their lawyers, Byrne and James stood before Judge Mary Ann Howard to affirm the details and await her sentence.

The prosecutor could have thrown the book at the men. After all, the severity of the crime, the injuries, and the value of the books called for long sentences. But when the prosecutor interviewed the men and read their background—James' gambling debt and estrangement from his family, and the beating Byrne suffered as a child—she knew no jury would convict them.

There were also other extenuating circumstances. Although the guard had recovered from the neck wound, multiple scans during his hospitalization revealed early stage colon cancer. As bizarre as it might sound, Val James helped save the guard's life by nearly killing him. At the sentencing, the guard and his family told the judge they forgave Val for what he did. They hugged him and thanked him for saving their loved one's life from cancer. Val apologized, tears streaming down his face. The family cried as well. Even the judge was seen wiping away a tear.

"This is one of the strangest cases I've seen," Judge Howard said. "Despite the hardships both suspects have suffered and the apparent good coming out of the attack, your deeds can't go unpunished. Mr. Byrne, I sentence you to six months in the county jail, six months home confinement, then another twelve months of community service talking to families about intergenerational violence, and what happened to you. After you complete this sentence, you will continue probation for five years."

"I will suspend three years of probation, Mr. Byrne," Judge Howard added, "if you agree to pay for the restoration of the Edward Curtis book that was stained with Mr. Delaney's blood during the attack."

"That's the least I can do, your honor."

"You can thank Detective Jansen for the reduced probation. It was her idea for you to use some of your wealth to benefit the library by paying for the restoration."

Byrne turned and smiled at Jansen. "I really appreciate it. I think it might even help me heal some wounds I suffered long ago."

Jansen choked back tears. She smiled and nodded.

"Your honor, may I say something?"

"Yes, go ahead, Mr. Byrne."

"I am a victim of intergenerational violence. Grandfather Byrne came back from his trek with Edward Curtis with a little money in his pocket and big plans for opening his own photography studio. Sadly, the Great Depression intervened. He had put down most of his savings on the studio for rent, but with the economy collapsing, no one was paying for portraits. Grandfather Byrne figured Curtis would bail him out, allow him to use space in Curtis's studio, as well as loan or give him money to help pay the mortgage on the family farm. When Curtis rejected William's plea for help, William's life spun out of control. He lost everything, became a drunk, and began taking his failure and frustration out on his wife and my dad, Peter. Peter was subjected to years of beating and abuse. He learned that behavior from his dad, William. Then my dad, Peter, took out his rage on my mother and me. The belt beating was the culmination of generations of violence and verbal abuse."

"So, what happened to me," Colin continued, "was because of Curtis' cruelty 100 years ago. Our family suffered while his work became famous and is now worth millions. My rage over learning about Grandad Byrne's life following Edward Curtis' rejection caused me to do what I did. I know it sounds crazy, especially from someone like me, who has lived a good life and given much back to the community. I have failed to live up to my own standards. I apologize to all I have hurt."

"Still, I believe no one should benefit from Grandfather Byrne's work," he continued. "If nothing else, public knowledge of our family history may well result in the recognition of my grandfather's contribution to helping record and preserve disappearing Native America culture."

"Thank you, Mr. Byrne," said the judge.

"Step forward, Mr. James, for your sentence."

A stern lecture followed, along with her recognition of how a gambling habit had wrecked Val's life and the life of his daughter and ex-wife. Val got three years of prison time, five years of probation, and 1,000 hours of community service to talk to young people about how a gambling addiction destroys lives and how to stop it.

"To the court and those I have harmed, including my wife and daughter, I am truly sorry," Val said. His wife and daughter had rallied to his side and were sitting behind him at the sentencing hearing. Colin's payment of the money owed to Val's bookies, plus tuition for Val's daughter to continue college, and the no-interest home mortgage for his ex-wife, helped smooth the family reunion.

Also in the audience was Billy Salishman. He was labeled a victim. The D.A. did not charge Salishman with a crime. He had recovered fully from the injuries. A deep scar from a laceration on his scalp would be a lifetime reminder of the role he played in the Byrne family drama.

When he had entered the courtroom, he raised his hand and waited for the judge to recognize him. "Mr. Salishman, the prosecutor has requested that you be permitted to offer a Native American prayer," said Judge Howard. "Given the fact this case involves books with culturally important images and information, I will allow it."

For the next few minutes, Billy chanted a shortened version of the Salish anthem, the prayer he offered daily in front of the Portland Train Station.

"Thank you," the judge said, when the prayer ended.

CHAPTER 37

1

Five weeks later...

The John Wilson Room in the Portland Central Library was abuzz in anticipation of a major addition to the rare book collection.

Bill Bowman was rocking from foot to foot nervously as the library board of directors stood around a long wooden table waiting for the unveiling.

"Ladies and gentlemen," Bowman said. His voice was steady and clear. "We are here today, thanks to history professor Bryan Byrne, whose great-grandfather William Bryan Byrne served as photography assistant to Edward S. Curtis during the creation of the last seven volumes of *The North American Indian*.

"We celebrate the addition of a major piece of history, recently discovered in a storage room containing Byrne family heirlooms. Our donor, founder and CEO of Byrne Estate Vineyards, Mr. Colin Byrne, is unable to attend our gathering. Mr. Byrne's son, Bryan Byrne, historian, author and professor at the prestigious private school, Canyon College, is representing the Byrne Family tonight."

The group applauded Bryan Byrne.

"Ladies and gentlemen, these journals," Byrne said, his hands reaching down and touching the books on the table, "give us fresh perspective and historical details of the Edward S. Curtis treks never known before. In them, my great-grandfather details his life with Curtis over the seven years they worked together. They contain an amazing amount of detail about the trials and tribulations of the Curtis expedition. The stories contained here will further illuminate Curtis, the man, and add weight to his legacy."

"One more thing," said Bryan Byrne. "You can thank the leadership of Bill Bowman for this day. He convinced me and my father that the John Wilson Special Collections is the best place for them."

The room burst into applause. Bowman turned red. He was embarrassed by the attention, but also full of pride for helping make the journal contribution a reality.

Bill Bowman thanked everyone for coming and recommended they move downstairs to finish the celebration while he locked up the journals. Chuck Grayson, who attended the ceremony, headed back to his home office to post a story about the event, and wrap up his coverage of the library theft and aftermath.

2

Vintner's Son to Take Over
Operations at Byrne Vineyards

By Charles "Chuck" Grayson
Editor, Urban Street PDX

PORTLAND, OREGON—Bryan Byrne, son of disgraced vintner Colin Byrne of the Byrne Estate Vineyards, has taken a leave of absence from his teaching position at an Arizona College to take over as interim CEO at the winery.

Bryan told this reporter the arthritic hip that threatened his career as a history professor has been replaced. He is walking without a cane and looking forward to exploring Old West trails that are the substance of his college lectures.

"Thankfully, the severe hip pain and the addiction to pain medication are behind me after completing a rehab program," said Byrne. "I am now ready to take the reins of Byrne Vineyards in my father's absence."

Bryan said he had worked summers between college semesters at the vineyards. He reportedly has experience with every part of the wine-making process, from pruning and picking grapes to helping with the crush, aging of wines, and bottling.

His dad, Colin, will be in jail another five months before he can regain oversight of the winery, which produces one of Oregon's highly prized pinot noirs.

Editor's note: Edward Curtis' The North American Indian, that includes more than 100 photos by his talented assistant, William Byrne, is must-see. The portraits are stunning. Although some say Curtis fell short of his lofty goal to create a comprehensive record of Native American culture in North America, his work was a major contribution. I'll give him—and William Byrne—credit for that.

Please leave your comments here:

"All is well that ends well." — Molly P, Newberg, Oregon

3

Despite his love for a good scoop, Grayson left out another part of the story with a happy ending: Bryan Byrne and Stella Mason agreed to a paternity test to determine if Bryan was the father of Stella's daughter. The test came back positive. They decided to marry. Still up in the air was whether Bryan would return to Arizona to continue teaching. Stella agreed to go with him, if that's what he wanted. He said he would wait until his dad was released from jail before deciding.

4

After the Curtis theft case was resolved, Mike Melrose retired from his job as chief of detectives and recommended Mark Larson as his successor. Although Larson had scant experience as a detective, he had been a patrol officer for 10 years before his promotion to detective. His management experience at Paragon Security, where he oversaw operations for the entire northwest and a multi-million budget, gave him the perfect qualifications for the administration-heavy chief detective job. One senior cop in a different division waiting for promotion grumbled. Otherwise, Larson was a popular choice to replace Melrose. He accepted the position and began dating Meghan McQuillan, who assumed ownership of McQuillan's Books after her dad, Bruce, transferred the business to her. Recovered from his heart attack, but still suffering from COPD, Bruce came in a couple of days a week to greet customers.

5

Jim Briggs continued his work doctoring the dogs of the homeless. Kim Jansen finally told Briggs she didn't have a maternal bone in her body. She was considering resigning from the police force and helping Briggs run his mobile dog clinic and pet crematory.

As they lay in bed one night spooning, Kim felt the deep scar on her abdomen. One more battle scar, she thought. No doubt she would suffer more in the future. She turned out the lights and slept soundly, her gutted trout dreams a thing of the past. They disappeared right after she made her decision not to have more children.

End

ABOUT THE AUTHOR

Photo by Dennis F. Freeze

Bruce Lewis was a crime reporter for several California daily newspapers where he earned six awards for best news and feature writing. Bruce is the author of *Bloody Paws*, a crime thriller from publisher Black Rose Writing. He also wrote the Master Detective Magazine cover story, *Bloody Murder in Beautiful Downtown Burbank*. In 2022, he and his wife moved from Northwest Portland to the San Francisco East Bay. He is currently working on *Bloody Feathers*, Book 3 in the *Kim Jansen Detective series*.

NOTE FROM THE AUTHOR

Word-of-mouth is crucial for any author to succeed. If you enjoyed *Bloody Pages*, please leave a review online—anywhere you are able. Even if it's just a sentence or two. It would make all the difference and would be very much appreciated.

Thanks!
Bruce Lewis

ALSO BY BRUCE LEWIS

BLOODY PAWS
A KIM JANSEN DETECTIVE NOVEL

Questions or comments to: BloodyThrillers@gmail.com

Shortly after losing her husband in a freak accident, Veterinarian Helen Williams is brutally attacked by a group of homeless men and left for dead.

Emotionally raw and physically battered, Williams accepts a job to manage a pet crematory and assist Veterinarian Jim Briggs—her college lover—with his canine mobile care business, including doctoring the dogs of the homeless for free.

As homeless people disappear without a trace and police fear a serial killer is on the loose, Mark Larson and Kim Jansen are assigned to the case. Led astray by confusing clues and personal relationships, they struggle to uncover the truth before the killer takes another life.

We hope you enjoyed reading this title from:

BLACK ROSE
writing™

www.blackrosewriting.com

Subscribe to our mailing list – *The Rosevine* – and receive **FREE** books, daily deals, and stay current with news about upcoming releases and our hottest authors.
Scan the QR code below to sign up.

Already a subscriber? Please accept a sincere thank you for being a fan of Black Rose Writing authors.

View other Black Rose Writing titles at
www.blackrosewriting.com/books and use promo code
PRINT to receive a **20% discount** when purchasing.

CPSIA information can be obtained
at www.ICGtesting.com
Printed in the USA
BVHW030623230522
637770BV00004B/167

9 781685 130046